THREAD END

DATE DUE	

#3523PI   Printed in USA

This Large Print Book carries the
Seal of Approval of N.A.V.H.

AN EMBROIDERY MYSTERY

THREAD END

AMANDA LEE

WHEELER PUBLISHING
A part of Gale, Cengage Learning

GALE
CENGAGE Learning

Farmington Hills, Mich • San Francisco • New York • Waterville, Maine
Meriden, Conn • Mason, Ohio • Chicago

LIBRARY OF CONGRESS CATALOGING-IN-PUBLICATION DATA

Lee, Amanda, 1967–
    Thread end : an embroidery mystery / by Amanda Lee. — Large print edition.
        pages ; cm. — (Wheeler Publishing large print cozy mystery)
    ISBN 978-1-4104-7382-0 (softcover) — ISBN 1-4104-7382-1 (softcover)
    1. Murder—Investigation—Fiction. 2. Large type books. I. Title.
PS3620.R4454T465 2015
813'.6—dc23   2014037029

Published in 2015 by arrangement with NAL Signet, a member of Penguin Group (USA) LLC, a Penguin Random House Company

Printed in the United States of America
1 2 3 4 5 6 7 19 18 17 16 15

For Tim, Lianna, and Nicholas

ACKNOWLEDGMENTS

A special thank-you to the Prairie Schooler (prairieschooler.com), who so generously allowed Marcy to sell her products in the Seven-Year Stitch! I'd also like to give a special shout-out to all the Irish wolfhound lovers out there who so adore Angus (especially you, Ann P. in the Netherlands)!

CHAPTER ONE

It was almost lunchtime on Friday, and I was pacing. The museum exhibit I'd been anticipating for two months was finally opening that evening! My boyfriend, Ted; my friend Rajani "Reggie" Singh; her husband, Manu; and I were all going together. The guys weren't overly excited about the Padgett Collection textile exhibit, but they knew we were — and they were great guys, so they were taking us. Reggie was the library director for Tallulah Falls's one and only library, Manu was chief of police, and Ted was his head detective. I almost felt that we should be VIP guests, given the extra security Reggie and I would be bringing along.

Angus, my Irish wolfhound, could sense my excitement, and he paced with me. I perched momentarily on one of the red club chairs that helped make up my embroidery shop's sit-and-stitch square, and he sat and placed his head on my lap.

"It's all right," I said soothingly as I scratched his head. "I'm just excited about tonight. Reggie will be here to see you soon. Yes, she will! She's bringing lunch!"

His shaggy gray tail wagged, but he kept his head in my lap and enjoyed the scratching.

I smiled as I glanced around my little store. I owned the Seven-Year Stitch embroidery specialty shop, and it had been especially busy this morning. A busload of seniors had stopped by quaint Tallulah Falls on their way along the Oregon coast. They'd blown in and out like a storm, but I'd made several sales and had been able to tidy up the shop again within an hour of their departure. The candlewick-embellished pillows had been plumped and rearranged on the two navy sofas that faced each other across an oval maple coffee table, the ottomans had been returned to the fronts of the red club chairs, and the red-and-blue braided rug that lay beneath the table had been swept. In the merchandise part of the store, I'd dusted and restocked the shelves, straightened the embroidery projects that lined the walls, and righted Jill's straw hat, which had somehow been knocked askew.

Jill was a mannequin who looked an awful

lot like Marilyn Monroe. She stood near the counter of the Seven-Year Stitch, silently greeting patrons — although I had heard more than one shopper speak to *her* on occasion. I couldn't blame them. She was pretty realistic-looking. I often dressed her in embroidered outfits to match the season or the current weather. It was a way to make her look trendy and an excuse to make and display more of my embroidery. Today she wore a pair of white shorts emblazoned with crewel sea turtles along the slash pockets, a green tank top, and a sun hat. It was the second week of June, and Jill appeared to be getting ready to hit the beach.

Anyway, I'd had a great start to, hopefully, an even better day and evening. The bells over the shop door jingled, and Angus and I jumped up in unison. It was Reggie with lunch — chicken salad croissants from MacKenzies' Mochas. MacKenzies' Mochas was just down the street from the Seven-Year Stitch and was owned and operated by my best friend, Sadie MacKenzie, and her husband, Blake. In addition to coffee, they served delicious baked goods and deli items. The chicken salad croissants were my absolute favorite.

I hurried over to help Reggie before Angus knocked her down in his enthusiasm over seeing her.

"I'm sorry, Reggie. I should've put him in the bathroom before you got here," I said.

"If you had, I'd have been angry," she said, handing me the food boxes and bending to hug Angus. "He's precious. Yes, he is . . . part of the family . . . just a sweet little baby."

I smiled. Weighing in at around a hundred and fifty pounds, Angus was called a "little baby" by only a few people. Reggie and I were two of them.

I took the food boxes into my office and set them on my desk. "If you don't mind, grab us a couple drinks from the mini fridge. I'll post on the door that I'll be back in thirty."

"Diet soda?" she called over her shoulder.

"Yeah, that'll work." I took my tiny cardboard clock from behind the counter and moved the hands to indicate that I'd be back in half an hour. I didn't lock the door, but I hoped the sign would allow Reggie and me to eat undisturbed.

"What are you wearing tonight?" I asked as I returned to the office and sat down across from Reggie.

"A coral sari," she said.

"That'll look gorgeous," I said. "And Manu?"

She shrugged. "Black suit."

Unlike Manu, Reggie preferred her native Indian style of dress.

"What about you and Ted?" she asked.

"Ted is wearing a navy suit, and I'm wearing a royal blue dress. It's a short dress but long-sleeved, with the sleeves and top portion of the bodice made of lace."

She smiled. "You'll look great." She opened her box. "Sorry to make you feel as if I'm rushing you, but I have to get back to the library to make sure everything is taken care of for the weekend."

"Of course." I opened my box and picked up half my croissant. "I hadn't realized how hungry I was until I smelled these." I took a bite. Chicken, mayo, white seedless grapes, pecans, basil, sea salt, buttery bread . . . delicious.

"We had a little lull this morning, and I looked — for about the thousandth time — at the Web site for the exhibit," she said.

"I'm so thrilled our tiny museum managed to score such an elaborate collection," I said.

"Me, too. Most of all, I'm looking forward to seeing the kilim rugs." She sipped her soda. "They have a vintage Sivas kilim with threads in varying shades of orange, brown, blue, and lavender. I'm sure the Web site photo doesn't do it justice."

"Sivas . . . that means the rug is from Turkey?" I asked.

She nodded.

Although often lumped together with Oriental rugs, kilim rugs were actually very different. Oriental rugs were pile rugs, whereas kilim rugs were made by interweaving designs into wefts and warps to create a flat weave. Common patterns woven into kilim rugs included the ram's horn, hands on hips, fertility, eye, star, dragon, amulet, comb, burdock, running water, and scorpion. If my memory of the exhibit's Web page was correct, the Sivas kilim featured the ram's horn design.

In addition to floor coverings, kilim textiles included wall hangings and even furniture. All of the kilim rugs that would be on display at tonight's exhibit were to be hanging, probably behind thick glass . . . which would be good, considering how badly textile lovers like Reggie and me enjoyed feeling the texture of the pieces.

I tore off a piece of my croissant and tossed it to Angus, who was waiting patiently. "Did we decide to meet at the museum or at my house? I recall our going back and forth, but it's been such a crazy week that I've totally forgotten."

"We decided to meet at the museum and then return to your house afterward," she said.

I smiled. "That's right. For coffee, dessert, and gossip."

She chuckled. "Right. Is Vera coming to the exhibit's opening?"

"I believe so. I haven't seen her yet today, but I'm pretty sure she'll be there," I said. "There isn't much happening in Tallulah Falls that Vera misses out on."

"That's true. She has certainly broken free from her cocoon and learned to spread her wings," said Reggie.

When I'd first moved to Tallulah Falls, Vera Langhorne was a dowdy woman under the thumb of her manipulative husband. Now widowed, she'd had a complete makeover and was enjoying a much happier life. She was even dating again. Her boyfriend, Paul Samms, was a journalist.

Reggie and I finished our croissants, and then she hurried back to the library. I tidied my office back up and went to take the clock off the front door. Not ten minutes after I'd done so, a young woman came in to buy some needlepoint canvas.

"Do you mind if I ask what you're making?"

"Not at all," she said. "I'm making some

coasters for a friend." She frowned. "On second thought, should I get plastic instead of canvas?"

"Either will do fine," I said. "But the plastic would be sturdier."

She nodded, obviously still contemplating which would be the best.

"I'll show you both, and maybe looking at them will help you make up your mind." I led her to the needlepoint supplies.

"Are you going to that museum exhibit tonight?" she asked.

"I am," I said with a smile. "Are you?"

She shook her head. "I don't particularly care for the guy who runs the place. My older sister went out with him once or twice. Shame, though. I'd like to see those vintage fabrics."

"Then go," I urged. "Don't let someone else deprive you of something you'd enjoy. You don't have to associate with the curator."

"You really think so?" She tucked a wayward strand of her long light brown hair behind her ear.

"I know so. There'll be a lot of people there. You can just blend into the crowd," I said. "Or, better yet, look for me. I'm going with friends, and we'll make sure no one harasses you."

She gave me a shy smile. "Well, I might just do that. Even though I don't think he'd harass me . . . I'd prefer to avoid him. Thanks."

In the end, she chose a light blue canvas and said she'd buy some corkboard tiles on which to mount her finished designs. She said the blue background would save her some work and complement her pattern. I told her it sounded as if she'd made a wise choice. As I rang up her purchase and slipped it into a periwinkle Seven-Year Stitch bag, I wondered to myself just what the museum curator could have done to the young woman's sister to make her want to avoid him. Was he a love-'em-and-leave-'em kinda guy? Or maybe too clingy? Now I was eager to meet the man.

"There's an interesting story there," I told Angus after the young woman had left.

He woofed. At first, I thought he was agreeing with me. But then he ran to the window, and I could see that his excitement was caused by Vera Langhorne approaching the shop. Tail wagging, Angus pranced back and forth from the window to the door until Vera came in.

"Good afternoon, Angus," she said. "Sit down, and I'll give you the treat I brought you."

He dutifully plopped his behind onto the floor, and Vera dug in her large purse and brought out a granola chew bone. She gave it to him, and he went running to the sit-and-stitch square with it.

I laughed. "You've made his day."

"I'm glad. How are you, Marcy, dear?"

I stepped out from behind the counter. "I'm great." I gestured toward my office. "May I get you something to drink?"

"I'd love a mango juice, if you have one." She set her purse on the floor and dropped into the red club chair closest to the counter, smoothing out her crisp white linen slacks.

I hurried into the office, grabbed a bottle of juice, and then rejoined her.

"Thank you," she said as she accepted the juice. "It's mighty warm out there today. Now, tell me what's so great about you . . . as if I didn't already know."

"I'm so excited about the textile exhibit opening that I can hardly stand it." I sat on the navy sofa facing the window. Near my feet, Angus lay crunching his granola bone contentedly. "Are you going?"

"Are you kidding?" Vera asked. "Of course I'm going. Get this: Paul managed to speak with the owner of the collection for an article he's working on to correspond with tonight's event, and the owner might — just *might* — be willing to part with a piece or two."

"Wow. It'd be wonderful if the museum could afford to buy even one to keep on permanent display."

Vera's brown eyes widened. "The museum . . . Of course."

"Isn't that what you meant?" I asked.

"I was thinking it could be a good opportunity for a personal collector, but sure, the museum would really benefit from being able to hold on to a piece of history, too."

I hid a smile. Vera's late husband hadn't allowed her free rein with the finances, even though the bulk of their wealth had belonged to her. She'd been making up for that ever since his death.

"I can't afford to buy," I said. "I'll be happy to simply look."

"The prices were more reasonable than you might think," she said. "I was surprised really. If there's anything that strikes your fancy, let me know so I can get the owner to quote a price for you."

"All right," I said, knowing full well that Vera's idea of a reasonable price and mine were as far apart as Mexico and Canada.

"Anyway, I'm wearing an elegant white

dress," she said, brushing a lock of her beautifully highlighted chin-length blond bob behind her ear. "It has spaghetti straps, so I'll need to get a spray tan when I leave here."

"Tan or no tan, I'm sure you'll look fantastic," I said.

She leaned her head back against the chair and gazed up at the ceiling. "I love getting all dressed up and going to parties. John never went in for that sort of thing." She sighed.

I wondered — but didn't dare ask — if she ever missed her husband. There had been a lot of animosity between them before he died, but she'd loved him once. I wondered if the good memories ever outshone the bad.

As quickly as the melancholy had descended, Vera sent it packing with a resolute smile. "I really had better get going. I just wanted to drop in before going to the tanning salon . . . and then on to the beauty salon."

"You'll be the belle of the ball," I said with a grin.

"I doubt that." She winked. "But I won't be halfbad." She stood. "See you there!"

"See you, Vera!"

Angus left his granola bone long enough

to see his friend to the door. She turned and hugged him before stepping out into the balmy afternoon.

After quite a bit more pacing and waiting on a few more customers, I heard my phone ring.

"Good afternoon! This is the Seven-Year Stitch. How may I help you?"

"Have you heard from Ted?" asked Reggie.

My heart dropped. "Don't tell me they're canceling on us!"

"No," she said. "But Manu just called and said he'd heard from the FBI. The bureau is sending someone down from their Portland office because they suspect a known art thief will show up at the exhibit."

"Why would an art thief bother with an antique textiles exhibit in an itty-bitty town like Tallulah Falls?"

"Who knows?" Reggie huffed. "But they've sent down photos of the guy so that Manu and Ted — along with the rest of the department — can be on the lookout for him at the exhibit tonight."

"Aw, it won't be so bad," I said. "They'll be discreet, and it'll give them something to do while we're mooning over the textiles."

"I guess you're right," she said. "I just wanted us to have one night out when our guys would truly be off duty."

21

CHAPTER TWO

Ted arrived at my house at about a quarter past six o'clock. We were to be at the museum at seven, and I was still putting the finishing touches on my makeup. I had short platinum hair, so I liked to take special care in playing up my eyes when I was getting dressed up and wanted to feel glamorous.

"Come in," I called from the top of the stairs, mascara wand in hand, when Ted rang the bell. "I'll be right down!" I hurried back to the vanity in the bedroom so Ted wouldn't see me before I was "finished."

"Anything I can do to help?" he called from the foyer.

"Would you mind letting Angus back inside?" I asked.

"Will do!"

I was fortunate that my master bedroom was big enough to accommodate a vanity. Sure, it was a little crowded, but it was worth it. Having a mom who was a Hollywood costume designer meant that my entire life I'd wanted a vanity like those I'd seen in dressing rooms. I didn't have a vanity reminiscent of the ones in a makeup and wardrobe department, though. Mine was even better. It was a small distressed white table with an eyelet skirt around the bottom. Baskets with dividers held makeup and other beauty products. There was a basket attached to either side of the vanity. The top held my mirror — regular on one side and magnifying on the other — a pencil cup filled with makeup brushes, and a bottle of my favorite perfume.

I quickly finished applying my mascara and started to brush a rich red lipstick onto my lips. But then I realized I'd like to kiss Ted hello first without either or both of us ending up looking like clowns, so I dropped the lipstick into my beaded clutch and went on downstairs.

I found Ted and Angus in the kitchen. Angus was giving Ted high fives, and Ted was feeding the dog bacon-flavored treats.

Ted turned and gave a low whistle when he heard me approach. "Wow. You look fantastic."

"Thank you." I smiled, thinking he looked gorgeous as I took in his glistening black

23

hair, his incredible blue eyes, and the suit that looked as if it had been tailor-made for him. "I haven't put my lipstick on yet."

He flipped Angus the last bacon treat he'd been holding and walked slowly toward me. "Really? Why's that?"

The smile tugging at the corners of his mouth told me he knew exactly why that was, and my heart did a little tap dance. I laughed softly.

He pulled me into his arms. "I've wanted to do this all day." He lowered his head and kissed my mouth until my knees went weak. Then he kissed my neck, and my knees nearly gave out completely.

As his mouth moved back to mine, I murmured, "We really should go."

"Do we have to?"

"Manu and Reggie will be waiting."

Ted kissed me one last time and then raised his head. "You're right. We'll have to continue this later. How quickly do you think we can get rid of the Singhs tonight?"

I playfully tapped his shoulder. "You're so mean!" But as I looked into his eyes, I said, "Reggie probably has to work tomorrow."

"So do you," he reminded me.

I grinned. "The Stitch doesn't open as early as the library does."

"Now who's mean?"

■ ■ ■ ■

When we pulled into the museum's parking lot, there were almost no empty spaces.

"Let me drop you off at the door," Ted said. "I might have to park in the municipal lot across the street, and you don't need to walk that far in those heels."

I was wearing five-inch pumps. Even at that, I only came up to Ted's shoulder. "I appreciate your concern, but I'll be fine. I didn't dream there'd be such a huge turnout for the exhibit, though, did you?"

He shook his head. "The museum staff had better take measures to stay within the maximum-occupancy fire code."

I laughed. "You're worried about maximum occupancy when there's an art thief on the loose?"

"Hey, safety and emergency-exit procedures are no laughing matters." He pulled into an available space, put the car in park, and shut off the engine. Then he turned to me. "So Reggie told you there might — and the key word here is *might* — be an art thief nosing around the exhibit?"

I nodded. "You aren't concerned?"

"Not particularly," he said. "I don't think the man suspected of being in the area will burst onto the scene with guns blazing and try to steal the pieces on exhibit."

"Actually, I can't see any art thief worth his salt doing that," I said. "The risk of damaging the art would be too high."

"Precisely, my Inch-High Private Eye. You're learning."

"Yeah, well, I prefer leaving the investigating up to you," I said.

"Since when?" He chuckled. "However, if you should happen to see this man . . ." He took a photo from his breast pocket and handed it to me. "Then please quietly let me know."

I dutifully studied the photo of the small, balding man with large round glasses, but I knew full well that if the man came anywhere near the museum tonight, Ted would be the first to spot him. My guy never missed anything.

"He looks nice enough," I murmured. "Timid, too. He doesn't seem the heist-y type."

"As far as we know, he only stole one painting, but it was priceless. Before he turned to a life of crime — or, in this case, an *incident* of crime — he was an art history professor somewhere in Canada."

"Wonder what it was about that one painting that made it so irresistible to him," I said.

"I don't know. He stole the piece in Seattle and left a note saying he simply couldn't stand to see the painting in the hands of such a boorish, unappreciative collector," Ted said.

"What was the painting?"

"It was an early work by Cézanne," he said. "It was similar to his skull paintings. Are you familiar with those?"

"I seem to recall he liked doing still-life paintings with skulls in them," I said.

"Yeah. The man apparently had a touch of the macabre. Professor Vandehey was in Seattle authenticating the painting."

"He must've been sure it was the real thing to have given up everything for it," I said.

"He must have." He suddenly smiled and waved. "There are Manu and Reggie. Sit tight." He got out of the car and came around to open my door.

Chivalry is alive, well, and sexy, I thought as I took his hand.

Reggie and Manu were heading toward us. She looked lovely in her coral sari. It had silver beading and sequins and was very elegant. Reggie was even wearing low-heeled silver sandals. She typically wore flats, and I couldn't remember ever seeing her in heels before.

"You look beautiful," I said.

"So do you," she said with a warm smile.

Manu cleared his throat.

"And you look dashing, Manu," I said.

"Thank you." He adjusted his black tie. He really did look nice in his black suit and white shirt. He even had a white pocket square. I was accustomed to seeing him in jeans and plaid shirts, so this was a nice change.

"Oh, yes, smooth out his ruffled feathers," Reggie teased. She looked around the parking lot and then at the crowd gathering at the door. "I had no idea there were so many people interested in textiles."

"They're not," said Manu. "We live in a small town, and there's nothing else to do."

"Well, I don't know about that," Ted said. "There are some pretty decent reruns on TV tonight."

"Then what are we standing around here for?" Manu asked.

"Ha-ha," Reggie said, taking his arm and heading toward the entrance.

"Ted's worried about maximum-occupancy laws," I said.

"You've got to be kidding me!" Reggie

shook her head. "Manu said the exact same thing!"

"It's our duty to serve and to *protect,*" Manu said. "That includes getting your butts out of there safely in case of an emergency."

"As well as everyone else's butts," Ted added. "Can you imagine what a field day the press would have if there were some sort of emergency here tonight, fire codes weren't being followed, and Tallulah Falls's chief of police and head detective were on the scene?"

I squeezed his hand. "It would be all right. We'd have Vera's boyfriend spin it."

"I'll spin you," he said with a wink.

"Promise?" I grinned.

"Aw, get a room!" Manu said. "By the way, that's something *else* we could be — ow! Stop pinching me, woman. I was only kidding . . . sort of."

"Please behave yourself," Reggie said. "I've been looking forward to this night for weeks, and I know Marcy has been, too."

Manu turned to Ted and me and shrugged like a chastised schoolboy. Then, just as quickly, he turned serious. "Those two guys at the door had better be counting. I'm going to ask when we get up there, and they'd better know exactly how many people are in

29

that building."

Before we went inside the museum, Manu showed the men his badge and asked how many people were in the building. One of the men gave a satisfactory answer and assured Manu that when they neared the maximum-capacity limit, they would keep people out until others exited. Once inside, Manu and Ted excused themselves and went to speak with the head of the security staff.

"They're going to make sure the staff is aware of . . . the professor," Reggie said.

"Good. That gives us some time to linger over the pieces we like best without feeling that we're boring them to death," I said.

My favorite was a biblical tapestry depicting the battle between David and Goliath that dated back to the early 1500s. It was a large piece that — when the panels were placed side by side as they were displayed — was seventy-five feet long and ten feet wide. The information card reported that it had been woven in the Flemish city of Arras. It comprised three panels. One panel showed the Israelite army encamped on one mountain looking anxiously into the valley. The center panel was, of course, that of David poised to throw a stone from his sling at the jeering giant. The third panel showed the Philistine army on the other mountainside gloating over what they presumed would be a quick victory for Goliath.

Although Reggie loved the Sivas kilim she'd seen on the Web site, her favorite was a vintage Sharkoy kilim rug from the Balkans. It had been woven in shades of brown, blue, cream, and rose, and it had burdock and amulet motifs.

"That rug would go beautifully in my living room," Reggie said.

"Well, Vera said the collector was willing to sell a few of the pieces," I said lightly. "You could ask."

She laughed. "As if I could afford to pay whatever the asking price would be for an antique rug . . . and then put it on my floor and walk on it."

"But you could always hang it up."

"Of course I could. Maybe I can get Manu to cash in his pension," she said.

We were laughing at that thought when Manu and Ted joined us.

"You two are having entirely too much fun at this staid gathering," Ted said, putting his arm around me and pulling me against his side.

"I'm trying to talk Reggie into buying this rug," I said.

Manu's eyes bulged. "Oh, no, you aren't!"

"This stuff isn't really for sale, is it?" Ted asked.

"Vera said Paul interviewed the collector and that some of the pieces are," I said. "In fact, she told me to let her know if I saw anything I liked. I said that the museum might be interested in acquiring something to display full-time but that I certainly couldn't afford anything."

"Neither can we," Manu said.

"I know, my darling," Reggie said. "We were only joking around."

"Do you two feel confident that the museum is secure?" I asked.

"We do," Ted said. "The FBI even sent someone from their art theft division down from Portland to keep an eye out for Professor Vandehey."

"And there are a group of people waiting outside for someone to leave so they can come in," Manu said. "I think the security team here is on top of things."

"It wasn't that we really *doubted* them." Ted's glance at Manu belied his words. "But we knew they'd never handled an exhibit of this size before."

"Exactly." Manu nodded. "Everything here is under control, and we can all enjoy the exhibit."

I noticed the young woman who'd been in

my shop earlier in the day walking around looking uncomfortable and out of place. I got her attention and waved her over.

"Hi! I'm glad you decided to come." I introduced her to Ted, Manu, and Reggie. "And this is . . . ? I didn't get your name this morning."

"It's Kelly," she said. "Kelly Conrad. It's nice to meet all of you."

Everyone exchanged pleasantries, and then the curator joined us. He was a short, trim man, fairly attractive, with neatly cut auburn hair and green eyes.

"Good evening," he said. "I'm Josh Ingle. Are you enjoying yourselves?"

"We are," I said.

"Glad to hear it," Josh said. "If you need anything, please let me know." He looked pointedly at Kelly. "Good to see you."

She nodded.

"I'd like to talk with you later, if you have time," he said.

"I was actually on my way out," Kelly said.

"Wait," Josh began.

"Thanks, Marcy," she said. "See you soon." With that, she hurried off through the crowd.

Josh frowned after her and then turned back to us and smiled. "Again, I'll be around should you guys need anything.

Back to mingling."

"That was odd," Ted said after Josh had walked away.

"Yeah, wonder what that was about," Manu said. "Must be some history there."

"She told me when she came into the shop this morning that she wanted to come tonight but that she preferred to avoid the curator," I said. "She said he went out with her sister a couple of times."

"Those must have been a few terrible dates," Reggie said.

CHAPTER THREE

I'd stayed up too late the night before; but
even sleep-deprived, I was chipper as Angus
and I pulled into our usual parking spot
outside the Seven-Year Stitch. I had seen
Vera and Paul only briefly at the museum
exhibit, so I supposed Vera would be in
sometime today. I hoped she would, anyway.
It would be fun to relive the evening with
her . . . going over the pieces we'd liked
best. I wondered if she'd made the collector
any offers. I grinned. Knowing Vera, she
probably had.

I hopped out of the Jeep and snapped
Angus's leash onto his collar. He jumped
out and sniffed the sidewalk while I unlocked the front door. As soon as we got
inside, I took the leash off. Angus bounded
over to the sit-and-stitch square where he'd
left his favorite toy — a Kodiak bear Vera
had brought him back from a trip she'd
taken a few months ago.

I relocked the door. I still had about half an hour until the shop opened, and I liked to have the shop tidy and restocked when customers started coming in. The first order of business every Saturday morning was to take the trash out. The sanitation truck ran at noon every Saturday, so all the shops on our side of the street scrambled to get their garbage out to the receptacles before then.

Fortunately for me, the Seven-Year Stitch didn't generate a lot of trash . . . especially when compared to MacKenzies' Mochas. That shop produced more garbage in a day than the Stitch did in a week. In fact, Blake had to take their garbage out twice a day — double-bagged so the food scraps wouldn't attract bears.

I was thinking about bears, Blake, Sadie, and how Sadie had talked me into coming to Tallulah Falls and opening my shop — for which I would be forever grateful — when I stepped out the back door with my bag of trash. I tossed the bag into the bin, turned, and then gasped as I saw something lying against the wall.

For the world, the . . . thing . . . looked like the kilim Reggie had admired so much last night at the exhibit. But it couldn't be . . . could it?

I crept closer. It *was* the rug — I recognized the colors and the unmistakable patterns. But what was it doing *here*?

I took another step toward the rolled-up kilim and saw that it was badly stained. Had someone bought it, got something all over it, and left it here for the sanitation crew to dispose of? Surely not.

Maybe Vera had bought it, gotten it stained, and then left it here at the back of my store to see if I could clean it. No, that didn't make any sense to me either, but I was really grasping at straws.

I took one more step closer and nudged the rug with my foot. I wasn't about to touch such a valuable kilim until I found out why it was lying outside my shop.

When I pushed it, the rug rolled slightly. Then I spotted something . . . a *hand*! And the hand was attached to a body . . . that was attached to a face . . . a face that looked vaguely familiar.

With trembling hands, I fumbled my cell phone from the front pocket of my jeans and called Ted.

"You've got to come," I said when he answered. "Here . . . to the shop . . . please. There's this guy . . . a *dead* guy . . . wrapped up in Reggie's rug."

"What? Babe, you aren't making sense."

37

I couldn't answer. I'd begun to hyperventilate.

"Sweetheart, I'm on my way. Sit down and put your head between your knees," he said. "Is anyone with you?"

When I didn't answer, he repeated that he was on his way.

I became vaguely aware that Ted had ended the call, and I returned my phone to my pocket. I didn't know what to do. Maybe the man wasn't dead after all. I guessed I could take his pulse to see. Or I should probably wait for Ted. The gray cast to the man's skin made me fairly certain that there was nothing I could do to help him. And it wasn't a stretch to assume that the stain on the rug was blood. I'd wait for Ted.

Suddenly, I heard footsteps pounding up the alley behind me. I whirled around, stumbled, and would have fallen had I not been righted by Blake — he whose thundering footsteps had startled me while he was sprinting toward me with a white paper bag in one hand.

"Ted called," he said, panting for breath. "Are you all right? He said you were hyperventilating. Here — breathe into this. Let's get you inside."

I was sort of wondering if maybe Blake didn't need the paper bag more than I did, but I simply nodded. With one strong arm around my shoulders, Blake started to lead me back into the shop.

As he turned, he noticed the body. "What the — ?"

"Exactly," I said. "Let's go inside until Ted gets here. This is freaking me out."

"You and me both."

We went inside. Blake was now every bit as shaken as I was but was determined to be strong for me.

Angus was thrilled to see Blake and immediately bounded up to him.

"In a minute, boy," Blake said softly. "First, let's get Marcy settled on the sofa."

Sensing something was wrong, Angus sat down and began to whine.

"It's okay," I told him as I sank onto the sofa. "Everything's fine."

Blake took a seat on the red club chair diagonal to the sofa. "Seriously, breathe into the bag."

I shook my head. "I'm fine."

"What happened?"

"I have no idea," I said, petting Angus's head in an effort to soothe us both. "I took out the garbage, and when I turned to come back into the shop, I saw the rug. I thought it strange that someone would throw it away like that, and then I saw the hand and re-

39

alized someone was wrapped up in the rug."

"That's all you saw? A hand?" He shrugged. "Do you think maybe it could be a mannequin?"

"No. I saw the man's face, too. He was real." I glanced at the front door and realized it was still locked. "I've got to unlock the door."

Blake jumped up from the chair. "I'll get it. You sit there and rest."

"Thank you. The keys are on the counter."

He unlocked the door. "Do you want me to leave the sign as *Closed*?"

"No. Change it to *Open,* please," I said.

"Are you sure you're up to having customers today?"

"Positive." I smiled slightly. "I'll take any normalcy I can get right now."

He returned to his seat. "Are you feeling okay?"

"I'm still shaky — and I'm sorry for that poor man lying outside — but I'll be all right."

Sadie hurried through the front door carrying a large to-go coffee cup. "Marce, how are you?"

I assured her that I was fine. "I'm even better if that's a low-fat vanilla latte with a dash of cinnamon."

Sadie saw how my hand shook as I took

the cup, and her big brown eyes flew to Blake's blue ones. He gave her a nod, and they communicated volumes merely by holding each other's gaze for a few seconds. They've only been married for five years, but you'd think they'd been together forever. Like every other couple, they'd had their share of hardships. But they'd always persevered . . . and always would. They'd be lost without each other.

I took a sip of the warm, delicious coffee, and Sadie sat beside me on the sofa.

Angus, still confused and upset by the anxiety in the room, sighed and plopped his head onto his paws.

"Aw, look how pitiful he is," Sadie said. "Now I wish I'd brought him some biscotti." She spoke to Angus. "I'll bring you back some biscotti, sweet boy. Yes, I will."

Angus wagged his tail. He wasn't convinced everything was okay yet, but he knew it was getting there.

Sadie took my free hand and gave it a squeeze. Like Angus, she didn't seem confident she knew what was going on, either. But she wanted me to know that she was there. Dog and human best friends share that trait. I quickly filled her in on the situation.

At last, Ted strode through the door. As

41

he took my latte, set it on the coffee table, and gathered me into his arms, I finally felt that everything was truly going to be all right. So, naturally, I began to weep.

"I'm so glad you're here," I whispered against his shoulder.

"Everything's okay, babe. I've got you."

I didn't know why suddenly feeling secure would make me weep, but it did. Looking back, I usually did hold up fairly well in the midst of a critical moment and fall apart when it was over. Okay, so looking back on my call to Ted, maybe I *didn't* hold up that well in the critical moment. But what would you have done if you'd found a dead guy wrapped in an antique kilim in *your* alley?

Ted sat on the sofa, pulling me onto his lap. He gently wiped the tears from my cheeks and kissed my forehead.

Angus sat up and placed his head on my knee, making us all laugh. He could be such a clown.

"We should go on out back," I said to Ted.

"Not yet. Manu is there. He said he'd handle that situation while I made sure you were okay."

"I'm fine," I said. "Really. You should go —"

"Ted, come out here!" Manu called from

the back door. "You're not going to believe this!"

I got up. "Come on."

"I think you should stay in here," Ted said, standing and taking my hand.

"He's right," Sadie said. "You've had enough of a shock for one day. Who knows what Manu has discovered out there?"

"Besides, you need to be here to wait on your customers," Blake said. "Speaking of which, I'd better get back down the street."

Ted shook Blake's hand. "Thanks for being here for Marcy."

"Anytime."

"Yeah, Blake, thank you for coming to my rescue," I said as Ted headed for the back door. "And you, too, Sadie."

Sadie stood and gave me a hug. "I need to get back to the shop as well. But call me if you need anything."

I promised her I would, and then Angus and I were alone in the sit-and-stitch square. I waved to Sadie and Blake as they passed the window en route to MacKenzies' Mochas. Then I picked up my latte, sat down on the sofa, and sighed.

"Big morning, huh, Angus?"

In response, he moved closer to me and lay at my feet.

I took a drink of the now lukewarm latte

and mused aloud to my faithful hound, "I wonder who that guy out there is. And why did he look familiar."

I fell silent as Angus rolled onto his side for a nap, and I searched my memory for a different image of the balding gentleman who'd been wrapped in a rug and dumped in the alley behind the Stitch. The man didn't work in any of the local shops. The museum — was that where I'd seen him? I tried to recall the faces of the people I'd mingled with at the exhibit opening last night, but I couldn't place the victim's face. Still, I kept fixating on the museum. Then it dawned on me — the photograph. The victim was Dr. Vandehey, the professor turned art thief.

I scrambled out of my seat, startling Angus, and hurried to the back door. He came chasing after me, but I didn't allow him to follow me outside. He jumped up so he could peep out and bark at all the excitement.

"Isn't that the man from the picture you showed me last night?" I asked Ted. "The art thief?"

"The *alleged* art thief," Manu said.

"But didn't he confess?" I asked.

Ted took me gently by the shoulders. "You're right about the identity of the victim, but I still don't think you should be out here."

"Right," said Manu. "You could accidentally contaminate the crime scene."

"Crime scene?" I slumped against Ted. "This doesn't mean you have to close down my shop, does it?"

"No, sweetheart. We'll just cordon off this part of the alley. The inside of your shop will be business as usual."

"Thank goodness," I said. "I suppose I should go back in. My being out here is driving Angus crazy."

A black SUV rolled right up to the yellow crime scene tape, and a short man wearing a dark suit stepped out of the vehicle. He had a "standard-issue" buzz cut and sunglasses. I think all of us — me, Ted, Manu, and the crime scene technicians, heck, maybe even Angus — knew before he'd introduced himself that he was FBI.

He flashed a badge. "Special Agent Floyd Brown of the Portland office of the Federal Bureau of Investigation's Art Theft Division. What have we got here, and why did I have to hear about it over the police scanner rather than through a personal phone call from the chief of police?"

Manu drew himself up to his full five feet seven inches. He was taller than Agent

Brown by at least two inches — maybe three. "Agent Brown —"

"*Special* Agent Brown," the man interrupted.

"You weren't notified because we haven't made a positive ID of the victim yet," Manu continued. "Therefore, we don't know that an investigation of this death falls within your jurisdiction."

"It looks like Vandehey to me," Special Agent Brown said.

"Well, just because it looks like him doesn't mean it is," Manu said. "Now I respectfully request that you step back and allow our crime scene techs to do their jobs."

Since Angus was still barking and scratching at the door, I excused myself to go back inside.

"Wait," said Special Agent Brown. "Who are you?"

"I'm Marcy Singer. This is my shop."

"Are you the one who found the body?"

"I am."

"Then I'll come inside and take your statement," he said.

Manu started to protest, but I shook my head slightly. If Brown was in the shop taking my statement, he'd be out of Manu's and Ted's hair.

"Right this way," I said.

I opened the door and took Angus's collar, gently moving the dog back so Special Agent Brown and I could get inside.

"Come on, Angus," I said. "Special Agent Brown, would you like some coffee? It won't take but a minute to put on a pot."

"No, thank you," he said, ignoring Angus, who was snuffling his pant leg.

I led the agent to the sit-and-stitch square, and he sat down on the sofa facing the window. I took the red club chair.

"Is there something you can do with him?" He jerked his head toward Angus, who was now checking out the man's jacket pocket.

"I can put him in the bathroom, but he'll bark so much, we won't be able to hear each other over the racket," I said. "If you'll pet him, he'll probably go on and leave you alone."

Special Agent Brown sighed, patted Angus's head, and said, "Nice dog. Now, go away."

I picked up Angus's yellow tennis ball and gave it a toss. The dog loped after it and brought it back for me to throw again. As I played fetch with Angus, I relayed my statement to Special Agent Brown.

"So you recognized the rug and the professor," said Special Agent Brown.

"I *thought* I recognized the rug," I said. "And it only dawned on me a few minutes ago that the victim looked like a man in a photo I'd seen last night. As Chief Singh pointed out, we can't be sure of anything until the crime scene technicians and the medical examiner have gone over all the evidence."

"Yeah, well, I don't set much store in co-incidences, Ms. Singer. I tend to take things at face value."

"Have you spoken with the museum curator and confirmed that one of the rugs from last night's exhibit is missing?" I asked.

"No," he said. "I came right here." He narrowed his eyes. "Why hasn't your esteemed police chief taken care of that?"

"I'm sure he has someone looking into it," I said. I wasn't really sure of anything except that Manu was thorough. I knew that as soon as he arrived, he'd put his team into motion. I figured that included sending a deputy over to the museum.

"Well, that's not good enough for me. I'll go over there myself. But first I want to know why this man was dumped behind your store, Ms. Singer."

"Beats me. I imagine it's because the museum is one street over and that if the rug is indeed the one from the exhibit, then the victim was dumped here because it was convenient."

"We'll see about that," he said. He got up, plucked a dog hair from his jacket, and left.

Chapter Four

After Special Agent Brown left, Ted came inside and sat on the chair near Angus.

"Was Brown respectful to you?" Ted asked, rubbing one of Angus's ears. "He struck me as something of a jerk."

"Yes and yes," I said with a grin. "He was respectful but also a jerk. Anyway, I gave him my basic statement — took out the trash and found a dead guy — and then let him know that nothing had been definitively proven yet about the identity of the victim or even the rug, for that matter."

Manu arrived in time to hear the last part of my statement. "How'd he take that news?"

"He was going straight to the museum to see what he could learn there," I said.

"I figured as much," Manu said. "Deputies Dayton and Moore are there. I'd better warn them that he's on his way." He stepped into the hallway so he could have some privacy.

"So, why do you think Special Agent Brown is being so disagreeable?" I asked Ted. "He acts as if he doesn't trust what you and Manu are telling him and doesn't even want your help on the case."

"He doesn't want our help. This case is very personal to him," Ted said. "When Professor Vandehey stole that painting a few years back but was never caught, he made Special Agent Brown look like a fool. Worse yet, that was the first case Brown had been allowed to oversee."

"So he got in a lot of trouble?"

"He got demoted." He picked up Angus's tennis ball and rolled it, grinning when the dog scampered after it. "Brown wasn't allowed to head up another case for over a year. I even heard that some people in the bureau thought maybe Brown was an accomplice because he botched the investigation so badly."

"What do you think?" I asked.

"I believe it was a combination of Brown being inexperienced and Vandehey being clever and covering all his bases."

"Okay, so Agent Brown — ahem, *Special* Agent Brown — has a vendetta against Vandehey." I spread my hands. "We're pretty

51

sure the professor is our victim, right? Then what's left for Brown to be mad about?"

"Well, Inch-High Private Eye, think about it. Brown shows up last night because the bureau got a tip that Vandehey might come to this exhibit. . . ."

"And the next day, Vandehey is dead," I finished. "You don't think Special Agent Brown is the killer, do you?"

"You know what I always say — everyone's a suspect . . . at least, until we uncover the truth."

The bells over the shop door jingled, and I whirled around, half expecting a knife-wielding maniac. Instead, it was a Chanel-purse-wielding Vera Langhorne.

"Gracious, darling! What's happening in the alley?"

"Excuse me." Ted gave me a quick kiss and said that he should probably get back outside since Manu had undoubtedly finished his call and gone back out himself.

With that, my noble lawman escaped, leaving me to Vera's inquisition.

"What is it?" she asked. "What's going on?"

I quickly — and with as little drama as possible — explained that I'd taken the garbage out this morning and discovered

52

someone wrapped in a rug lying in the alley.

"Was this a *dead* someone?" Vera asked.

I nodded.

"Again?"

"Again?" I huffed. "What do you mean, *again*? I've never found a body in the alley before!"

"I know, I know, darling." She sat on the sofa facing away from the window and put her purse on the coffee table. "I guess I'm thinking of the time you found that man in your storeroom. That was dreadful." She petted Angus and cooed, "Hello, my sweet boy," before looking back up at me. "Was finding this person as bad as that?"

"Of course it was," I said, sitting on the sofa across the square from Vera. "Who gets used to stumbling over dead bodies?"

"Police, I imagine," she said. "Maybe journalists, too — I'll have to ask Paul — although neither of those groups find many dead bodies on their own, do they? They're notified of the occurrence beforehand so they have a few minutes to steel their nerves or what have you. But not you, darling. Time and again, you get surprised by . . . . well, you know."

I merely listened to Vera's rambling and stroked Angus's wiry fur.

53

"So, this person you found," she continued. "Was it anyone we know? Or *knew,* rather?"

"Um . . . no. No positive identification of the body has been made yet, but I don't think we knew the man. At least, I didn't know him."

"And you say he was wrapped in a rug?" she asked. "What kind of rug?"

I was carefully weighing my answer to that question when Vera's journalist boyfriend, Paul Samms, came rushing into the shop.

"What's the story with the body in the alley?" Paul asked in lieu of a greeting. "I was halfway between here and Lincoln City — on my way to do a piece on a clambake — but turned around when I heard over the police scanner that there was a body found in the alley behind the Seven-Year Stitch. This story is clearly much better than a clambake."

Not for the guy in the alley, I thought. I blinked twice. The similarities between Paul and Vera were becoming more apparent by the second.

He seemed to notice his beloved at last. "Hello, Vera, love. So, what's the scoop?"

"We were just getting to that," she said. "Marcy?"

Once again, I told my tale of the garbage

drop discovery.

Paul sat on the sofa beside Vera and took out his pen and notebook. "Which sounds better? *Mysterious Body Found Dead in Alley Behind Embroidery Shop* or *Man Reaches His Dead End Behind the Seven-Year Stitch*?"

"The second one is catchier," Vera said. "You need to be sure the reader understands that the man *is* the dead end, though."

"Do you have to mention my shop? I mean, at least in the headline could you say something like . . ." I scrambled to come up with a clever headline that didn't implicate my embroidery shop as the scene of the crime. "How about *Dead Man Found Near Museum*?"

"I thought you found him in your alley," Vera said.

"Right . . . but the alley is only one street over from the museum," I said.

Paul tapped his pen against the notebook. "You think this murder has something to do with the museum? With the textile exhibit?"

"What aren't you telling us?" Vera leaned over so far that she could've placed her elbows on the coffee table.

I bit my lip. "I'm not at liberty to say. Nothing — not even the identity of the victim — has been verified yet."

"But who do you think it is?" Paul asked.

When I hesitated to answer, he added, "You know I won't print anything without confirming it with Manu first. Whatever you tell me right now is completely off the record."

"The police believe it *could* be someone named Vandehey," I said. "See? I don't even have a first name."

"Do you know whether or not this Vandehey is — or was — an art history professor?" Paul asked.

"Ted did call him Professor Vandehey."

He nodded. "Geoffrey — with a *G* — Vandehey."

"You said it was off the record!" I protested as he wrote the name down.

"It is." He grinned. "Right now I'm not article-writing. I'm doodle-thinking. It helps me get my thoughts in order."

"Who is this Geoffrey Vandehey?" Vera asked.

"He is — or was, prior to his fall from grace — an expert in all forms of antique art," Paul said. "I'm talking jewelry, textiles, sculptures, pottery, and, of course, paintings. His doctorate was in art history, and he taught at some university in Canada." He frowned up at the ceiling. "I can't for the life of me remember the name of that school."

"You can look it up later," Vera said. "Get on with the story." She softened her tone and smiled. "Please."

"Of course." He smiled at me. "My gal loves a good yarn. So, our Professor Vandehey attended an art show in Seattle. While there, he met a buyer who invited Vandehey to lunch at his home. He wanted the renowned professor's opinion on a recent purchase."

"The Cézanne," I whispered.

Paul's eyebrows shot up. "I'm not the only one knowledgeable about Professor Vandehey."

"You've been holding out on us," Vera said.

"No . . . truly . . . I don't know much about the man at all," I said, inwardly cursing myself for the slip. "I merely heard something about a professor stealing a previously undiscovered Cézanne in Seattle some years back."

Vera narrowed her eyes, but she didn't contradict me.

This time, I was the one who urged Paul to continue his story.

"Well, you're absolutely right, Marcy. The painting the buyer had acquired was undisputedly a Cézanne. Vandehey couldn't bear for the painting to be hidden away by this man that he'd come to realize was terribly crass. He tried to talk the man into donating the painting to a museum, but, of course, the art buyer refused. Vandehey returned later and stole the Cézanne."

"Doesn't that make him every bit as selfish as the art buyer?" Vera asked.

"I don't think so. Poor Vandehey gave up everything he had in order to share the painting with the world — or a small part of it," said Paul. "The art buyer reported the theft to the police and said he strongly suspected Vandehey because the professor had tried to get him to either donate the painting to a museum or sell it to him."

"I wouldn't think a professor would earn enough money to go around buying Cézannes," Vera said. "Did he have a side job?"

"The professor didn't have a lot of money, which is why the buyer scoffed at his offer," Paul said. "Anyway, Vandehey went into hiding. But before doing so, he wrote a letter to the police from his hotel saying that he was donating the painting to a facility where it could be enjoyed by more than one person."

"Was the painting ever recovered?" I asked.

Paul shook his head. "And if the victim

you found this morning was, in fact, Geoffrey Vandehey, then it might never be."

Ted came in through the back door, greeted Paul, and then told me that he and Manu were going over to the museum. "Deputies Dayton and Moore are fairly new to the department, and although we're confident they can handle themselves, Special Agent Brown is a bit much to ask of them — or anyone, for that matter — to deal with on their own." He turned to Paul. "Manu will be giving a press conference this afternoon at the station."

"I'll be there," Paul said.

"Paul was just regaling us with a story about Professor Geoffrey Vandehey," Vera said.

Ted's eyes flew to mine.

"It wasn't Marcy's fault," Paul said quickly. "She told me that nothing had been verified."

"I did say — off the record — that the victim *might* be Professor Vandehey," I said.

"If it *is* Vandehey, then I might be able to point you in the direction of a viable suspect," Paul said.

"Who's that?" Ted asked.

"Chad Cummings, the buyer from whom Vandehey stole the Cézanne. He was at the exhibit last night."

Ted's eyes widened. "Are you kidding me? How did I not know that?"

"Why would you?" Paul asked. "There's no reason Cummings would be on your radar. He hasn't done anything wrong."

"Well, maybe he hadn't before last night," Vera said. "Wait. Did I meet this Cummings fellow?"

"No, dear. I believe you were talking with that aromatherapy lady." Paul frowned. "I find her terribly off-putting."

I could understand that. Ever since I'd opened my shop, Nellie Davis — proprietress of the aromatherapy shop two doors down from the Seven-Year Stitch — had all but tried to have me run out of town. She'd even hinted to a reporter once that my shop was cursed. I'd been half expecting her to show up with a flaming torch and a pitchfork for months now. In fact, this latest discovery might lead her to round up a gaggle of angry villagers this very night.

"I don't care for Nellie all that much myself," Vera said. "But she does carry some good products in her store."

"Back to Cummings," Paul told Ted. "I'd done an article on him several months before his acquisition of the Cézanne and the matter with Vandehey, so when I spotted him, I went over to say hello. His wife is an embroidery enthusiast, so he brought her to Tallulah Falls for the weekend to enjoy the exhibit."

"Thank you, Paul," said Ted. "I think you just earned yourself an exclusive."

CHAPTER FIVE

After everyone left, Angus napped and I was bored. Ted and Manu were gone. Vera and Paul had left almost immediately after Ted and Manu. I wouldn't be surprised to discover that Barbara Walters and Sam Donaldson had trailed after the police in order to get "the scoop."

There weren't even any customers dropping in. On a Saturday! I wondered if they'd heard about the body in the alley and had stayed away because either they assumed the shop would be closed or they were creeped out about the murder.

I sighed. And even though he was half-asleep, Angus heaved a sigh of his own. What loyalty.

Still, if my life were a musical, this is the point where I'd begin to dejectedly sweep the floor. As I swept, I'd sing, of course — a slow and sultry tune — the Gal Who Found the Murdered Guy Blues.

After the first verse, Jill would come to life and harmonize with me. Suddenly, we'd be in evening gowns dancing around with a gorgeous cast of characters. And then the song would fade. The lights would go down, leaving me alone in a spotlight. I'd be dressed in my jeans again. I'd toss aside the broom, hug my dog, and belt out the ending of the song.

Did I mention that my mom was a costume designer? Having a parent entrenched in Hollywood was pretty much a guarantee that I'd have a rich imagination. I felt I'd outdone myself with my musical number, though. In fact, I was just getting ready to call Mom and fill her in — together, we probably could even have come up with words to the song! — when a man walked into the shop.

He was above-average height, a little too thin, and had shoulder-length, wavy brown hair streaked with gray. He had a prominent nose, and he strode with his chin lifted as if he were sniffing the air.

Angus slowly stood but did not approach the man.

"Oh, my," the man said in a British accent. "Is he aggressive?"

"No." I smiled at the man as I stroked Angus's back. "He was sleeping, and you must've startled him." The dog sat at my side and watched the newcomer.

"So sorry about that." He reached into the pocket of his linen blazer and handed me a business card. SIMON BENTON, ART COLLECTOR.

"Welcome to the Seven-Year Stitch, Mr. Benton. I'm Marcy Singer. How may I help you?"

"I understand you made an unpleasant discovery here this morning." Before I could respond, he raised his hands. "Please don't be alarmed. I'm not an investigator or a tabloid reporter or any of that nonsense. I'm merely concerned about the rug. It was an antique kilim, was it not?"

"It appeared to be."

"Was it from the exhibit that premiered at the museum last night?" he asked. "You *are* familiar with the textile exhibit, I presume."

"Yes," I said. "I attended the opening."

"I imagined you would, with your interest in" — he waved one arm airily — "this sort of thing. So . . . what of the rug?"

"What about it?" I was hedging. I wasn't prepared to answer this stranger's questions.

"Was it one of the kilims displayed at the museum?"

"I have no idea, Mr. Benton."

"Well, then, more important, do you

believe the rug can be restored?"

"Again, I have no way of knowing that," I said. "When I saw the rug, it was rolled up. It appeared to be badly stained, but I couldn't see the extent of the damage."

"Ah . . . well . . . that's too bad, isn't it?"

"Yes, it is." I shook my head. "And as much as it pains me to say it, that lovely kilim is most likely a lost cause. It's now evidence in a police investigation. Even if it *could* be cleaned, it won't be."

"Yes, I see your point. I wasn't thinking past saving that antique rug."

"We don't *know* that the rug was an antique," I said.

"Of course we don't. . . . Not yet, anyway. The museum hasn't gone public with any news of a theft."

I drew my eyebrows together. "Gone public? Do you know something I don't?"

"I went to the museum this morning. It was closed, and there were a couple Tallulah Falls deputy police cars there," he said. "There were a few journalists there as well. That's where I first heard of your grim discovery, whispers about the museum having been burgled, and the likelihood that the kilim you saw had been taken from the exhibit."

"All of that is mere speculation right now

— except for the fact that I did indeed find a body in the alley outside my shop this morning. I hope the museum exhibit is safe and sound." I was pretty certain that it wasn't, but I desperately hoped I was wrong. It would be a shame for the museum's first major event in recent history to end in disaster. Who knew if Tallulah Falls Museum would *ever* get another exhibit to display?

"That is my hope also," said Mr. Benton. "However, I'm not optimistic about that. Back to the rug — do you think you could re-create it?"

"Re-create it?" I echoed. "You mean, draw you a picture of the rug I saw?"

"No, silly girl. I'm asking if you could make a rug like the one you saw."

"For one thing, I didn't see the rug lying flat." Unless it *was* the kilim from the museum exhibit, but I wasn't going to tell Mr. Benton that. "And, for another thing, even if I had seen and could reproduce the pattern, I don't weave rugs."

"Hmmm . . . too bad." He wandered around the shop then, looking at the projects I had placed on the walls and shelves. "You did all these?"

"I did."

"You appear to be quite the accomplished

66

needle crafter." Mr. Benton turned back around to face me. "You do no weaving at all?"

"Well, I might've woven a potholder or two at summer camp at some point, but I've never woven a rug."

"And you don't know of anyone who does?" he asked.

"No, I'm afraid I don't." I wondered about his fascination with the kilim. Even if I — or anyone else — could whip up a rug exactly like the one in which Professor Vandehey had been wrapped, it still wouldn't be *that rug.* It would be nowhere near as valuable, especially if it were the rug from the museum exhibit.

As if reading my mind, Mr. Benton said, "Not only am I a collector. I'm a bit of an entrepreneur. I help others create prints and replicas based on original works of art . . . for a percentage of the profits, of course."

"What a wonderful idea."

"I agree." He lifted a shoulder in a half shrug. "It makes beautiful art available to the masses and helps perpetuate appreciation for the original. Unfortunately, Mr. Ingle, the museum curator, doesn't seem to be open to such a venture."

"Maybe he simply doesn't know how to go about creating a collection based on the current exhibit," I said. "You have to admit, textiles are more difficult to duplicate than paintings."

"That's true." He smiled slightly. "And yet, for one so young, Mr. Ingle seems to be very much — how do I say this? — of an old mind."

I laughed. "I guess he prefers traditional curating methods."

"Do you know him well?"

"No. I met him for the first time last night."

With his hands shoved in the pockets of his khaki pants, he strolled over to the counter. "You have a charming boutique here, Ms. Singer."

"Thank you."

"Would you have dinner with me?"

My eyes widened. Had I heard him correctly? One instant we were talking about Josh Ingle, and the next Mr. Benton was inviting me to dinner? "Excuse me?"

"Would you . . . and your husband or whoever . . . like to dine with me this evening?" he asked. "I'm only in town for a few days. At this point, I'm primarily awaiting word on the status of the museum exhibit. I know hardly anyone here, you seem pleasant enough, and I detest sitting alone in a restaurant."

I had no idea when Ted and Manu would finish up for the day; plus, I didn't know how Ted would feel about my accepting an invitation for both of us to have dinner with a stranger. "I'm sorry, Mr. Benton, but we already have plans this evening."

"Very well. Perhaps another time." He nodded and left.

The entire encounter was odd, and I felt mildly unsettled as I sat back down on the sofa. Picking up on my mood, Angus sat close to me and placed his head on my lap. I caressed his ears and then leaned over to give him a hug.

"Could today get any weirder, Angus? Wait. Don't answer that." I was half-afraid he might.

I glanced at the clock and saw that it was nearly four o'clock. A few customers had filtered in but not nearly as many as on a typical Saturday. I walked around the store with a feather duster, flicking it over the shelves. Angus lay by the window watching the few people on the sidewalk pass by. It dawned on me that it wasn't just the Seven-Year Stitch that was experiencing a lull. The entire town seemed dead today. Maybe everyone was at the beach. That seemed like a wonderful place to be, in my opinion. If

Ted finished up with work in time, it would be great to take Angus to the beach. The frisky pup could romp in the sand and play at the edge of the water while Ted and I enjoyed a leisurely stroll.

I took my phone from the front pocket of my jeans and called Ted. I was going to ask how he felt about a picnic by the sea, but the call went straight to voice mail. I left a message saying I was thinking about him and hoping the investigation was going well.

Then I called Mom. I had a sudden need to vent and was thankful when she answered on the first ring.

"Hello, darling. Is everything all right?"

I hesitated.

"Oh, Marcella . . . there hasn't been another murder in Tallulah Falls, has there?"

She'd said it almost lightly, as if she were joking but scared that what she was asking would be verified.

"There *has* been another murder, Mom. I found the body this morning in the alley behind the shop."

"No! Oh, my darling, I'm so sorry. How are you?"

"I'm fine. . . . Really, I am . . . at least, as fine as can be expected," I said. "I mean, I am sad for the man who was killed and for his family, if he had any. . . ." I blew out a breath. "But why did he have to be dumped behind the Seven-Year Stitch?"

"I'm sorry," Mom repeated. "What is up with that place? It seems that sleepy little town of yours has more crime than all of San Francisco — maybe San Francisco and L.A. combined!"

"I'm sure it only looks that way because Tallulah Falls is so small. Whenever anything happens here, it's a big deal and everyone knows about it . . . whereas that's not so much the case in San Fran."

"I guess you're right," she said. "Still, the number of incidents happening in or near your shop is unusually high. I wonder if you should call an exorcist."

I chuckled. She didn't. "Wait. Are you serious?"

"No," she said quickly. "That is, unless you think it might be a good idea. I'm almost positive I have the number of a director who became close friends with a priest after he came and cleansed . . . or blessed . . . or did whatever needed to be done to scare away some evil spirits that were plaguing a movie set."

"Huh." I mulled that over for a moment, trying to picture the scene in my mind. The only thing I could come up with was something like a witch doctor from a Saturday morning cartoon show. I knew exorcists didn't go around dressed as witch doctors, but I thought the costume would make things more dramatic somehow. It would step it up a notch from the priest all dressed in black with the exception of his white collar.

"So do you want me to give the director a call?" Mom asked.

"No." I shook myself out of my reverie. "I was merely imagining how something like that might work. I've been pretty whimsical today." I told her about the musical number I daydreamed.

"That sounds positively charming! Maybe you should try your hand at screenwriting, Marcella."

"I might . . . one of these days," I said. "I'd better clear this latest hurdle before I even think about anything else."

"My sweet girl . . . you sound so melancholy. Do you need me to come to Tallulah Falls?"

"No, Mom. I don't think you're a hundred percent recovered from your last visit yet." The last time Mom had visited Tallulah Falls, she'd gotten embroiled in her very own murder mystery. She was even a prime suspect!

"Nonsense. If you need me, I'll be on the

next plane headed your way."

"I know, and I love you for being so supportive. But everything is fine," I said. "Ted and Manu already have some terrific leads. I'm sure they'll have the investigation wrapped up in no time."

"Okay . . . but if you need me to fly out —"

"If I do, I'll let you know." I paused. "Is it horrible of me to wish the poor man had been found by anyone else and anywhere except behind my shop?"

"Of course not, darling. That's only human." She sighed. "But try to look on the bright side — you could've found him outside your *house.*"

"That's the best you could do for a bright side?" I asked. "Really?"

"I didn't have much to work with," she said. "Did you know the man . . . the man who was killed?"

"No, I'd never seen him before."

"And you don't have any idea why he was killed?"

"Although they haven't made a positive ID yet, the police believe the man was Professor Geoffrey Vandehey," I said. "I'm not entirely sure what the motive for his death may have been, but it's possible it was a heist gone wrong. The professor had confessed to stealing a painting — an early Cézanne — a few years ago."

"So you think maybe he was involved in some heist, and then his partners killed him to take his share?" she asked.

"I believe that's possible. Get this — the professor was wrapped in a rug, and the rug looked an awful lot like an antique kilim on display at the Tallulah Falls Museum's newest exhibit, which opened last night."

"Doesn't that negate your theory, then? Why would his killer wrap him in an antique kilim, thus destroying a valuable piece of art?"

"I'm guessing the murderer didn't know the value of the rug, if it was indeed a kilim from the exhibit," I said. "That, or else he stole the entire collection and didn't feel that one rug made much difference."

"Either way, wouldn't a museum robbery narrow the suspect list down to the museum staff?"

"Not necessarily. But the last I heard, the museum theft was only speculation. Besides, in Tallulah Falls, nothing is ever what it seems at face value."

CHAPTER SIX

I was turning off the lights in the back of the shop when I heard the bells over the door jingle.

"I'll be right there!" I called. I didn't know whether to be glad I had a customer or apprehensive that it was a Nosy Nellie coming to find out more about the body found in the alley. Worse yet, it could be Nosy Nellie *Davis* from the aromatherapy boutique. She might have gathered up enough villagers, torches, and pitchforks to pay me a visit. Come to think of it, she might be willing to take Mom up on the offer of an exorcist because she thought my *cursed* shop was bad for business.

To my relief, when I emerged from the back of the store, I saw Ted playing with Angus.

I laughed. "I'm so glad to see you!"

Ted straightened and pulled me into his arms. "How glad?"

I drew his mouth down to mine and kissed him passionately.

"Wow." He grinned. "I'd have to say you're delighted to see me."

"I am."

He hugged me tightly. "I'm glad to see you, too, sweetheart. It has been a long, exhausting day."

"I was going to suggest a picnic on the beach," I said. "Now I'm thinking pizza and a movie rental might be better."

Ted cupped my face in his hands and gave me a tender kiss. "You know, I think I'd prefer the picnic if you're still up for it. That sounds like the perfect way to unwind."

"I agree. Want to walk down to MacKenzies' Mochas with me and get the food?"

"Sure. I don't want you to forget the brownies," he said. "And we should probably get a peanut butter cookie for Angus."

At the sound of his name, Angus burrowed between us.

Ted laughed. "I think we can take that as a *yes, we should.*"

Ted and I stepped out the front door, and I locked it. As we walked past the window, Angus barked at us and paced back and forth. I held up an index finger and promised him we'd be back in "one minute."

"Do you think he understood that?" Ted teased.

"Of course I do. He understands everything I say. We have an almost telepathic relationship." I looked up at his handsome profile. "You don't believe me, do you?"

"Actually, I do," he said with a smile. "The more I see the two of you together, the more I realize what a special bond the two of you have."

"Did you ever have a dog growing up?"

He shook his head. "My mom had a poodle, but it died when I was a baby. I can remember having goldfish, a frog, a turtle . . . and my sister had a rabbit . . . but we never got another dog."

"That's sad. I mean, do you think your mom just never got over the loss of her poodle?"

"I think she didn't want the responsibility," he said. "It was all Mother could do to take care of Tiffany and me."

"Does she have any pets now?" I asked.

"Nope. She lives in one of those upscale condos where she can make the staff do all her bidding. She loves it."

At that point, we were at MacKenzies' Mochas.

Ted opened the door. "After you, my lady."

Blake was standing at the counter. "Hey, now! Don't let Sadie see you treating Marcy like a queen! She'll expect me to step up my game."

We laughed. Ted and I both knew that Blake already treated his wife like royalty.

"You're in a punchy mood this afternoon," I said.

"Sadie and I took the evening off," he said. "We'd planned on attending the museum exhibit tonight, but we heard it's been shut down."

Ted nodded. "Manu is giving a press conference. The museum was robbed, and the majority of the Padgett Collection was taken."

"That's terrible. I hope you find the thief. . . . Still," Blake continued, "a night off is a night off. I'm looking forward to it, no matter what we do."

Ted and I exchanged glances. I could tell we were wondering the same thing — *should we invite Blake and Sadie to go to the beach with us?* I felt it was entirely Ted's call. He was the one who'd spent the day investigating a murder while I'd merely meandered around the shop waiting for the nonexistent customers to come in. On the other hand, Blake had rushed to my side this morning immediately after getting Ted's call.

"We came by for some food to take on a beach picnic," Ted said. "Would you guys like to join us?"

"That sounds like fun," Blake said. "Let me check with Sadie."

When Blake left to find his wife, Ted turned to me and whispered, "I hope you don't mind."

"Not at all. I was thinking the same thing but thought you might be too tired to entertain another couple."

"Angus will entertain all of us," he said. "Besides, I get the feeling it'll be a short night, anyway. Blake probably wants to be alone with Sadie almost as much as I want to be alone with you."

When Blake returned, he was wearing his mock serious expression. He would draw his eyebrows together to try to look severe, but the twinkle in his blue eyes and the fact that his dimpled smile was bursting to reveal itself ruined the effect for him.

"We'll go on one condition," he said. "We provide the food . . . no charge."

"We didn't invite you along in order to take advantage of your generosity," I said. "I insist that we pay."

"And I insist that you don't. Besides, the invitation really came from Ted."

"That's true," Ted said, with a grin. "And

I have no problem whatsoever taking advantage of MacKenzie's generosity."

I playfully smacked Ted's arm while he and Blake shared a fist bump.

"My boy, Angus, wants you to bring him a peanut butter cookie," Ted told Blake. "So make sure that generosity extends to including a cookie."

"I'll bring two just to show you how great a guy I am," Blake said. "Tell Angus I'll fix him right up. Do you guys want to meet at the lighthouse in about half an hour?"

"That sounds good," I said. "I have to feed Angus before we go. If I don't, he'll wind up stealing the entire picnic."

"Then, by all means, feed the little guy, but make sure he saves room for dessert." Blake winked.

We arrived at the lighthouse right on schedule. Ted was driving my Jeep while I held on to a stack of blankets and Angus hung his head out the window sniffing the salty air. Blake and Sadie were already there setting up our picnic beneath a tent.

"Wow, you guys really outdid yourselves," I said as I got out of the car and clipped Angus's leash onto his collar.

"Hey, we like to be prepared for anything," Blake said. "You want a picnic? I can throw one together for you" — he snapped his fingers — "just like that."

"Only because we bought that tent to use at a Lincoln City Summer Fair last year and Blake keeps a card table and some folding chairs in the van," Sadie said.

"To be prepared for anything," Blake repeated, shaking his head.

"I think you did a great job," Ted said. "This is a pretty sweet setup. You must have been a Boy Scout, MacKenzie."

"Since when did you two become the Lone Ranger and Tonto?" Sadie asked.

"What do you mean?" Blake frowned. "We've always been friends."

I could see Sadie's point. There had been times in the past when Ted and Blake did not always see eye to eye. But, unlike Sadie, Blake had been more accepting of my relationship with Ted.

When I had first moved to Tallulah Falls, Sadie and Blake tried to fix me up with their friend Todd Calloway. He and I had become friends and gone out on the occasional "date," but I had always had more of a connection . . . more chemistry . . . more everything . . . with Ted. I think Blake had been able to see that all along, but Sadie had held on to her hope that Todd and I would heal each other's bruised hearts and live happily ever after. But I wound up with Ted, and soon after, Todd began dating Deputy Audrey Dayton.

Angus suddenly drew everyone's attention away from the small talk by chasing after a seagull. It was especially captivating since I was still holding his extend-a-leash, and he dragged me with him for a few feet until I could get him stopped. He'd had obedience training, but sometimes in his excitement that discipline went out the window.

"Please don't chase the birds," I told him once I had him sufficiently distracted by the peanut butter cookie Blake had handed me. The guy really *was* prepared for anything.

"I don't know," said Blake. "He has a point in running them off. Those pesky little guys can ruin a picnic in a hurry."

"Plus, it's against the law to feed them," Ted said. "So it's best that you avoid temptation, Marcy."

"Oh, that is so true," Sadie said. "When we were roommates in college, Marce fed everything. She would even leave bread crumbs on the windowsill outside our room for the ants."

"It was just that one time! Don't you ever forget anything?" I asked.

"You have to admit, that was pretty unforgettable," Sadie said, laughter bubbling up in her voice.

"I need to hear more of these college stories," Ted said.

But as we sat down on the lightly padded blue chairs and began to fill our plates, our conversation turned more serious.

"Someone came into the coffee shop this afternoon and said the textile exhibit had been shut down because the museum was robbed," Sadie said to Ted. "Is that true?"

Ted nodded. "I was filling Blake and Marcy in on it earlier." He squeezed a packet of mustard onto his ham sandwich while Angus watched with extreme interest. "I'll save you a bite, buddy."

"So the rug that was in the alley this morning" — my appetite waned at the memory — "it *was* the kilim from the exhibit?"

"Yes," Ted said. "And the victim was Dr. Vandehey."

Sadie paused with her cup of peach tea halfway to her lips. "Vandehey . . . why does that sound familiar?"

Ted explained how Dr. Vandehey had stolen the newly discovered Cézanne, had confessed to the crime and been pursued by federal authorities, but had avoided capture.

"No, that's not it. That's a good story, but

I'd never heard it before," Sadie said, turning to Blake. "I think Vandehey was the name of the man Josh was complaining about the other day."

"You're right," Blake said. "Josh called him Professor Know-It-All."

"Are you talking about Josh Ingle?" Ted asked.

"The museum curator?" I added.

"Yeah," Blake said. "Josh thought this Vandehey guy was really obnoxious."

"Playing devil's advocate, though, Josh can be pretty sensitive when it comes to his job," said Sadie, sipping her tea and then putting the cup back down on the table. "See, Josh is working hard on his master's degree at night, but he currently only has a bachelor's degree in art history. The board of directors wanted someone with a master's degree for the position when their current curator retired after thirty years to move to Arizona, but Josh's uncle persuaded them to give him a chance."

"Josh's uncle has deep pockets and is a strong patron of the arts," Blake said.

"Apparently, Professor Vandehey had a doctorate in art history and — to hear Josh tell it — the man either was or thought he was a genius," Sadie said. "He corrected Josh on several points while they were walking around the museum, and it not only made Josh feel dumb, but it made the poor guy fear that the board had brought Vandehey in to take his job."

Ted got out his notebook and pen, flipped the pad open, and wrote something. "I need to find out how long Josh Ingle has been acquainted with Professor Vandehey. If that man has been living in Tallulah Falls under all our noses . . ." He expelled a breath.

"Oh, no, man." Blake waved a hand. "I don't think it was like that at all. Josh didn't start bellyaching about the guy until two . . . maybe three . . . days ago. I think that's when this Vandehey guy blew into town and started making Josh feel inferior."

"Do you think Vandehey came to Tallulah Falls to case the museum?" I asked.

"I believe that's a strong possibility," said Ted.

"Why would he do that?" I tossed Angus a piece of ham from my sandwich. "He was able to stay under the radar for all this time. . . . I mean, he practically got away with stealing a priceless Cézanne. . . . Why would he risk his freedom by coming here and stealing something else?"

"Maybe he ran out of money," Blake said. "Who knows how much he got for the Cézanne, but I'm certain it would be nowhere near what the painting was worth since he couldn't sell it to a legitimate buyer."

"That's true," said Sadie. "And he could hardly apply for a job using his real name and credentials since he was a wanted man."

Ted was shaking his head. "From what the FBI has divulged to us, Vandehey never sold the Cézanne. He is believed to have given it to a small library somewhere. So far, the bureau has been unable to find it, but they believe it's in either Canada or Mexico."

"Then, unless he's independently wealthy, he would definitely need money," said Blake.

"Even if he *was* a wealthy man, the government would freeze his assets to force him out of hiding," Sadie said. "Right, Ted?"

"That's right." He handed the final bite of his ham sandwich to Angus, as promised. "I suppose the library that became the unknowing beneficiary of a stolen piece of artwork might have paid Vandehey a small stipend, but it couldn't have been much."

"Obviously, I never met the man, but it doesn't appear to me that Professor Vandehey was a bad guy," I said. "Yes, he stole a painting. But from what I understand was written in his confession, he simply couldn't stand for it to be in the home of the unappreciative boor who'd acquired it. Was his taking it wrong? Of course. But it doesn't strike me as the action of a greedy man."

"What are you saying?" Sadie asked.

"He doesn't strike me as the type of person who would come to Tallulah Falls after being on the run for years to steal for the sake of stealing," I said. "There had to be a compelling reason for him to come here."

"I agree," said Ted. "And that reason is what I need to find out in order to determine who killed him."

"I think when you find your museum thieves, you'll find your killer," said Blake.

"You're probably right," Ted said. "But I can't go solely on that presumption or else I might overlook something important."

"True," I said. "It could be that Vandehey didn't have anything to do with the theft but that he was recognized and killed because he wouldn't give up the location of the Cézanne."

"And it could be as simple as whoever was giving him the money to live on got tired of doing so," Ted said.

As Sadie and I packed up the picnic, Blake and Ted played ball with Angus. The three of them kept getting farther and farther away.

"I believe the guys are trying to see who can throw the ball the hardest," I said, with a laugh.

"They must be trying to impress Angus," she said.

"My guess is that Ted is trying to tire Angus out so there won't be a furry little face between us when we try to cuddle on the couch later."

"How are you . . . after this morning, I mean?" Sadie asked me.

"I'm okay." I gathered our trash into a small bag, tied it closed, and placed that bag in another one. "I might not be able to sleep tonight. . . . Hopefully, I won't see the professor's face every time I close my eyes. But mainly, I just feel sorry for Dr. Vandehey."

"What do you think happened?"

"I don't know," I said. "For some reason — and maybe it's nothing more than wishful thinking — I don't feel that Dr. Vandehey was here to rob the museum. Maybe he was here to prevent the theft . . . or something. I don't know. I really am grasping at straws. Every instinct I have is telling me that he was a good man caught up in a bad situation."

CHAPTER SEVEN

Both Ted and Manu were supposed to have been off duty this weekend, but my discovery of Dr. Vandehey in the alley and the museum theft had resulted in everyone at the police department working this Sunday morning. I called Reggie and invited her over for brunch. She said she'd be delighted, and that she'd come over in half an hour.

Before I began cooking, I allowed Angus to go into our fenced backyard for his morning romp. On nice days in the fall, winter, and spring, he enjoyed spending quite a bit of time outside. So far this summer, it had been too hot to let him go out for more than a few minutes except in the early morning and late evening.

After Angus went outside, I washed my hands, slipped on my comic-book-heroine apron, and got down to the business of making brunch. I started with blueberry muffins. While the muffins were baking, I set a cutting board on my blue granite counter-top and chopped broccoli and cauliflower to go on the veggie pizza. I then sliced apples, oranges, and kiwi and arranged them on a decorative plate. Once I'd taken the muffins out of the oven and put the pizza in, I made a pitcher of Bellinis and put on a pot of coffee.

I let Angus back in, filled his water bowl, and added a tray of ice cubes. I then refilled the ice tray and put it back ino the freezer. Angus lapped at his water and then retrieved one of the ice cubes and ran off to the hall with it. I could hear him crunching on it as I set the ash square table. Although I didn't have a formal dining room, the size of my kitchen more than made up for that fact.

I'd just taken the pizza out of the oven when Reggie arrived. She rang the doorbell, and Angus raced to the door ahead of me. He woofed a hearty greeting as I clamped my hand on his collar to restrain him from jumping on Reggie the instant I opened the door.

"You have perfect timing," I said. "I just put the finishing touches on our meal."

She looked relaxed and elegant in a white tunic and pants and silver jewelry. She carried a shopping bag. "Something sure smells delicious." She reached into the bag and handed me a small box of chocolate truffles. "Those are for you. And, of course, I didn't forget about Angus." She took out a mint-flavored bone designed to clean his teeth and freshen his breath. "I thought maybe he could use this after brunch."

I laughed as I took it out of the package and handed it to him. "Or, hopefully, it will keep him busy while we eat."

Angus took his treasure to the living room while Reggie and I went into the kitchen.

"We'll never be able to eat all this food," Reggie said. She picked up a blueberry muffin and inhaled its aroma. "Then again . . ."

"I thought that what we didn't eat we could save for Manu and Ted. I really hate that they had to work today."

"Me, too. But that's the life." She shrugged. "Had you made special plans for today?"

"We'd just planned to take a drive up the coast," I said. "It wasn't a big deal. I was looking forward to spending the day with Ted. . . . That's all. And then I had to stumble over a body in the alley!"

"Even if you hadn't discovered Professor Vandehey, someone would have. . . . Plus, the museum was robbed on top of everything."

We filled our plates and sat down. At her

request, I poured Reggie a cup of coffee, and I had a Bellini cocktail.

"Manu and Ted are fairly certain Dr. Vandehey's murder and the museum theft are connected, aren't they?" I asked.

She nodded as she put butter on her muffin. "Josh Ingle is, too. He's terrified he'll lose his job over this whole mess, even though he took a lot of extra security measures to protect the exhibit."

"What's your opinion of Josh?" I asked.

"I don't know him terribly well, but I like him all right. Why?"

"Well, I had a customer come in Friday before the museum exhibit opening, and she expressed a reluctance to go to the event because she was afraid she'd run into Josh," I said. "I encouraged her to go and told her she could hang out with us."

"Was she the young woman who introduced herself to us?" Reggie asked.

"Yes," I said. "And immediately after that, Josh came up and she took off."

"I remember that."

"So, based on her opinion and reaction to Josh, I was wary of him. But Blake and Sadie seem to think he's great," I said.

"I imagine he visits the coffeehouse quite often," she said. "So maybe they know him better than your customer does. It sometimes takes only one unpleasant encounter to ruin an entire relationship with someone."

"True. Blake and Sadie did mention that they believe Josh's uncle influenced the board of directors to give him his job as curator. Do you think he's competent?"

"I had no reason to think otherwise — nor did anyone else — before the theft," she said. "And he *had* taken more than adequate security measures. Still, I don't think anyone — Josh, the board of directors, or the security guards — really expected anything to happen Friday evening." She sipped her coffee. "I believe they thought the worst-case scenario would be someone getting drunk off the free champagne and making a scene."

"If you'll recall, the only concern Ted and Manu both really expressed was that the museum would exceed maximum occupancy." I took a bite of my pizza. The still-warm crust, tangy sauce, and crisp vegetables made a delicious combination. "Ted said the thieves stole the majority of the Padgett Collection."

"They did. There were a couple of the bigger pieces that they left behind," she said. "And it breaks my heart that they so carelessly ruined that kilim." Her eyes widened.

"And that they killed the professor, of course!"

I smiled. "I know what you meant, Reggie. It's all right to say that we're not only sad that a man lost his life but that an antique rug was destroyed as well."

"I guess. . . . It makes me feel callous to even think it, though."

"You're anything but callous." I tasted the refreshing Bellini. "Was anything besides pieces from the Padgett Collection stolen from the museum?"

"No. It appears the thieves were specific in what they wanted. They left everything else in the museum alone."

"That seems odd to me," I said. "If I wanted to rob a museum, I'd make the most of it and take everything I possibly could."

"Maybe they did. What if Vandehey wasn't in collusion with the thieves? He might've interrupted them in the midst of the heist and spoiled their plan."

"And got himself killed in the process."

"That's only one theory," Reggie reminded me.

"I know," I said. "What about the security cameras? Didn't they provide a clue as to who was behind the heist?"

"The cameras had been shot with paint-ball guns immediately. The person or persons who shot the lenses were masked, wore coveralls, and had on gloves."

"What about the alarm system?"

"It didn't go off at all," she said. "That's why no one knew about the theft until after you found Professor Vandehey wrapped in a rug taken from the exhibit. It was disabled also."

"That really sounds like an inside job, don't you think?"

"It seems that way. I believe Manu and Ted are spending the day interviewing all the staff and reinterviewing the security guards they spoke with yesterday."

"What about the art collector, Mr. Padgett?" I asked. "I mean, the collection was undoubtedly insured, but he has to be upset about the loss."

"I imagine so. I haven't heard anything about that yet, though."

"Is the museum offering a reward?"

"They want to," Reggie said. "The board of directors suggested that to Manu first thing when he spoke with them yesterday. They thought it would be a good way to pacify the collector and get the public to speak up if anyone knew anything about the heist or the missing items."

"I get the feeling there's a *but* in there somewhere," I said.

"Manu told them to wait. He said it would only muddy the waters at this point." She added more apple slices to her plate. "He told the board they should wait to see if the collection is ransomed back to them."

"You mean, like a kidnapping?" I asked.

"Exactly like a kidnapping. Art is usually stolen either to resell or to ransom back to the victim," she said. "If the thieves plan to ransom the textiles back to the museum, they'll call and make their demands within the next day or so."

"So Manu thinks that offering a reward would hinder the investigation somehow?"

She nodded. "Everyone and his or her brother would want that reward. Our police department is too small to follow every possible lead, especially those pulled out of thin air in the hope of reaping some of the reward money."

"I see."

"But if the leads they're pursuing don't pan out, he'll let them go ahead and post the reward." She bit an apple slice in half. "Maybe some students from the academy or the criminal science program at the community college will help out at that point."

After Reggie left, I spent the rest of the afternoon working on my latest project, a floral bouquet pillow. The piece had fuchsia lilies, white tulips, and pink roses. It would look lovely when it was made into a pillow. I had two quandaries, though: Did I want to put a gold tasseled border or a braided dark green border on the pillow? And did I want to keep the pillow here at home and place it on the white, overstuffed chair in my living room, or did I want to take it to the Seven-Year Stitch and place it among the candlewick embroidery pillows on one of the navy sofas? I was leaning more and more toward the gold border and displaying the pillow in my living room.

As I stitched and listened to the crunching noises Angus made while gnawing on his granola bone, I thought back to the conversation Reggie and I'd had over brunch. Could she be right about Professor Vandehey? Had he been killed because he'd interrupted the heist? Or had he been part of the robbery team from the very beginning and been killed so that the thieves didn't have to give him his share? The latter scenario made more sense to me. And yet I couldn't shake my feeling that the professor had been a good man at heart. Maybe that was it — maybe he'd agreed to take part in the robbery but had backed out, and the thieves had killed him to ensure his silence.

I determined to find out more about Dr. Geoffrey Vandehey. I'd start with a computer search later tonight or tomorrow morning. If that didn't satisfy my curiosity, I'd talk with Paul Samms.

I continued working on the pillow until Ted called.

"Hi, beautiful," he said when I answered.

"Hi, yourself. You sound exhausted."

"I am pretty beat. I just got home and I'm going to take a shower. Would you mind if I take a quick nap before coming over?"

"Why don't I come to you?" I said. "I can pick up some food and a movie."

"You're awesome," he said. "Bring Angus, too."

"Are you sure?"

"Positive."

"See you in a few," I said.

I placed my pillow, embroidery floss, and scissors in my tote bag so I could take the project to work with me tomorrow. Hopefully, business would be back to normal on Monday.

"Angus, do you want to go see Ted?" I asked.

He got up, tail wagging. He understood the word *go* and was always ready. Whether it was for a walk or for a drive, it made no difference to Angus. He pranced around impatiently while I put the tote away.

"Do you mind if I go upstairs and freshen up a little?"

When he saw me head toward the stairs, he sighed and flopped back down onto the floor as if I'd tricked him.

"We'll go in just a minute!" I called over my shoulder.

I knew some people would think me insane for talking to my dog as if he were a person, but why shouldn't I? For one thing, I was absolutely positive that he understood me. Besides, I talked to Jill sometimes, and she was a mannequin.

I hurried into the bedroom, changed tops, and reapplied my makeup. I slipped on a pair of peep-toe wedges and called the pizza parlor as I walked back down the stairs. I placed the order and grabbed Angus's leash, and he hurried over without my even having to call him. I told you we understood each other.

Fortunately, the pizza parlor Ted and I frequented had a movie-rental kiosk outside, so I was able to hop out of the Jeep and leave the engine running long enough to choose a movie and then get back in and go around to the drive-through window. That way, I didn't have to let Angus out of my sight.

After I'd paid for the pizza and placed it in the passenger seat, I was really glad there was a doggy barrier between the front seats and backseats. It still allowed Angus to put his big furry head over the seat, but it didn't give him enough room to snuffle the pizza box as he so desperately wanted to do.

When we arrived at Ted's apartment, he answered the door in jeans and a T-shirt. He was barefoot and his hair was still wet from his shower. He smelled yummy in a very masculine way.

He greeted me with a kiss before taking the pizza so I could unclip Angus's leash. Both the dog and I followed Ted into the kitchen. Unlike my country kitchen, Ted's was ultramodern. The appliances were stainless steel, the cabinets were glossy black with thin, tubular silver handles, and the countertops were dark gray granite. There were skylights and recessed lighting over the island and a chandelier over the table in the breakfast nook.

Ted placed the pizza on the table as I put my purse on the counter. We turned, and he took me in his arms for a more passionate embrace.

"I've missed you today," he said.

"I've missed you, too."

"Thank you for sending Reggie over with

the muffins. They were delicious."

"You're welcome," I said. "I happened to think that she was probably a little lonely, too, so I called and invited her to brunch. We went over our own theories on the robbery."

"Did you come to any conclusions, Inch-High? We could use all the help we can get on this one." After kissing me again, he went to the cabinet and took out some plates.

"We're fairly certain it was an inside job. I mean, it would *have* had to be, wouldn't it? The thieves knew where the cameras were, blacked out the lenses, disabled the security alarm. . . ."

"We feel pretty sure there was someone within the museum helping the thieves," he said. "But we can't rush to judgment. Locating the security cameras and discovering what type of alarm the museum used could have been done by someone on the outside." He opened the box and put slices of the pizza on the plates.

This pie was nothing like the veggie pizza I'd had this morning. This one was ham and pineapple.

"Would you like to eat while watching the movie, or would you prefer to eat here at the table?" he asked.

"Let's eat here at the table. I'd hate to get

pizza sauce on your sofa."

"Says she of the white living room furniture." He winked as he pulled out a chair for me.

I sat down. "Reggie told me you and Manu were questioning all the museum staff today, including the guards you spoke with yesterday."

"Yeah, we needed to make sure they were telling the same stories they told last night," he said.

"Did you go through their employment records? Had any of them been disciplined or anything?"

He chuckled. "Yes. Believe it or not, this isn't my first investigation."

"I know. I'm sorry. I didn't mean it that way. I just keep searching my brain for a solution of some sort."

Angus moved closer to me, so I tore off a piece of my crust and gave it to him.

"I know what you meant," Ted said. "Believe me, there's not a painted canvas or a chiseled piece of marble we've left unturned at that museum, and we still don't have anything other than guesses. The thieves apparently left no evidence whatsoever. I feel sorry for our crime scene techs. They're working around the clock to go over every inch of the museum so it can open

102

again by Tuesday."

"Reggie said that art thieves often ransom the art back to the museum or collector," I said. "I take it that hasn't happened?"

"Not yet. Did she mention that less than fifteen percent of stolen art is ever recovered?"

"No. That's depressing."

"It is," he said. "In Boston in 1990, thieves stole thirteen pieces of art from the Isabella Stewart Gardner Museum. The pieces were valued at more than three hundred million dollars and were never recovered. There's still an outstanding reward of five million to anyone who can provide information leading to the return of the works."

"Speaking of rewards, did Manu change his mind about allowing the museum to offer one?" I asked.

"Not yet. If no leads pan out and no ransom demand is given by Tuesday, he'll let the board of directors announce the reward."

"What about Dr. Vandehey? How do you think he figured into this entire plot?"

He shrugged. "Too soon to tell."

We finished eating and went into the living room to watch the movie. Fifteen minutes in, I heard Ted quietly snoring beside me. I extracted myself from his arms, covered him with the afghan from the back of his couch, and turned off the movie. I kissed him tenderly, and then Angus and I left.

CHAPTER EIGHT

Ted was adorably sheepish when he came by the shop the next morning. He even brought me a dozen red roses, which I accepted gratefully but told him was completely unnecessary.

"I felt like such a jerk when I woke up on my couch this morning and realized what had happened," he said. "Was the movie good?"

"I only saw the first few minutes, but it didn't seem to be as great as the commercials made it out to be."

"I don't remember any of it. I did go ahead and drop it back off at the kiosk, but we can rent it again if you'd like to."

I stood on my tiptoes and kissed him. "We'll see where the day takes us."

"I really am sorry I fell asleep on you," he said.

"I'm not. It was nice to see you all vulnerable and sweet." I grinned at his eye roll.

"Besides, I've fallen asleep on you before."

"That's different."

I shook my head. "It only proves that the man of steel is human."

He raised an eyebrow. "So now I'm Superman?"

"You always have been to me."

He pulled me closer. "Oh, I like that." He lowered his head and gave me a toe-curler of a kiss.

Then, naturally — and probably a good thing since we shouldn't be providing a PDA for everyone on the sidewalk — duty called and Ted had to leave. He did say he'd try to be back for lunch.

Not long after Ted left, a cheery woman in a bright pink pantsuit came into the shop.

"Good morning and welcome to the Seven-Year Stitch," I said.

"Hi," she responded a bit breathlessly. "What a wonderful dog! Hello, my dear! How are you? Are you a good boy?"

Angus sat in front of her and even offered his paw when she held out her hand.

She laughed. "Yes, you are a good boy! You are!" She patted his head. "I could tell he was a good dog the instant I walked in. You just know sometimes, don't you? And, of course, you wouldn't have a mean dog running around your shop. That would be bad for business!"

"Wouldn't it, though?"

"Of course, a young woman like you needs some sense of security being here by yourself," she said. "I heard about that dreadful business of a body being found in your alley. What's the world coming to?"

She barely gave me time to admit that I had no idea what the world was coming to before she plowed on, apparently no longer as concerned about the fate of the world as she was about the project she had in mind.

"Do you have some of that perforated cross-stitch paper I've been hearing about?"

"Yes, it —"

"I teach a Sunday school class, and each September some of my students move up to an older class, and I like to give them some sort of little graduation gift — nothing big, just a token really . . . something to remember me by more or less — and this year I'd like to make each of them a bookmark." She looked at me expectantly.

I gave her a second to make sure she wasn't just taking a breath.

"Perforated paper would be excellent to use for bookmarks," I said. "Let me show you what I have."

She and Angus followed me to the corkboard where the fourteen-count perforated paper was hanging. She chose an ecru that "would go with anything" and then bought several skeins of floss.

"Do you think they'll like them?" she asked me as I placed her purchases in a small periwinkle bag.

She was so earnest that I wanted to step around the counter to hug her. "They'll love them. And I'm sure they love you and that you've made an impression on their lives that they'll never forget with or without the bookmarks. But they *will* love the book-marks."

She beamed. "Well, aren't you the sweet-est thing? Thank you!"

"Thank *you,*" I said. "Please stop back in and give me a progress report. And, by the way, I offer needlework classes Tuesday through Thursday. There's a flier in your bag with more information."

"All right. I'll take a look at it."

"Even if you aren't interested in taking a class, the sit-and-stitch square is always open during operating hours," I said.

"Thank you, my dear. I'll be back."

After the lady left, I smiled at Angus. "Today is getting off to a much better start than Saturday did!"

As soon as Vera walked in, she noticed the

flowers on the counter. She hugged Angus and then went straight to smell the roses . . . something Vera always took time to do these days.

"Is it a special occasion, or is he in the doghouse?" she asked me.

I laughed. "Neither."

Vera placed her hand over her heart. "I might swoon."

"I think he actually *thought* he was in the doghouse because he fell asleep on Angus and me while watching a movie last night, but I really didn't mind at all. I knew he was exhausted."

"Poor dear," Vera said. "Paul told me this investigation would be intense. There are so many variables: Was Vandehey's death tied to the theft, or was it a timely coincidence? Had Vandehey been involved in the heist? Were the thieves associated with the museum? There's simply so much to consider."

"I know. I believe Manu, Ted, and their deputies have questioned nearly everyone in Tallulah Falls at least once."

"And they're no closer to having any answers . . . or, if they are, they're keeping their information under wraps."

Before we could discuss the situation further, a tall, thin woman with dark hair in a pixie cut walked into the shop. Her eyes were so unnaturally green that I wondered if they were colored contacts. The woman moved almost timidly in her lacy yellow sundress, and I thought she was afraid of Angus.

"Don't worry," I said. "He's very friendly."

"Oh, I'm not afraid." She smiled slightly but still wore that deer-in-the-headlights expression.

"Welcome to the Seven-Year Stitch. I'm Marcy Singer."

"Yes, well . . . are you open?" she asked. "I heard about your . . . misfortune . . . on Saturday. I thought maybe the shop was a crime scene or something."

"Nope. Everything is business as usual," I said. "The misfortune happened out back in the alley. I think the police still have an area out there blocked off."

Vera sat on the navy sofa facing away from the window and patted the seat beside her. "Why don't you come on over and introduce yourself?"

"Please," I added. "And would either of you care for some coffee or bottled water?"

"I'd love a bottle of water, Marce," Vera said. "Honey, you want something?"

The woman shook her head, but she did sit down beside Vera.

I got Vera a bottle of water from the mini

fridge in my office. When I returned, Angus was sitting by the deer-slash-woman with his head on her knee. She was stroking his ears.

"As I was telling your friend Vera, my name is Sissy . . . Sissy Cummings," she said. "My husband hates my name. My sister started calling me *Sissy* when I was born, and it just stuck. Everyone calls me that . . . except my husband. He calls me Portia — which is my real name, of course — but I prefer Sissy."

"Nice to meet you, Sissy," I said.

"I love needlepoint and embroidery," she said. "I even did some latch-hooking when I was a little girl. When I heard about your shop, I knew I had to get myself here as soon as possible and get some stuff . . . especially since we're staying the week."

"I'm so glad you came in," I said.

"Were you here for the exhibit?" Vera asked.

"Yes, my husband, Chad, is an art collector. He'd heard the collector might be willing to part with some of the pieces, so we came down from Seattle to spend a week or so. Chad was hoping the collector would be here, and he could negotiate with him."

"I imagine the collector will be here soon," Vera said. "I know I certainly would be if *my* collection had been stolen."

"That's why we're still here," said Sissy. "Chad thinks the art collector will come in from Denver or wherever it is he's from and they can do some other wheeling and dealing."

"Who was the collector?" I asked. "I can't recall his name."

"I believe it was Padgett," Vera said. "Anderson Padgett."

"That's right. I remember seeing his name in the paper now." I turned to Sissy. "Are your husband and Mr. Padgett friends?"

"No . . . and I highly doubt they will be after they talk art, either," Sissy said. "Chad is really very sweet, but he can have an overbearing way about him sometimes, especially where art is concerned."

"How about Simon Benton?" I asked. "Do you know him?"

"Vaguely," she said. "Chad and I met him at the exhibit Friday evening. *He* knows the collector from Denver. Apparently, they're good friends."

"He came into the shop Saturday morning," I told Sissy and Vera. "He wanted to know if I thought the rug — the one wrapped around the body of Geoffrey Vandehey — could be restored. I told him that even if it could, the rug was now evidence in an investigation."

"Wow. I guess he was just concerned for his friend's collection," Sissy said. "He'd said that his friend — Mr. Padgett — was older and not in good enough health to come to Oregon, so Benton was here to make sure everything went okay with the exhibit."

"I feel sorry for Mr. Padgett," said Vera. "He's unwell and now has to make a trip to what — file a claim?"

"I wouldn't think he'd have to come to Oregon to file an insurance claim," I said. "Maybe he just wants to come and check things out for himself."

"Probably." Sissy opened the small straw purse she carried and took out her phone. "Oh, no, it's nearly twelve. I have to meet Chad at twelve for lunch. May I come back in later and get some things?"

"Of course," I said.

"I have a list of floss numbers that correspond to my new pattern," she said. "Could you maybe gather those up for me?"

"Certainly. It'll be my pleasure."

Sissy gave Angus a final pat and then hurried out the door.

Vera turned her speculative gaze on me. "There's a woman who's scared to death of her husband. I used to be one of those women, so I recognize the signs when I see them."

"I believe you could be right. Did you notice how she referred to the art belonging to *Chad* instead of *us*?"

Vera nodded. "I wouldn't say Chad Cummings is an abusive husband, but his wife definitely knows who's boss. When she comes back for her embroidery floss, try to get her to come to tomorrow evening's class. I'd like to talk with her some more."

"All right." I was a little wary about what Vera wanted to talk with Sissy about, but I'd still invite her.

Ted arrived with lunch — club sandwiches and kettle-cooked chips — at a quarter past twelve. We went into my office to eat, and I grabbed us a couple sodas from the fridge.

"Vera was in earlier," I told Ted as I sat down across the desk from him. I kept my desk very tidy, partly because it was also our lunch table. "She asked if it was a special occasion or if you were in the doghouse. When I said *neither,* she said she thought she might swoon."

He laughed. "Actually, I wouldn't mind being in Angus's doghouse. I thought I might pop by there after work and take the two of you to the beach . . . this time just the two — I mean, three — of us."

"That sounds like fun. Should I pack a picnic?"

"Definitely not." He opened his chips. "Then all of Tallulah Falls would be tagging along."

"Blake and Sadie are not *all of Tallulah Falls,*" I said. "Besides, they have to work this evening."

"I'm only joking. But I would prefer to keep you to myself tonight." He popped one of the chips into his mouth. "Mmm. These are good."

I tried one. They were. "Yum. Taste this, Angus." I tossed him a chip, and he gobbled it up.

We were unwrapping our sandwiches when the bells over the door jingled.

"Darn," I hissed. "I forgot to put the *Be Back Soon* clock on the door. I'll take care of this customer and then put up the clock."

I hurried out into the shop with Angus on my heels despite the fact that there was ham, turkey, and bacon right there on the desk near him. To my surprise, Josh Ingle was standing at the counter.

"Good afternoon, Mr. Ingle," I said. "How may I help you?"

"I'm actually here to see Ted Nash," he said. "Someone at the police station told me he was probably here."

Ted emerged from my office wiping his mouth on a napkin. "Ingle, what's up?"

"May we speak privately?" Josh asked. "The three of us?"

I looked at Ted, undecided whether I could or should talk with the museum curator about something private, which I took to mean the heist and/or the murder of Geoffrey Vandehey. But when Ted nodded, I put the clock on the door that told customers I'd be back in half an hour.

The three of us, along with Angus, returned to the office. I moved the sewing machine chair over near the desk, and Josh sat down.

Ted and I returned to our seats, and Angus sat down among us, obviously wondering where this new person weighed in on the issue of sharing food with pets . . . or, more specifically, this pet.

"Please continue eating," Josh said. "I don't want to interrupt your lunch."

"What did you want to talk with us about?" Ted asked. "If it's about the theft, I can come by the museum as soon as I leave here."

"Please . . . can I just talk with you now?" He ran a hand over his high forehead. "Here's the deal. That FBI guy came back

116

to the museum just a few minutes ago and asked me why Geoffrey Vandehey had been in Tallulah Falls for the past week. I said I didn't know, but I swear he acted like Vandehey and I were big buddies or something."

"Mr. Ingle, we've already discussed this," Ted said. "Special Agent Brown is trying to bully you into a confession. If you have nothing to confess, don't let him bully you."

"Well, that's just it," said Josh. "What if I did something . . . but I didn't *mean* to?"

"I can give you two some privacy if you'd like," I said.

"No, please stay." He sighed and rubbed his forehead again.

"Mr. Ingle, may I get you a drink?" I asked. "Water? Soda?"

"Water would be nice," he said. "And call me Josh, please."

I got up and got Josh a bottle of water. When I handed it to him, he immediately uncapped it and drank half of it.

Ted looked a bit irritated at having his lunch disrupted, but I felt sorry for Josh Ingle. The young man was terribly agitated.

Ted continued eating his sandwich.

"Why do you think you did something unintentionally?" I asked Josh when he at last lowered the water bottle.

A smile tugged at the corners of Ted's lips,

117

and I could imagine him calling me *Inch-High Private Eye* in his mind.

"You see, Vandehey *did* come in on Tuesday," said Josh. "The exhibit didn't arrive until Wednesday, so I didn't have any reason to think he was there to steal it. I mean, all right, people *knew* the exhibit was coming — it had been in all the papers and stuff — but I didn't dream that old man was *casing* the museum! The only thing I thought he was interested in stealing was my job!"

Angus woofed slightly, alarmed by Josh's agitated outburst.

"Is he okay? Is he gonna bite me?" Josh asked.

"No," I said. "But please calm down. He hates it when people get upset. So why did you think the professor wanted your job?"

"The guy knew *everything,* okay? It was like from the minute he walked into the museum, I was on a quiz show," he said. "He'd say things like 'Of course, you're aware that in the twelfth century the Western Sudanese were creating some amazing terracotta figurines.' And then he'd look at me, and I'd get the quiz. He'd say, 'Do you recall where those were produced?' When I couldn't answer, he'd fill in the blank — 'Ah, I remember — Jenne-jeno, that's it.' Who the hell has ever heard of Jenne-jeno?

118

I haven't!"

Angus emitted a low growl this time, and I called him over to soothe him. "It's all right, Angus. Mr. Ingle is just upset." To Josh, I said, "Maybe he simply wanted to talk with someone who had similar interests."

Josh shook his head. "He had me take him on a tour of the entire museum. The whole time, he kept testing me — seeing if I had as much knowledge as he had. And, of course, I didn't! He had a doctorate! I'm struggling to get through my master's degree!"

"I'm with Marcy," said Ted as he finished up his sandwich. "I think you were being paranoid about Vandehey. Furthermore, I think you're being paranoid about Brown."

"That's easy for you to say," Josh said. "You're not the one with your back to the wall here. And it turns out, I *wasn't* being paranoid. Maybe Vandehey wasn't after my job, but he could very well have been casing the museum for a band of thieves." He turned to me. "Did you find anything on or near the body that you might've forgotten to tell the police about?"

Ted and I shared a look that said *puhleeze.*

"Actually, yes," I said. "I found a note saying that after you led him on a guided tour of the museum and allowed him to figure out how to foil all security measures, he and his band of merry men — listed and described individually — were going to steal the textiles, sell them, and give the proceeds to the indigent of Jenne-jeno."

"You're being sarcastic," said Josh, "but that's exactly the type of thing he would do! That guy — Chad Cummings, the art collector whose Cézanne Vandehey stole — told me yesterday that Vandehey had offered to *buy* the painting so he could donate it to a museum and share it with the world. He thought Cummings had no appreciation for it."

"I've spoken with Cummings," Ted said. "I don't think he has much appreciation for anything, with the possible exception of money."

Josh sighed. "Well, I have to agree with you there." He looked at Ted. "Please tell me what to do."

"Don't let Brown get under your skin," Ted said. "Staying calm is the best — but probably the most difficult — thing you can do."

"I swear to you, I didn't help that man . . . or anyone . . . rob the museum," Josh said. "I didn't even know who Vandehey was when he came in on Tuesday."

"Do you drink, Josh?" Ted asked. "If you do, and if you're on foot, maybe you could go over to the Brew Crew and have Todd Calloway give you a shot of whiskey. It might calm your nerves some."

Josh nodded, stood, and wiped his hands down the sides of his pants. "I might do that." He turned to me. "By the way, how do you know Kelly?"

"I don't really," I said. "She came into my shop for the first time on Friday morning, and we talked about the exhibit. How do *you* know her?"

"I went out with her sister until I met Kelly," he said. "I liked Kelly better and asked her out, and she wouldn't go." He shrugged. "It wasn't like her sister and I were close or anything. I mean, we'd been to dinner and a movie once and then to a concert. It was no big deal."

"Maybe it was a big deal to Kelly's sister," I said.

"Huh . . . I never thought of that."

It appeared to me that Josh Ingle did a lot of things without thinking.

CHAPTER NINE

After Ted and Josh Ingle left, I took Angus for a walk. When I returned, I gathered the fourteen skeins of embroidery floss Sissy Cummings had requested and placed them in a small periwinkle Seven-Year Stitch bag. Then I retrieved my laptop and performed a search for Geoffrey Vandehey. I wanted to know more about this man I'd found in the alley wrapped in a stolen antique rug.

Naturally, the top search engine results for Professor Geoffrey Vandehey were accounts of the Cézanne he admitted to stealing from Chad Cummings in Seattle. Very little was given about his background other than what I already knew — he was a college professor and an art history expert who had been solicited by Cummings to authenticate and appraise the Cézanne.

I went further into the search pages. At about the middle of page five, there was a link to an article on Dr. Vandehey when he was elected as an associate into the Royal Canadian Academy of Arts. I clicked the link and saw a photo of a younger Dr. Vandehey shaking hands with an older gentleman who was listed as the academy's president. The article stated that Vandehey enjoyed a distinguished career as an art professor, historian, and appraiser. He had two children, George and Elizabeth. The children's ages were not given, and no mention was made of their mother. I supposed that had Geoffrey Vandehey been a widower, the article would have said so; so I was guessing he was divorced.

I wondered what George and Elizabeth had thought when their dad had stolen a painting and gone on the lam. Had they been estranged before that? Had Dr. Vandehey written them to let them know what he was doing or had done?

I studied the younger Dr. Vandehey in the grainy photograph. He had been . . . well . . . not unattractive. His face wore a friendly, open expression. I wasn't a body language or facial expression expert by any stretch of the imagination, but I would never have guessed from this photo that Dr. Vandehey would someday steal a Cézanne and go on the run from federal authorities. Had he been desperate for money and had nowhere else to turn?

"What's your story, Professor?" I mused aloud.

Following the money angle, I wondered what an early Cézanne might be worth. It was entirely possible that Vandehey had appraised the Cézanne owned by Chad Cummings and found it to be worth much less than Cummings had expected. After all, Vandehey had mentioned in his letter to the feds that he wanted the painting to be appreciated. Every account I had of Cummings was that he wouldn't appreciate anything that didn't have an exorbitant monetary value.

I went back to the home page of the search engine and typed in *Cézanne minor work.* I hit ENTER and then began to scroll through the links. Within the next half hour, I learned about Cézanne's dark, Impressionist, mature, and final periods. I also found that the artist was prone to depression. That fact wasn't too hard to figure out, given his penchant for skull still-life art. One article indicated that the skulls illustrated Cézanne's resignation to death in his final period. But Cummings's painting had featured a skull and was said to have been believed to be one of Cézanne's earliest works.

I ran across an article about Cézanne's *The Boy in the Red Vest,* which had been stolen from the Foundation E. G. Buhrle in Zurich, Switzerland, on February 10, 2008. That painting had been valued at between ninety-one and a hundred and nine million dollars and was recovered in Serbia in April of 2010. The article pointed out that Cézanne seldom bothered to date or sign his work, but the date he created *The Boy in the Red Vest* was believed to have been between 1894 and 1895 because the young man had been in earlier works and the work had been done in Cézanne's Paris studio in Rue d'Anjou.

I returned to the search engine's main page and found another link to Cézanne's earliest works. According to an Impressionist Web site, Cézanne showed dramatic violence, romanticism, and the desire to revolt against academic standards in his paintings.

I was dwelling on how difficult it must have been for Dr. Vandehey to evaluate the painting, given the fact that Cézanne was reluctant to sign his work, when the bells over the door alerted me to the fact that someone had come in. I closed my laptop and stood to greet Sissy Cummings.

"Welcome back," I said.

Angus trotted over to greet her, too.

"Thank you," Sissy said. "Did you have time to get my order together?"

"I sure did." I went to the counter and retrieved the small bag that held her skeins of floss. "Is there anything else you need?"

"Not that I know of, but I'll look around as long as I'm here." She smiled. "I'm sure to find something I'll fall in love with."

"That happens to me every time I get a new shipment in," I said. "By the way, I offer needlework classes every Tuesday, Wednesday, and Thursday evening. If you're in town and looking for something to do, please drop in either to observe or to participate — on the house."

"What classes are you currently offering?" she asked.

"I have crewel classes on Tuesday. My friend Reggie Singh is teaching *chikankari* — Indian embroidery — on Wednesday. And I'm giving beaded embroidery classes on Thursday."

"They all sound wonderful," said Sissy. "I'll have to see if I can slip away one evening. I'd especially like to watch your friend demonstrate the Indian technique." She started when the bells over the shop door rang.

A paunchy man wearing jeans, a polo,

loafers, and a Gucci cap came into the shop.

"Just finishing up," she told him.

"Take your time." The man held a hand out to me. "Chad Cummings."

I shook his hand. "Hello, Mr. Cummings. I'm Marcy Singer. It's a pleasure to meet you, and it has been delightful chatting with your wife."

I noticed that Angus stayed with Sissy rather than coming over to greet Mr. Cummings.

"She's a thoroughbred, all right." Mr. Cummings gazed around the shop. "Nice place. You franchised?"

"No, sir."

He took his wallet from his back pocket, removed a business card, and handed the card to me. "If you ever decide to expand, call me. I might be interested in investing. The name's catchy, you'd make a cute spokesperson, and the needlecraft business is booming."

"Um . . . all right," I said.

"Chad, look," Sissy said, holding up a counted cross-stitch project of a train. "Wouldn't this be perfect for Chad Junior's room?"

He gave the piece a cursory glance. "Whatever you think, Portia."

"I think it would be lovely," she said. "I'm

127

getting it. Maybe I can get it made for him before Christmas."

"You the one who found Vandehey in the alley?" Mr. Cummings asked me.

"Yes, sir."

"I should pay you a finder's fee." He barked out a humorless laugh. "He didn't happen to have my Cézanne on him, did he?"

"Not that I know of," I said. "I heard about him stealing your painting, and I'm sorry for your loss."

"It was insured."

"How did you acquire the painting?" I asked. "Had it been passed down through the family?"

"Nah, I picked it up at an auction for a fraction of what it was worth," said Mr. Cummings. "The guy I was with was what you might call an art connoisseur. He didn't know who'd done the painting, but he figured it was worth a lot more than that Podunk auction house realized. So I had it insured for ten times what I paid for it." He laughed again. "Vandehey practically did me a favor when he stole it — I made over twenty million dollars on it."

"Wow. It's good you weren't attached to the painting, then," I said.

"I don't get very attached to anything," he

said. "A man can buy a whole lot of paintings for twenty million, most of them prettier than the one that was stolen. Still, I didn't appreciate the thought that I'd entertained a thief in my own home. So I had a private investigator on the lookout for him. He showed up here a few days ago."

"Marcy, I'm ready to check out," Sissy said.

I went over to the counter and rang up her purchases.

"By the way, I went into that aromatherapy shop — Scentsibilities — and bought you some more of that neroli oil," Chad told his wife.

Sissy's lips tightened, but she didn't say anything.

"I know you think it's too expensive and a waste of money, but it really helps when you get in one of your moods," he continued. "I told Ms. Davis she should franchise, too. There's money to be made here if you want it. Give me a call, Ms. Singer. Portia, I'll be in the Bugatti."

I handed Sissy her bag. "I hope you and Chad Junior enjoy the train."

Her face softened. "Oh, he loves trains." She took her phone from her purse, pressed a couple of buttons, and showed me a photo of a smiling boy wearing a conductor's cap.

"He's precious," I said. "How old is he?"

"He's seven now. He was five when this photo was taken." She turned the photo back toward herself and looked at it lovingly. "It's one of my favorites."

"Is he with you here in Tallulah Falls?" I asked.

She shook her head. "Chad said this was a business trip and that he would be a distraction. We talk at least twice a day through the computer, though."

"That's good. I'm sure he misses you."

"I certainly miss him. I'll be glad to get back home."

"Don't forget to stop back in if you have the chance," I said. "It's always great to have a fellow stitcher to talk with."

She smiled. "It is. Thank you, Marcy."

After Sissy left, Angus and I returned to the sit-and-stitch square. I picked the laptop back up off the coffee table, opened it, and unlocked the screen. I went to the top of the search engine page and typed in *Chad Cummings*.

As I suspected after he wanted to franchise both my and Nellie Davis's shops, Chad Cummings was a venture capitalist. His father had been a real estate developer and made a ton of money, and Chad had followed in his footsteps. I wondered if Chad

Junior with his conductor's cap would be some sort of tycoon, too. I figured he probably would.

Angus came over and dropped his tennis ball at my feet. I tossed it, and he scampered across the floor to get it.

He was on his way back to me when Todd Calloway came into the shop. Angus decided to give Todd a turn with the tennis ball.

"Thanks, Angus," Todd said as he threw the ball and then joined me on the sofa. He turned toward me and raised his eyebrows, looking comical and boyish in his jeans and faded blue T-shirt. His wavy brown hair was going in every direction, and there was a bemused expression in his chocolate eyes.

"What?" I asked.

"Why did you and Ted send Josh Ingle over to the Brew Crew to get wasted?"

"We didn't!" I searched my brain to recall the details of the conversation we'd had with Josh. "Ted was trying to get him to calm down and suggested he walk over to the Brew Crew for a shot of whiskey. At no time did either of us suggest Josh go get wasted." I frowned and bit my lip. "Is he wasted?"

"No. He was working on it, but I cut him off."

Angus returned the tennis ball to Todd,

and Todd tossed it back toward the mer-chandise part of the shop.

"That little dude is a wreck, though," Todd said. "He was still nursing that last beer when I walked over here. Maybe I can send him up to Nellie Davis's shop to sniff some . . . whatever calms people's nerves."

"Apparently, neroli oil does that," I said. "Chad Cummings bought some for his wife for *when she gets in those moods.*"

"He actually said that? In front of you and everything?"

"Yep."

Todd nodded. "What did he say when he came to?"

I laughed. "Nothing. She looked as if she didn't appreciate the comment, but I get the impression that Chad Cummings says whatever he wants whenever he wants to whomever he wants. He wants me to fran-chise the Seven-Year Stitch, by the way."

"Really? Baby Stitches all over the West Coast?" He turned his mouth down at the corners. "How do you feel about that?"

"No, thank you. I believe I was meant to enjoy a quieter life than the Cummingses," I said. "He mentioned that he told Nellie she should franchise Scentsibilities too. Hasn't he come over and tried to win you over to the dark side yet?"

"Not yet, but if he does, I might go."

"Are you serious?" I asked.

"I'd seriously like to have a Bugatti like the one he was driving." Todd winked. "Wouldn't you? I can see you and Angus buzzing down the highway with the wind in your hair . . . both of you sporting a pair of matching sunglasses."

I hit him with one of the candlewick pillows.

He laughed. "It's something to think about."

"Maybe so, but I have enough to deal with without worrying about my mansion being broken into and my priceless art stolen while I'm out cruising around in my Bugatti."

"Speaking of priceless art, I heard you found an antique rug . . . and a person . . . in your alley on Saturday," Todd said.

"Yes, I did. And before you ask, I did not knock over the museum, nor did I wrap said person in the rug and dump him in the alley."

"I'm glad. I'd hate for you to execute a caper like that without me."

"This from the man who's dating a deputy," I said.

He spread his hands. "Hey, I'd just like to think that no matter who either of us is dat-

133

ing, if you decide to commit a federal offense, you'd at least let me audition as the getaway driver."

"Of course I would," I said. "But after seeing Chad Cummings's Bugatti, I think I'd ask him first. Those things are fast."

"That's true. I couldn't blame you there," he said. "If you decide to *steal* the Bugatti, though, call me."

"Oh, first thing," I said.

He grinned. "Seriously, are you all right? I started to call you Saturday night, but I figured Wyatt Earp was taking care of you."

"I'm fine. I feel sad for Professor Vandehey, though. I looked him up on the Internet earlier, and he had two children."

Todd's grin faded. "Don't do that to yourself, Marce. You had nothing to do with that man's death. You merely stumbled across him lying behind your shop. Stop obsessing and move on."

"I'm trying, but . . ." I sighed.

He leaned over and kissed my temple. "Try harder."

I smiled. "I will."

"Want to come to the Brew Crew and get wasted?"

"Not particularly," I said. "I've never understood how getting so drunk I feel like death the next day will help me resolve

134

anything today."

"You might have mentioned that to Josh Ingle instead of suggesting he have a shot to calm his nerves," Todd pointed out.

"In my defense, it was Ted who suggested the drink. But at the time, it *did* seem like a good idea. The guy was a wreck."

"Still is. Only now he's sloppy drunk and telling anyone who will listen that the board pulled off this heist to oust him from his job."

"Do you think there could be any truth to that?" I asked. "It appears that the robbery *was* an inside job."

"It might've been, but I seriously doubt the board had anything to do with it," Todd said. "This is a real black mark on the museum's reputation. I'd think if they wanted to get rid of Ingle, they'd simply fire him."

"Yeah, you're right. There are much easier ways to get rid of a curator."

Todd said he'd better get back and check on his pitiful little patron.

"Sorry," I said.

"It's all right," Todd said. "And Ingle will be fine."

Todd left, and I thought about poor Josh. I wondered why he was so paranoid about his job. Did he really think the museum's board of directors would stage a heist just to get rid of him? I decided to take him some sort of care package tomorrow to apologize for suggesting he get a drink . . . and to find out his true thoughts on the museum heist.

I also wanted to ask Ted what he'd found out from the board. Not that he'd tell me confidential details of an investigation, of course, but I'd like to know if the board had truly detested Josh Ingle or if that was merely a figment of Josh's paranoid imagination.

My mind drifted back to Josh talking about Dr. Vandehey's visit to the museum. Had the professor not been scoping out the security equipment for the robbers, then why was he at the museum asking for the grand tour?

So many questions . . . And yet today, all I wanted to do was enjoy my time with Ted and Angus on the beach. I texted Ted and let him know that I was leaving fifteen minutes early so I could go by the market and get the stuff I needed to pack us a picnic. Then I held my breath that he wouldn't call and tell me he wouldn't be able to come.

CHAPTER TEN

It was half past eight on Tuesday morning, and I would normally have still been at home puttering around in my pajamas instead of running errands. But rather than feeling bothered, I couldn't keep from smiling. My mind kept drifting back to last night and the wonderful time I'd had with Ted.

I'd gone home after work and packed a picnic basket with tuna salad sandwiches, baked chips, apple slices, sodas, and macadamia cookies. As we'd done with Blake and Sadie, we had eaten near the lighthouse. But then we'd taken the long way home. We'd stopped at a dog park beside a playground, and while Angus had romped with a golden retriever, Ted and I had hit the swings. Then the golden retriever and her owner had left, and Ted, Angus, and I had played with Angus's flying disk. After that, we'd indulged in frozen yogurt.

I was still smiling when I reached my first

destination — MacKenzies' Mochas — and got out of the Jeep. I'd called ahead and was glad to see that the muffin basket I'd ordered was ready.

Blake appraised me with mock severity. "You're looking mighty chipper this morning . . . *too* chipper. Where are you headed with that basket of muffins? To engage in some sort of mischief perhaps?"

I giggled. Blake could not do "gruff" to save his life. "I'm actually trying to make up for some mischief I might have been a party to yesterday."

"Ah, yes. Todd mentioned something about a certain museum curator drowning his sorrows."

I groaned. "Has Josh been in for coffee this morning?"

Blake nodded. "He did look a little green around the gills, but I've seen worse. Heck, I've *been* worse. He'll be fine."

"I still feel the need to apologize . . . and to see what else he might be able to tell me about Geoffrey Vandehey's visit to the museum."

"Take the man his muffins, but leave the investigation to the police," Blake said. "As much as I enjoy our chats in the alley over a dead body, I'd prefer to keep them to a minimum. And I *definitely* don't want one of us to be the one wrapped in the rug."

Before I could respond, a couple of customers came into the coffee shop. I recognized one of them as Kelly Conrad.

"Hi, Kelly," I said.

"Hey, Marcy. Those muffins sure look good," she said.

"Thanks. I'm taking them to the museum." I paid Blake for the muffins and turned to go.

"Yeah, I feel really bad for Josh," Kelly said.

"So do I," I said. "I think he could really use all the friends he can get right now." I had no idea what had happened between Josh and Kelly, but I hoped they could at least be friends.

"I guess so," she said. "I might go by and talk with him after I get off work today."

"I'm sure he'd appreciate that," I said.

Although the Tallulah Falls Museum and Historical Society had officially reopened, there were no patrons there when I arrived with my muffins. The museum felt ominous in the quiet semidarkness. I was wearing rubber-soled flats, and they squeaked on the tile floor as I made my way to the curator's office.

Before I reached the door, Josh Ingle

139

stepped out, barking, "Who's there?"

"It's Marcy Singer." I held up the muffin basket. "I have a peace offering."

"Yes, I see you now," he said. "I just . . . heard the squeaking . . . and I thought . . ." He trailed off, but I knew what he meant. He thought someone had been slipping up on him . . . which technically I had been, but not for any nefarious purpose.

"I should have called first and told you I was coming," I said. "I'm sorry."

He smiled. "That's quite all right. I guess I'm just a little jumpy."

"That's understandable."

He invited me into his office, which could be described as *overcrowded* if one were being charitable or *a mess* if one were not. There was one large white desk near the window. There was a large black leather executive chair behind it. A flat-screen computer monitor and a mouse resting on a desk calendar took up the center of the desk. A double-stacked in-box was to the right of the monitor, and its twin out-box was on the left. Both were overflowing. The rest of the desk was covered in business cards, sticky notes, pencil cups, and paper clips. A phone, stapler, tape dispenser, coffee cup from MacKenzies' Mochas, and pack of gum rounded out the clutter. Josh even had a Rolodex. I thought everyone kept their contact information and addresses on their computers or phones these days.

There was a cubicle within the office that housed another desk, phone, computer, and single in-/out-box, but it was neater than Josh's space. There were file cabinets and a large copier to the right of Josh's desk, and floor-to-ceiling bookshelves lined the walls. In addition to books, the shelves contained many three-ring binders, what appeared to be scrapbooks, and file folders.

"What is all this?" I asked.

"Maps, historical documents, newspaper clippings, providences . . . you name it, I probably have it here somewhere," he said.

"Wow. You have a lot to keep up with."

"I do." He nodded toward the cubicle. "Of course, I have help. My assistant, Diane, is here three days a week."

"That's good." I handed Josh the muffin basket. "These are for you. I'm sorry Ted and I suggested you should drink yesterday. I know it didn't help matters, and it probably made them worse."

He smiled and set the muffin basket on the copier. "Ah, it wasn't that bad. Thank you for the muffins, though. I won't turn those down." He pulled out his assistant's chair. "Have a seat."

"Thank you." I took the chair as Josh moved around his desk to his own chair. "I looked up Geoffrey Vandehey online yesterday. All I'd known about him before then was what I'd heard about the Cézanne theft."

"I hadn't even known that until after he died," Josh said. "I mean, I knew someone named Geoffrey Vandehey had stolen a Cézanne in Seattle three or four years ago, but I didn't know that the man who walked into this museum was Geoffrey Vandehey. What kind of museum curator does that make me?"

"It makes you an excellent curator but a lousy detective," I said. "Why on earth would you expect Geoffrey Vandehey to ever resurface, much less here in your museum?"

He shrugged. "I don't know, but that Agent Brown sure thinks I should have."

"What name did Vandehey use?"

"George Elsbeth."

"His children's names are George and Elizabeth," I said.

"He just walked in and wandered around looking at the exhibits. As I would do with anyone, I greeted him and offered him a guided tour," he said. "The man could've refused, but he seemed to welcome the company. Then, as I elaborated on some of the exhibits, it became apparent to me that he was more knowledgeable in some areas than I was."

"In *some* areas, maybe, but not all. You're too hard on yourself."

He blew out a breath. "I guess. But still . . . Here's an example. Have you ever heard of A. C. Gilbert?"

I shook my head.

"He was born in Salem, Oregon, and was a toy inventor," said Josh. "Actually, he created toys that were designed to entertain as well as educate. One of his most popular toys was the Erector Set."

"Cool," I said.

"Right. Anyway, while we're looking at the antique toy exhibit, Elsbeth — I mean, Vandehey — starts to chuckle. Then he tells me that when he was a little boy, he had one of Gilbert's Atomic Energy Laboratories. The toy came with a working Geiger counter, an electroscope, and low-level-radiation sources."

My eyes widened. "Please tell me he was joking!"

"No, he wasn't!" Josh laughed. "I looked it up. The thing came with alpha, beta, and gamma particles as well as four uranium-bearing ore samples!"

I joined in his laughter. "How in the world did that *toy* go through all the government regulations?"

"Apparently very well," he said. "There was a book included with the Atomic Energy Lab teaching kids how to prospect for uranium, and the U.S. government offered a ten-thousand-dollar prize to any successful prospector."

"That's hilarious. These days just about everything poses a choking hazard. It sounds like the Atomic Energy Laboratory could've turned kids into the Incredible Hulk." I shook my head. "I'm not surprised I haven't heard of it. It couldn't have been on the market long. . . . Was it?"

"No. It was only produced between 1950 and 1951."

"So Professor Vandehey was more knowledgeable than you about the Atomic Energy Lab," I said. "In my opinion, that's a *good* thing!"

"Yeah, I guess it is," said Josh. "But it was more than that. He knew about the antique-embroidery exhibit . . . that one piece in particular likely originated from the Amish settlement in McMinnville. The sampler was done by someone named Mary Miller and was dated 1899."

"It doesn't sound as if he knew for certain,

though."

"No, but he knew *lots* of things. To be honest, I didn't really care where the sampler came from," he said. "From the time I took the job as curator here, I set out to improve upon the museum's collections. I didn't do a lot of research or give a lot of thought to what we had but to what we *could* have."

"I think that's admirable, Josh. You've made many improvements and got in a lot of new exhibits since I've been here . . . and I've not even lived in Tallulah Falls for an entire year yet. Getting the Padgett Collection was quite a coup."

"Yeah, and look how that turned out for me."

"It started out great. Everyone I talked with was so excited about the new exhibit," I said. "It isn't your fault that the collection was stolen."

"Isn't it? While I was giving Geoffrey Vandehey, alias George Elsbeth, the grand tour, wasn't I letting him get the information he needed to rob the museum?" he asked.

"You know, for some reason, I don't think so. Maybe it's because I'm the one who found his body in the alley and I felt sorry for him, but I honestly don't think he was in on the scheme to steal the Padgett Collection."

Josh looked skeptical.

"I could be completely wrong," I admitted. "But I have a hunch that Geoffrey Vandehey wasn't a bad person."

"He stole a Cézanne right off Chad Cummings's wall," Josh said.

"True . . . or, at least, he *allegedly* stole the painting."

"Now, you don't think he even did that?" Josh asked. "Should we recommend Dr. Vandehey for sainthood?"

"Don't go getting snarky with me when I'm only trying to help you feel better," I said.

"You're right. I'm sorry. Dr. Vandehey *allegedly* stole the painting."

"The confession could have been forged." I huffed. "Or maybe he *did* steal the painting and the confession wasn't forged. I met Chad Cummings this morning, and I get the feeling that anything Dr. Vandehey did could very well have been because he was provoked."

"I have to agree with you there. Chad Cummings is a piece of . . . work," Josh said. "And I highly doubt he had any appreciation whatsoever for the Cézanne."

"Oh, he appreciated it, all right. He absolutely *cherished* the twenty million dollars he made on it."

Josh raised his eyebrows. "Twenty million?"

"That's what he told me he made off the painting," I said. "Cummings had apparently insured the painting for that much."

"Wait. . . ." He rubbed his forehead. "Cummings should have had the painting appraised before he had it insured."

"He should have, yes."

"But wasn't Dr. Vandehey there to appraise the painting?" he asked.

"Yes, he was. So if the painting was already insured, then maybe the professor was there to offer a second opinion or something."

"I guess that's possible."

"You don't sound so sure," I said.

"I'm not."

As I returned home to pick up Angus before going to the Seven-Year Stitch, it began to lightly rain. I turned the windshield wipers on the delay mode and thought about my conversation with Josh Ingle. I was coming back from my trip with more questions than answers.

First of all, even though the museum was once again open to the public, I didn't see another single person when I walked inside. Where were the security guards? I'd thought the board of directors — or, at least, the chairman — had offices at the museum. Was I mistaken?

Of course, there hadn't been any patrons, either, but I could understand that. The few who might have been interested in attending the museum first thing on a Tuesday morning could have been under the assumption that it was closed because of the theft.

The lack of staff was what struck me as odd. No receptionist had greeted me when I'd walked in or had left. Did Josh answer the phone, provide the tours, head up acquisitions, and take out the garbage? Hmmm . . . that sounded like *my* job. But, then, I'm an entrepreneur . . . a sole proprietor . . . not a curator at a small museum. It made me wonder if perhaps the board of directors was considering closing down the museum. Josh had been so sure at first that Dr. Vandehey was there to take his job and then that Special Agent Brown was trying to tie him to the crime. I was reminded of the quote by William Burroughs: "A paranoid is someone who knows a little of what's going on." What "little" did Josh know? And, of course, the bigger question might be, what did he *not* know? If someone on the board wanted to close the museum, having the collection stolen was certainly a step in the right direction.

Then again, maybe I had it all wrong. Maybe the museum had a sizable staff, but it just so happened that no one was there today. I knew extra security had been hired for the Padgett Collection exhibit's opening night, in addition to the four guards employed by the museum. It could simply be that Josh Ingle's paranoia was contagious.

I pulled into the drive, and Angus pushed back the living room curtain to peer outside. He seemed delighted to realize that I hadn't left him home alone for the day after all. By the time I got to the foyer, he was racing back and forth from the living room to the foyer.

"Are you ready to go?" I asked. As if he needed to pack a lunch or something . . .

He trotted to the door.

Our drive to the Seven-Year Stitch, despite the drizzle, was happy and carefree. When we got there . . . not so much. I could've sworn I heard the commingled themes to *Jaws* and *Psycho* swelling as I saw Nellie Davis standing on the sidewalk. Nellie "Scentsibilities" Davis, who had no sensibilities. There she stood, short gray and white hair sticking out in all directions, red glasses sitting cockeyed on her beaklike nose, fists on her hips.

From the time I arrived in Tallulah Falls, she'd been trying to drive me away. It wasn't my fault that a few people had met their untimely ends in or near the Seven-Year Stitch. It also wasn't my fault that I leased the shop before Nellie's sister decided she'd like it for herself. Every encounter I'd had with this woman had been unpleasant.

I pretended to search for something in my purse. My intention was to wait her out. Darned if she didn't knock on my window! Naturally, that made Angus bark.

"Just a second!" I called to Nellie.

As usual, Nellie was dressed all in black. It emphasized her paleness . . . and her thinness . . . and made her seem sort of like a mime. I half expected her to do that sideways shuffle mimes do when I got Angus out of the car.

"What can I do for you this morning, Nellie?" I unlocked the door, unclipped Angus's leash, and let the dog go on inside.

"Who was that man you found in the alley?" she asked.

"His name was Dr. Geoffrey Vandehey," I said. "Don't you read the newspaper?"

"Yes, I read the newspaper . . . when I have time." She compressed her lips before continuing. "And I saw the article Paul

150

Samms wrote. He said the body was found near the museum, but everybody knows it was behind your shop."

"Technically, it was behind your shop, too." I went inside, and she came with me. "We do share an alley, you know."

I could tell by the way her eyes bulged behind those big glasses that she hadn't liked that at all.

"Still, *you* found him, not me."

"What's your point, Nellie?"

"Did I ever tell you that before you leased this shop my sister wanted it?" she asked, looking all around the room.

"I seem to recall hearing something about that."

"Well, now I'm glad she didn't take it."

"Because you believe it's cursed?" I asked. "My mom is thinking along those lines, too. She suggested I consult an exorcist."

"Maybe you should," she murmured.

"I might just do that," I said. "Thank you for your concern. I truly appreciate it."

"You're welcome."

Sarcasm was completely lost on this woman.

She began fidgeting with the hem of her shirt. "You should be more careful whether you get someone to do an exorcism or not."

She was beginning to scare me . . . even for her.

"I will. Thank you." I watched her closely, but she refused to meet my eyes. "Is there something you aren't telling me?"

"I was here late Friday night. I had a shipment come in late, and I wanted to get it all displayed and ready before Saturday morning. I have a lot of customers who come in first thing on Saturday," she said. "Sometimes they're even waiting when I get here."

I was thrilled that her business was booming, but I didn't think that was why she was telling me to be careful. "Did you see something? Hear something?"

"No . . . um . . . of course not. I'm just saying that it could've been dangerous had one of us been working whenever this . . . this incident took place."

Like the Bard, methinks Nellie doth protest too much. "Nellie, are you *sure* you didn't see or hear anything while you were here Friday night?"

She nodded. "Of course I'm sure. Do you think I'm a ninny? Why wouldn't I be sure?" She grabbed my arm. "Please don't let it get out that I was here at all on Friday night. I'm so afraid someone will find out and think I saw something. But I didn't. I swear, I didn't see a thing."

CHAPTER ELEVEN

Sadie came over just after Nellie Davis left.

"Is everything okay?" she asked. "I saw Nellie leaving."

"Yeah, it's fine," I said. "She was actually civil today."

Sadie had bent down to pet Angus. Now she straightened. "That makes me suspicious."

"Me, too."

"What aren't you telling me?" Sadie asked.

"I'll have to swear you to secrecy," I said.

She rolled her eyes. "Spill it."

"Nellie was working late at her shop on Friday night."

Sadie's eyes widened. "Did she see anything? Does she know who murdered Geoffrey Vandehey?"

I tilted my head. "She *says* she didn't see anything . . . but the way she kept saying it over and over makes me wonder. Plus, she doesn't want it to 'get out' that she was here

153

that night."

"She knows something, Marce."

"I believe she does, too," I said. "Getting her to admit that and to tell the police what she knows is something else entirely. You know what else? She told me to be careful. Me! The person voted *Hopefully Most Careless* by Nellie Davis."

"You have to find out what she knows." She looked at her watch. "I have to get back. But I'll be thinking on this . . . and I'll put Blake on it, too."

"I'm wondering if the museum doesn't have some sort of security camera that would show footage of our alley," I said.

"I hope they do," Sadie said. "I'll check back with you later."

I restocked the flosses and embroidery kits while Angus lay in the sit-and-stitch square gnawing on his Kodiak bear. I glanced toward the door and saw someone getting ready to come inside. At first, I was startled because I just saw the thin, black-clad figure and thought Nellie Davis was coming back. But when my visitor opened the door, I could see that it was Simon Benton, the art collector.

"Good morning, Mr. Benton."

"Hello, Ms. Singer."

Angus got up and came to greet Mr.

Benton.

"I brought something for you today, young man," Mr. Benton said. "Perhaps it will make you more agreeable toward me." He reached into his pocket and took out a shrink-wrapped dog biscuit. He handed it to Angus. Angus sniffed it but was reluctant to take the treat.

"Thank you," I told Mr. Benton, taking the treat. "That was thoughtful."

I stepped behind the counter, got a pair of scissors, and cut away the shrink wrap. Then I handed Angus the biscuit. He took it and returned to the sit-and-stitch square to eat it.

"I learned — as likely you did — that the rug in question was indeed the kilim that belonged to my friend Anderson Padgett," said Mr. Benton.

"I did. I'm sorry . . . about the entire collection. Do you think there's any hope of it being recovered?"

"I don't know. At this point, we can only hope."

"How's your friend taking the news?" I asked.

"He was rather stoic over the phone, but I imagine he'll be upset when he arrives and the reality of the loss strikes him," he said.

"He's on his way to Oregon, then?"

"Yes. I'm to pick him up in Portland later today."

"I hope the trip won't be too taxing for him," I said, remembering Mr. Benton saying that Mr. Padgett was in poor health.

"Yes. Well, from your mouth to God's ear, eh?"

"Could I get you a cup of coffee or a bottle of water, Mr. Benton?"

"No, thank you, dear. I merely came by to reiterate my offer to dine," he said. "This evening is out of the question, or course, but would you care to have lunch with Andy — Anderson Padgett, that is — and me tomorrow? I'd like for your young man — the detective — to join us also."

"I'll have to check with Ted as to his plans, but I'd enjoy meeting Mr. Padgett and discussing textiles with the two of you," I said. "By the way, how did you know I was dating a detective?"

"Someone mentioned it. The museum curator, I think." He thought a moment. "Yes, I'm sure it was he. That chap doesn't seem to have any luck in the romance department. Shame." He smiled. "Anyway, Andy and I shall be able to do double duty if you both are available. We can thank Detective Nash for his hard work and have an engaging chat with a lovely young lady.

Can't beat that, can we?"

"Thank you," I said, not knowing quite what else to say to that. "What time would you like to meet?"

"Will eleven thirty suit?" Mr. Benton asked. "Andy tends to be a late riser, and that will definitely be the case tomorrow. I imagine our lunch will be his breakfast."

"That'll be fine. Could we eat next door at MacKenzies' Mochas?"

"Of course. We'll look forward to seeing you then."

After Simon Benton left, I got the laptop from the office to look up Anderson Padgett. If I was going to be having lunch with him tomorrow, I wanted to find out more about him. I pulled up my favorite search engine and typed in his name. From the extensive list of links that popped up, I chose the top three.

Anderson Padgett had made his fortune as an architect. He'd married at age twenty and remained married until his wife died four years ago. He had been eighty at the time, so the couple had been married for sixty years.

"Wow, maybe that's why he's a billionaire," I mused aloud. "What do you think, Jill?"

No, I didn't actually believe my man-

157

nequin could talk, but, like the dog, I sometimes conversed with her anyway.

I'll say, Jill said silently in her breathy Marilyn voice. *Most Hollywood billionaires would have had to be paying alimony to at least four wives by the time they were eighty.*

"True. I don't think they marry as often as they used to, though."

You know, I always said — or, at least, Marilyn said — the public doesn't mind people living together without being married, provided they don't overdo it.

"Hmm . . . and what do you think about the Padgetts being married sixty years?"

I think it's very sweet . . . very special. Don't you? Or are you worried that you won't have that? Are you afraid that you and Ted won't see sixty years of bliss?

"Hush, Jill. You're a mannequin. You aren't supposed to be talking." That was the thing about Jill. Since she was essentially a manifestation of my subconscious, I could never be certain what she might say.

I went back to reading about Anderson Padgett. His extensive art collection included textiles, such as those displayed at the Tallulah Falls Museum and Historical Society; Japanese art from the Meiji period; modern sculpture, including a piece by Jeff Koons; and fine art photography by Richard Prince.

I didn't get much further along in my reading before a customer came in and had me show her how to make a queen stitch. That was all right, though. I felt I had enough information to be able to talk with Mr. Padgett intelligently.

The three hours from the time the shop opened until Ted came for lunch seemed to have flown by. I was thrilled — as was Angus — when he got there.

"I brought chef's salads today," he said, holding the bag he carried out of reach of Angus's nose. "I hope that's all right. I didn't have time to text and ask you about it, but after spending time around some of those unhealthy people who were at the museum exhibit premiere, I wanted healthy food."

I laughed. "Sounds great. So, did you have to talk with everybody who attended the premiere?"

"The deputies did," Ted said as we walked into my office. This time I had not forgotten to put the clock on the door. "The ones who remembered seeing something the deputies thought important were sent on through to Manu or me."

"I wasn't questioned."

159

He put the bag on my desk and pulled me to him for a kiss. "You have an airtight alibi."

"Oh, yeah." I went to the mini fridge. "Water all right?"

"Water is fine. In fact, bring me two." He took off his navy jacket and hung it over the back of his chair. "The rain cooled things off a little, but not a whole lot."

"Especially not when you're wearing a suit."

"Rub it in, Miss Jeans-and-T-shirt." He grinned.

"At least, I'm not wearing shorts or a skirt."

"I wouldn't mind that in the least."

I blushed and then changed the subject. "You said the deputies had been talking with everyone who attended the museum event Friday night, right?"

"Yes." He uncapped the first bottle and drank deeply. "Why?"

"They talked with the shop owners here in the square, too, didn't they? About Geoffrey Vandehey?"

"Yes." He drew out the word, which made me think he wanted me to get to the point.

"Nellie Davis came to see me this morning. She wasn't her usual battle-axy self, and she mentioned that she was here Friday night," I said. "I think she saw something,

Ted. Are there any surveillance cameras — maybe from the museum — that cover our alley?"

"There is one that partially shows the alley. We've looked at it, but the footage is lousy."

"It didn't show *anything*?"

"We saw a van leaving the alley at one point. But since it only partially covers the area and we had a side view of the van, we can't get a plate number to question the driver or anything." Ted finished off his bottle of water before opening the lid to his salad. "I'll go have a word with Nellie before I return to the office."

"She was so jumpy, Ted. I think she knows more than she's willing to let on."

"You're probably right. But please leave the sleuthing to me. You have enough on your plate right now."

"Speaking of plates, would you be able to have lunch tomorrow with Anderson Padgett and Simon Benton?" I asked. "I've already accepted for myself, but I didn't presume to speak for you. We're eating at MacKenzies' Mochas."

"I can do that." He frowned. "Why would Padgett and Benton want to have lunch with us?"

I scoffed. "Because we're wonderful!"

"I *know* that, but I'm looking for the ulterior motive."

"You're always looking for ulterior motives," I said.

"It's my job," he reminded me.

"Well, according to Mr. Benton, they want to thank you for your hard work."

"Which means they want to drill me about the investigation . . . informally, of course. Makes sense."

"I imagine that is why they invited you," I said. "As for why they invited *me,* I'm charming and a fabulous conversationalist."

"True."

I giggled and squeezed a packet of dressing onto my salad. "Sometimes you're hard to tease."

"No . . . not always," he said, his voice suddenly low and seductive. "You often tease me without even realizing it."

Lovely! He was making me blush again.

"Mr. Padgett is coming in tonight," I said. "Mr. Benton is picking him up at the airport in Portland and said our lunch would likely be Mr. Padgett's breakfast."

"George Vandehey was flying in this morning. He should be in the office sometime this afternoon." He wiped his mouth on a napkin. "I might not get to see you until after your class tonight."

"That's okay." I frowned. "I read that Dr. Vandehey had two children. Isn't the daughter coming?"

He shook his head. "Elizabeth Vandehey Hart was in an accident and paralyzed from the neck down shortly before Vandehey stole the painting from Chad Cummings."

I gasped. "That's why he did it, then! He was trying to pay for her medical expenses!"

"I suspect you're right about that. The feds looked into the Vandehey children's bank accounts, and during the months after the robbery, a deposit of fifty thousand dollars was placed in George's account and a deposit of one hundred fifty thousand dollars was added to Elizabeth's account."

"See? I *knew* he was a good guy." I took a sip of my water. "He only stole the Cézanne because he was desperate."

"That doesn't explain why he offered to buy it, Inch-High."

I took another drink. I didn't have an answer for that one . . . yet. "Maybe he didn't want Mr. Cummings to think he needed money. That would throw Cummings off his guard so that Vandehey could steal the painting."

"Maybe." Ted went back to eating his salad.

"And maybe *that* was why Vandehey was

163

back in town," I said. "Maybe Elizabeth was out of money and needed more care. Maybe Dr. Vandehey was in on the heist after all . . . which doesn't make him a bad man, only a desperate one."

"Why is it so important to you that Dr. Vandehey be a good man?" he asked.

"I don't know. Because I found him in the alley wrapped in a rug?"

"Wouldn't you feel better if you thought him to be a *bad* man, then?"

I tilted my head as I gave that some thought. "But he wasn't. I knew that the instant I saw him."

Ted smiled. "I love that you always find the best in people."

"I don't always," I admitted. "In fact, in all the months I've lived in Tallulah Falls, I could never find anything good to say about Nellie Davis. I couldn't even tell you anything nice about her shop, because I haven't ever stepped foot in the place. But today, I felt downright sorry for her."

"You must've felt downright sorry for Josh Ingle, too," he said. "You know, it wasn't our fault that he went to the Brew Crew and got drunk."

"Who told about the muffin basket? Blake or Sadie?" I asked.

He laughed. "Blake. He said I might have

some competition." He took my hand and caressed the back of it with his thumb. "Do I?"

"You know better." I grinned. "Come to think of it, though, a muffin basket might not have been the best gift to give someone recovering from a hangover. But, on the bright side, I saw that girl Kelly in MacK-enzies' Mochas and she said she might stop by and see Josh this afternoon."

"You didn't tell *him* that, did you?"

"Of course not. I was afraid she wouldn't show," I said. "Why? Do you think she was lying?"

"I don't know if she was *lying,* but she might change her mind," Ted said. "From what Josh said yesterday, he didn't have a clue about why one sister wouldn't date him after he dumped the other one."

"I'm kind of on the fence about that one myself," I said. "Granted, I have no siblings, but in the case of Kelly and her sister and Josh — from what I understand — Josh only dated the sister a time or two. Two dates do not a relationship make. Therefore, Josh was okay in asking out the sister. Am I right?"

"I think so. The Bro Code is more about not dating someone your friend was in a relationship with." He shrugged and speared a chunk of turkey with his fork. "I'm not up

165

on the Bro Code or any of that stuff these days. I'm off the market."

CHAPTER TWELVE

Ted had been gone only about five minutes when an attractive woman in her late fifties to early sixties walked into the Seven-Year Stitch. She had light gray hair cut in an angular bob, and she wore a turquoise sheath dress and nude pumps. Even though it was cloudy, she wore tortoiseshell sunglasses. When she took them off, I could see that she had gorgeous blue eyes. She placed the sunglasses in the straw purse dangling from her left wrist.

Angus ambled over to say hello, and the woman immediately held up her right hand, sending half a dozen gold bangles of varying widths sliding to her elbow.

"Sit," she said.

He immediately obeyed the command.

"Hi, there," I said. "Welcome to the Seven-Year Stitch. I'm Marcy Singer. Is there anything I can help you find?"

"No, thank you." She strolled over to the

167

pattern books. "I'm merely browsing for now." She plucked one of the books off the rack and began thumbing through it. "I've heard a lot about you, Marcy."

"Good things, I hope."

"Mostly." She didn't look up from the book.

I was dying to ask her from whom she'd heard these *mostly* good things, but before I could ask she began talking again.

"Beautiful roses," she said.

"Thank you."

"From someone special?"

"Yes," I said.

"Where did you come up with the name of your shop?"

"Well, it took me seven years to finally realize my dream of opening my own embroidery specialty shop," I said. "And I'm a movie buff, so when I started trying to think of clever names, the Seven-Year Stitch just sort of clicked."

She nodded. "And that's why you have a life-size Marilyn Monroe doll standing by the counter? Because of the tie-in to *The Seven-Year Itch*?"

I suddenly felt silly. Did the woman *intend* to be condescending? Or was I taking offense where none was meant?

I was getting ready to explain that Jill —

the *mannequin* — was sort of a shop mascot and that I display some of my embroidered clothing on her, but Special Agent Floyd Brown sauntered into the shop. There was sweat beading on his forehead just below his spiky hairline. He'd forgone his dark sunglasses today, and his brown eyes looked puffy and tired.

"I'm sure you remember me, Ms. Singer. I'll allow you to conclude your business here, and then I have some questions for you."

The woman glanced up from the pattern book she was holding. "Then you should probably have a seat. I might be a while."

Special Agent Brown drew himself up to his full height but was still half a head shorter than the woman I was now calling the Ice Queen in my mind.

"I respectfully request that you conclude your business here as quickly as possible and leave so that I can speak privately with Ms. Singer, Ms. —"

"You may call me Veronica," said the Ice Queen. "And what may I call you?"

"Special Agent Floyd Brown of the Federal Bureau of Investigation." He puffed out his barrel chest.

"Thank you." The Ice Queen gave him a tight smile. "And to whom should I report you for barging into this young woman's place of business and harassing her in front of her patrons?"

Special Agent Brown gaped. My jaw dropped, too, but I quickly closed my mouth. Angus still sat where the Ice Queen had issued her command, but now he wagged his tail.

"I'm not . . . I didn't . . . !" Special Agent Brown sputtered at the Ice Queen for a moment, and then he turned to me. "Am I harassing you?"

I looked from him to the Ice Queen — who arched a brow — and then back to Special Agent Brown. "I *am* with a customer at the moment. And unless this is an emergency, you could wait patiently for us to conclude our business. Furthermore, there was no need to embarrass me in front of a patron."

The Ice Queen gave me a small nod of approval.

"I-I'm sorry," said Special Agent Brown. "I'll wait." He went to the sit-and-stitch square and sat on the sofa that faced the window.

I was still looking at the Ice Queen with a mixture of amazement and admiration. Nobody intimidated *this* woman!

"I definitely want this one." She handed

170

me the pattern book she held. "And I might want at least one other." She resumed her leisurely perusal.

Ted returned to the shop then. I guessed he was returning to tell me what, if anything, he had learned from Nellie Davis. As soon as he walked through the door, he stopped in his tracks.

"Mother? What are you doing here?"

The Ice Queen turned and smiled warmly. "Hello, love. I thought I might try a new hobby."

"Those eyes! I should've recognized those eyes!" I cried.

"Why should you?" asked the Ice Queen, whom I supposed I should really refer to as Veronica, seeing as she was Ted's mother. "Lots of people have blue eyes."

"Not as striking as Ted's," I said.

"That's true," said Veronica.

"Mother, you didn't introduce yourself?"

"I wasn't sure you'd want me to," she said.

"Then, by all means, allow me. Marcy, this is my mother, Veronica Nash. Mother, this is Marcy."

Wait a minute. *Ted* was the person who'd told her *mostly* good things about me? What had he said that *wasn't* good?

Veronica shook my hand. Her grip was firmer than that of some of the men I'd

171

known. Somehow I was not surprised.

She looked back at her son. "Oh, by the way, the gentleman on the sofa is Special Agent Floyd Brown of the Federal Bureau of Investigation. He is waiting for Marcy and me to conclude our business so he can ask her some questions."

Ted took a step toward his mother. "What did you do to him?" he whispered.

Veronica splayed her hand on her chest and looked indignant. "Who says I did anything?"

"Experience."

"I simply reminded him to be mannerly," she said. Then she raised her voice back to a normal speaking level. "Would you like to go say hello to your fellow law enforcement professional while Marcy and I finish up?"

"I might as well." Ted wandered over to the sit-and-stitch square with Angus close on his heels. "Brown."

"Nash."

It wasn't *hello* and *how are you doing?* but it sufficed, I supposed.

"It's so good to meet you, Ms. Nash," I said.

"It's a pleasure to meet you. Please call me Veronica." She put the pattern book she'd had in her hand back in the rack and chose another. "This counted cross-stitch . . . is it hard to do?"

"As with all embroidery, there are varying levels of expertise," I said. "But I believe you could master anything you set out to accomplish."

"Why, thank you." She smiled.

"You'll probably want to start off with something simple and advance as you grow more comfortable with the technique."

"All right. And you can help me get started?"

"I'd be happy to." I gestured toward the seating area. "That's the main reason I have a sit-and-stitch square. People can come by to get help or to simply have a friendly conversation while they work. I also offer classes three evenings a week."

"That sounds fantastic," Veronica said. "I'm in. I'll take that pattern book you're holding, this one here, and one of those kits that has the needles and hoop and thread."

I convinced Veronica to take a complete beginning cross-stitch kit that included a stamped pattern to get started. "That way you can see if you like it before you've invested too much time and money into the craft. And I'll be happy to hold your pattern books behind the counter until you've decided if cross-stitch is right for you."

"No, I like them. I'll take them with me. I

believe I'm going to enjoy this new hobby." She glanced toward her son and Special Agent Brown. "They don't seem very friendly toward each other."

"I don't think they are," I said softly. "But then, when Ted is investigating a case, he's like a hungry lion with a steak. Don't get in his way. He was rather frightening the first time we met. I thought he was hard-nosed and strictly business."

"I don't know where that aspect of his personality comes from," she said.

Even though she appeared honestly perplexed, I couldn't help myself — I laughed.

She laughed, too. "I never was a shrinking violet . . . but I don't imagine I've ever frightened anyone."

My eyes immediately went to Special Agent Brown. Oh, no — this woman had never scared anyone in her life . . . except a federal agent!

I led Veronica to the counter. "Will that be all?"

"For now," she said. "I plan to begin on this kit this evening. If I get stuck or need more supplies, I'll be back tomorrow."

I rang up her purchases and she paid with a gold credit card. Then she waved in the direction of the sit-and-stitch square.

"A bientôt, mon coeur!" she called.

"*A bientôt,* Mother," Ted said.

As Veronica breezed through the door and down the street, I joined Ted, Angus, and Special Agent Brown in the sit-and-stitch square.

"I had no idea your mother had an interest in needlework . . . or that she was coming by the shop today," I told Ted.

"Neither did I." He turned to the agent. "Brown, do you mind if I stick around while you talk with Marcy? I have some information that should interest you."

"No," said Special Agent Brown. "Whatever."

I sat on the sofa beside Ted and petted Angus as I waited to see what Special Agent Brown wanted to talk with me about.

He took a notebook from the left pocket of his blazer. "Ms. Singer, I have reason to believe that Geoffrey Vandehey was involved in the theft of the Padgett Collection from the Tallulah Falls Museum and Historical Society."

I thought it was weird that he was being so formal, and I wondered if he was always this way or if he was getting ready to accuse me of something — like of being in cahoots with the thieves or something.

"When you — as you *allege* — stumbled upon the body in the alley, did you see

175

anyone else in the immediate vicinity?" he asked.

I remembered and felt empowered by Veronica Nash's refusal to kowtow to Brown. I lifted my chin. "As I told you on Saturday, Special Agent Brown, I took out my garbage. When I turned to come back inside the shop, I saw what appeared to be a kilim from the Padgett Collection. I stepped closer and saw that there was someone wrapped up in the rug. I instantly called the police. And no, I do not remember seeing anyone else in the alley until Blake MacKenzie came to my assistance." I leaned forward. "Do you have any evidence to refute my statement in any way?"

"No, but —"

"Then please do not refer to it as an allegation," I said.

Ted lowered his head and covered his mouth with his hand.

"Very well," said Special Agent Brown. "Did you investigate the body?"

"No. I thought it best to leave that to the professionals."

"Yes, but you *did* see Geoffrey Vandehey's face, did you not?" he asked.

"I did, though at that time I didn't know who he was," I answered.

"Right. Did you notice and perhaps pick

up any paper or other debris lying near the body?"

"Of course not!" I grimaced. "Why would I do that?"

Special Agent Brown flipped his hands palms up. "I don't know. I was merely hoping that you'd seen something . . . maybe a slip of paper . . . and that you'd carried it inside and laid it down somewhere when you came in and then forgot about it. I'm looking for anything that would give me a clue as to who Vandehey was working with."

"I'm sorry," I said, taking a kinder tone. "I've told you all I know."

"Our crime scene techs were on the scene within twenty minutes of Marcy's discovery of the body," Ted said. "You've seen everything they found on or near the corpse."

"I know." He rubbed his eyes.

"But, hopefully, Nellie Davis might be of help," Ted said. "Ms. Davis owns the aromatherapy shop two doors down."

The shop between mine and Nellie's was currently for lease.

"Ms. Davis came by and told Marcy this morning that she was working in her office late Friday night," Ted continued. "She said she didn't know what time it was, but I got her to admit that she was here until the wee hours of Saturday morning. That fits with the coroner's timeline for Vandehey's death."

"So this Davis woman was here at the time Vandehey's body was dumped in the alley?" Special Agent Brown asked.

"I think so," said Ted. "When we began talking, she said at first that she didn't see or hear anything. But when I promised her protection, said I'd try my best to retain her anonymity, and impressed upon her the fact that the slightest detail could help, she told me that she'd peeped out the window when she heard a vehicle engine start up. A black van was speeding away."

"But you already knew that from the surveillance video," I pointed out.

"True, but I'm hoping she'll remember something else. Even a couple numbers from the license plate would help," he said.

"A black van . . . That's not much, but at least, it's something," Special Agent Brown said. "Thanks, Nash. I appreciate your sharing that information with me. I think I'll pay Ms. Davis a visit myself." He stood, thanked us both for our time, and left.

Ted cocked his head toward me and gave me a bemused grin.

"What?" I asked.

"How long were you with my mother to learn that lesson in boldness?"

I giggled. "Not long. I don't know, Ted. . . . Special Agent Brown came in here ready to throw his weight around, and she politely let him know that he could throw his weight right down on the sofa and wait his turn."

He arched an eyebrow. "Politely?"

"Pretty much," I said. "She wasn't about to let him browbeat her into leaving, and she let him know that. I was impressed."

"I was impressed with you," he said. "You handled yourself exceptionally well. Brown will bully you if he can, but he'll back down quickly if he knows he can't."

"You and your mother favor each other," I said. "Now that I know she's your mom, I can see the resemblance so clearly. I don't know how I missed it at first."

"Like you and I both said earlier, we didn't know she was dropping in today . . . or any day."

"Why hadn't you introduced me to her before?" I asked.

"As you saw, Mother can be a bit hard to take." He looked away and scratched Angus's head. "I didn't want her to jeopardize our relationship."

"She won't. Our relationship is all about you and me — no one else."

"That's easy to say, but I've seen miserable family relations create stress between

179

more than one couple," he said. "Add that to existing stresses, and it can tear them apart."

"Do you and your mom have a miserable relationship?" I asked.

"No. I believe we have a fairly good relationship, but we don't share the closeness you and Beverly have." He shrugged. "And Mother can be hypercritical, especially until she gets to know and like a person."

"I can believe that," I said, thinking back to her comment about the Marilyn Monroe doll. "When she first came in and I introduced myself, she said she'd heard *mostly* good things about me. What did she mean by that?"

"Beats me. I say only great things when I talk about you," he said. "When she introduced herself, she didn't tell you her name?"

"No. Of course, Special Agent Brown came in shortly thereafter. Maybe she just didn't have time."

"And maybe she didn't want to tell you her name until she'd seen the real you," he said. "She would want you to be yourself . . . not put on airs if you found out she was my mother. Not that you *would,* but she doesn't know you . . . yet."

"Yet," I echoed.

Ted chuckled. "The expression on

Brown's face when I walked in here was priceless. He appeared to have been put in time-out."

"He *had* been, more or less. All it took for your mom to put him there was a veiled threat."

Ted laughed again, but I didn't. I felt uneasy. Was he telling me the truth about why he hadn't "taken me home to Mother"? Was it that he didn't want her abrasiveness to scare me off? Or was it that he wasn't serious about our relationship?

And what about Veronica Nash? Did she want to be my friend or my enemy?

CHAPTER THIRTEEN

Angus and I had just got back to the Seven-Year Stitch after going home for dinner. My crewel class would be starting in thirty minutes, so I was putting hard candy in a bowl to go on the counter and making sure I had enough bottled water in the mini fridge.

I heard the bells jingle and knew someone had arrived. I turned to see Kelly Conrad walk in and greet Angus.

"Hi, Kelly," I said. "Are you here for class?"

"No, I was walking by and saw that you were here and just wanted to say hey."

"Well, I'm glad you did. You can come by and say hey anytime." I smiled.

"I saw Josh at lunchtime today," she said. "He's really down."

"I know. I feel bad for him."

"Me, too. He's so afraid he'll lose his job over everything that has happened."

"I'm worried about the entire museum," I said. "I mean, the theft has cast such a pall over it. When I took the muffins by there this morning, there was no one there. Had traffic picked up any when you were there during lunch?"

"There were a couple of people there, but I got the feeling they were more curious about the theft than they were about any of the exhibits." She sighed. "I don't particularly *like* Josh, but I hate seeing him hurt."

"If I'm not being too personal, why don't you like Josh?" I asked.

She bit her lip. "Right after he dated my older sister, he asked me out. I thought that was a totally inappropriate thing to do."

"Had he and your sister dated long?"

"No. In fact, they'd only been on two dates," she said. "But that breaks some sort of etiquette code, doesn't it?"

"I don't know. I don't have any siblings." I fluffed the pillows on the sofa nearest me. "Had you met Josh first, would you have gone out with him?"

"Oh, sure!"

I glanced up, and she blushed and lowered her eyes.

"I mean . . . probably," she said. "He was sweet, cute, funny . . ."

"I'm certainly no expert, and I'm not

familiar with sibling codes, but why don't you talk with your sister? If she's okay with your seeing Josh, I see no reason why you shouldn't."

"I'll think about it," said Kelly.

Riley Kendall — friend, mom, hotshot attorney — barreled through the door like a woman on a mission. "Freedom!" She noticed Kelly. "Oops. I thought I was the first one here."

"That's okay," Kelly said. "I'd just stopped by to say hi to Marcy. I was just leaving."

"Don't go on my account," said Riley. Her dark hair was piled on top of her head in a messy bun, and she wore shorts and a T-shirt.

"You know, Riley, I've never seen you look this . . . free," I said.

"You mean sloppy?" She grinned, kicked off her sandals, and put her feet up on the ottoman.

Angus went to check out Riley's toes.

I laughed. "No, I think *free* is the better word."

"It's certainly the more tactful word," she said.

"Riley Kendall, this is Kelly Conrad," I said.

The women didn't shake hands but exchanged the typical *nice to meet you*s.

"I wish you'd stay for class," I told Kelly. "The first one's on the house."

"No, thanks," she said. "I really need to be getting home. I might try a class some other time, though."

"I hope you will. Take care, Kelly."

She said good-bye and left the shop.

I turned back to Riley. "So, tell me about this freedom."

"I feel guilty to put it that way, but honestly, Marce, I've been exhausted lately. It's great to have some time just for me. Mom's with the baby, Keith is playing softball, and I have no obligations for the next couple hours."

"You shouldn't feel guilty about that," I said. "In fact, I'm flattered that you get a couple hours and choose to spend them here!"

"Well, I *am* going to enjoy a soak in a bubble bath and a nonfat, decaf latte when I leave here." She frowned. "Decaf. That's probably one of the reasons I've been so tired all the time lately — no caffeine because I'm breast-feeding."

"Or you *could* be exhausted because you have a bazillion cases and you're the mother of a five-month-old baby," I said.

She grinned. "Could be. But lack of caffeine definitely does not help matters."

185

"You wouldn't happen to have a recent photo of Laura, would you?" I asked.

"It just so happens that I do! I took one of her and Mom before I left the house." She pulled the photo up on her phone, and I smiled at the image of the chubby, grinning baby.

Then I noticed Riley's mom, Camille Patrick, and my eyes widened. "Your mom got her hair cut!"

"She did," Riley said. "Just a few days ago. Do you like it?"

"I do." The long hair Camille had usually worn in a severe updo had been cut and styled into flattering chin-length layers. "It makes her look ten years younger."

"I think so, too."

Before we could talk more about Riley's baby or her mother's hair, Vera joined us. It seemed as if Vera had come through the door in midsentence. In fact, I initially thought she was speaking into a phone headset, but she wasn't.

"— can't believe Anderson Padgett is coming here tomorrow, can you?" Vera was asking.

"I can," I said. "Ted and I are having lunch with him and Simon Benton."

"Well, I want to hear all about it when you get back," she said. "In fact, I'd like to meet Mr. Padgett myself. Do you think you can wrangle an invitation?"

"I don't know," I said.

Riley held up her hand. "Hold up. Why's Anderson Padgett taking you to lunch? I mean, no offense, but it would seem to me that the man would want to come here, meet with the police, offer a reward, and go home. On second thought, why is he coming here at all? He could have taken care of all of his business over the phone."

"You know, I've wondered the same thing," I said. "He was apparently too ill to travel and sent his friend Simon Benton to Tallulah Falls to make sure his collection was in good hands."

"Which is another weird thing," said Riley. "If he was concerned about the collection being in good hands, why did he agree to loan it to the museum in the first place?"

"From what Paul has told me, Padgett was looking to sell off a few of his pieces," Vera said. "He loaned the collection to the museum for the publicity and to get it seen by art collectors with deep pockets like Chad Cummings."

"Is Padgett in financial trouble?" I asked.

"Not that I know of," Vera said. "Paul says Padgett could just be selling off some of his collection to make room for more stuff."

"Or it could be that he's very ill and is liquidating his assets," said Riley. "Some people do that to make it easier to settle their estate."

"Well, that's grim," I said.

Riley laughed. "It's true!"

"It is," Vera agreed. "I heard once about a mother dying and her three daughters fighting over everything the poor woman had. The collections she'd gathered over the years were nothing all that valuable, not like Anderson Padgett's art collections — stamps, decorative teacups, a certain set of figurines — and the daughters divided and sold them. I suppose the mom thought they would each take one of her collections and treasure it, but they just wanted the money."

"I see that all the time," Riley said. "That's why it often makes more sense to liquidate. Then there is a set amount of money to be divided among the heirs."

"I'll bet it's still not that simple," said Vera.

"Not always." Riley took her project out of a canvas tote. "I didn't make much progress this week."

"It's coming along great," I lied. Okay, it wasn't a lie exactly. The squirrel in the daisy patch Riley was making for Laura's nursery was going to be beautiful. But Laura might have to put it in her college dorm room rather than in her nursery.

Vera took out her project and thrust it at me. "I can't get this couching thing down to save my life. My strawberries are looking more like raspberries."

"No . . . you're getting it," I said. "You just need a little more practice. Let's take this out, and we'll do it again . . . together."

"You do the first one, and I'll watch," said Vera.

The rest of the class began filtering in, so before I could undo Vera's raspberry, I greeted everyone and offered them some water. I had a feeling tonight's class was going to run long.

I'd been right — the class had gone over by half an hour. By the time Angus and I got home, I was dragging. It had been a long day.

I let Angus go out into the backyard to play for a few minutes, and I thought about Riley's plan to take a bubble bath and sip a latte. That sounded like a winner to me, so I went upstairs to run my bathwater. While the water was running, I came back downstairs and made myself an instant caramel latte. It wasn't decaf, but I didn't have any fear that the caffeine would keep me awake tonight.

I let Angus back in and then went upstairs to sink into the tub. I took the latte and the phone with me. Angus followed me and flopped down on the floor outside the bathroom. I think it's sweet that he feels the need to protect me from whatever might be lurking inside my powder room.

A sudden image of Geoffrey Vandehey wrapped in the kilim outside my shop made me shudder, and the thought of something dangerous being in my bathroom wasn't so fanciful anymore. I *had* locked both doors, hadn't I? Yes, I was sure I had.

I eased into the warm water, took a sip of my latte, and called Mom.

She answered on the first ring. "Hello, darling. How are you?"

"I'm tired, Mom. How are you?"

"I'm fabulous! I just got off the phone not ten minutes ago from a producer who's hiring me to do a television miniseries set in Kansas in the late 1800s."

"So you're packing to go to Kansas?" I asked.

"Nope. They're shooting the entire thing on a soundstage in Los Angeles. I'll get to practically work from home. Isn't that wonderful?"

"It is," I said.

"I'm really excited, even though the

190

miniseries is based on a dreadful true story."

"How dreadful?"

"The worst," she said. "The miniseries sets forth the events of the Bender family, also known as the Bloody Benders. Isn't that gruesome?"

I agreed that it was. "Why were these Benders so bloody?"

"They were serial killers. The mom and dad were real oddballs."

"Uh, yeah, Mom . . . they were *serial killers.*"

She laughed. "Let me finish. They weren't very sociable. But from what I understand, the daughter was dynamic and attractive. She also claimed to be a spiritualist and a healer. It was she who lured wealthy travelers to the Benders' inn. Then, when the guest was having dinner, either the father or the son would bash the traveler's head in with a hammer."

"How pleasant! I'm going to change your ringtone to a bloodcurdling scream as soon as we're finished talking."

"Well, what about you and your real-life drama? Did you ever find out the name of that man you found in the alley?" she asked.

"Yes. He was Geoffrey Vandehey. He'd been a professor of art history at a university in Canada, but a few years back he stole a painting."

"Vandehey . . ." She paused. "Was the painting a Cézanne?"

"Yes, it was," I said. "It was supposed to have been a very early work of Cézanne's."

"I remember hearing about that. This Vandehey fellow had gone to appraise the painting, hadn't he?"

"He had. But, you know, I was talking with the museum curator today, and he mentioned that Cummings — the collector from whom the Cézanne was stolen — should have had the piece appraised before he had it insured," I said. "But after it was stolen, the insurance company paid Cummings twenty million."

"That does sound a little fishy," Mom agreed. "Maybe the collector had come to doubt the painting's authenticity for some reason."

"That's possible. He could've thought the original appraiser misled him for some reason." I took another sip of the latte and then set it back onto the tile floor beside the tub. "I hadn't thought of that."

"People do strange things for strange reasons."

"Speaking of that . . ." I told Mom about Ted's mother's coming into the shop today. I described her appearance, her demeanor, and the fact that she said she'd heard "mostly" good things about me. "I mentioned that part to Ted, but he said he'd only told her great things about me."

"You don't sound so sure."

"Well, the whole incident made me feel — I don't know — insecure," I said. "For one thing, why hadn't Ted ever taken me to meet her before now? And for another, why did she come into my shop and not even tell me who she was?"

"I imagine she was doing a little reconnaissance," said Mom. "As for Ted, I believe either he was waiting for a good time or he hadn't given the matter that much thought."

"You don't think it's because he's not serious about me?"

"Oh, darling, that man is over the moon for you. He adores you. Did you ask him why he hadn't introduced you to his mother before now?"

"Yes. He said that he and his mother are on good terms but not as close as you and I," I said. "He told me that he didn't want his mother to jeopardize our relationship."

"Well, there you go."

"It's not that simple."

"How do you know it isn't that simple?" she asked. "It sounds to me as if it's extremely simple. The man has a domineering mom with a forceful personality, and he didn't want the woman to intimidate or try to bully the woman he loves and is considering spending the rest of his life with."

I was quiet for so long that Mom had to ask if I was still there.

"You think Ted wants to spend the rest of his life with me?"

"I believe that's a strong possibility," she said. "So don't see slights where there were none intended. Ted had a short-lived first marriage, right?"

"Right."

"How do you know his mother didn't do something to drive a wedge between him and his first wife?"

"I don't," I said. "In fact, he said he'd seen other family members add to existing stresses in people's relationships before. Maybe that's what he was talking about."

"Maybe so."

"I don't want her to drive a wedge between Ted and me, Mom."

"Then don't let her." She thought a moment. "But the same thing I told you about Ted applies to his mother — don't expect to be offended. It's possible she was simply curious about you and wanted to come and check you out for herself. Was she abrasive?"

"She was kind of critical." I told her what

Veronica had said about the Marilyn Monroe doll.

Mom laughed. "It sounds like she needs a little more fun in her life. You could be the breath of fresh air she needs."

"It didn't make me feel like a breath of fresh air when she said it. It made me feel like I was silly."

"Marcella Singer, are you silly?"

"Sometimes."

"Is there anything wrong with being silly?"

"I guess not."

"I *know* not," she said. "For goodness' sake, I dress people up — sometimes in the most ridiculous costumes you could imagine — for a living. How silly is that?"

"You're right. I shouldn't let anyone make me doubt myself."

"No, you shouldn't."

"She was just so self-assured," I said. "The minute she walked into the Stitch, Angus went up to her, and she lifted her right hand and told him to sit. He did, and he didn't get up until Ted came in!"

"She wasn't harsh with my grand-dog, was she?"

"Harsh, no. Authoritative, yes." I chuckled. "And she practically told Special Agent Brown to go sit in the corner!" I told Mom how Veronica had chastised Special Agent

Brown for barging into my shop and confronting me in front of a customer.

"Good for her. It appears Ms. Nash wouldn't stand for seeing you be disrespected."

"Yeah . . . and after she left and I did answer Special Agent Brown's questions, I stood up to him and didn't let him intimidate me. Ted teased me about his mom having given me a lesson in boldness." I sighed. "She bought an embroidery kit and two pattern books. I have a strong feeling she'll be back. I just don't know whether it's to befriend me or try to come between her son and me."

"Well, my darling, my advice is this: Keep both eyes open, but expect the best from her. All mothers want their children to be cherished. When she sees how much you care about Ted, she'll love you."

"I hope so," I said.

"I *know* so. Why do you think I'm so crazy about Ted?"

When we were finished talking, I immediately looked up *bloodcurdling scream* in my ringtones and gave it to Mom's number. Of course, I'd have to keep my phone turned down at work to avoid scaring my customers — and myself — silly. But

Mom didn't call that often . . . and it would be fun to freak out Sadie or Ted.

CHAPTER FOURTEEN

I'd been busy unpacking a shipment of ribbon-embroidery kits and let time get away from me. Now it was almost time for Simon Benton and Anderson Padgett to be here, and I hadn't taken Angus for his mid-morning walk yet.

I went to the counter and got his leash. At the sight of the leash, he hurried over to me. I snapped the leash onto his collar, put the cardboard clock on the door saying I'd be back in ten minutes, and took Angus right toward the square. The square was a large open grassy area with a tall wrought-iron clock in the center and benches around all four sides. It was a nice place to sit and catch your breath after shopping up and down both sides of the street, or to read, or to people-watch . . . especially on a sunny, warm day like today. I kind of wished Angus and I had time to linger, but we didn't.

We walked back down the street toward

the Seven-Year Stitch. As we passed Nellie Davis's shop, Scentsibilities, she was standing at her door.

"Hello," she said.

"Good morning, Nellie."

She held out a candle. "This is for you. It's for stress relief. I thought you might need it because of Saturday. I've been using one this week."

"Thank you." I took the candle and sniffed it. "I hope you're feeling better after talking with Ted."

"Ted, yes. That other man, not so much. What was his name?"

"Special Agent Brown?"

"Yes, that's him," she said. "He made me nervous. I burned my stress candle the rest of the day after he left."

"He makes me nervous, too. I don't like his attitude. He's so accusatory . . . like I've done something wrong."

"That's how he made me feel, too! Like I was hiding something after I admitted to seeing that van."

"Well, don't pay him any mind," I said. "Everything will be fine."

I heard a car door slam shut. Simon Benton was getting out of a car parked across the street from the Stitch.

"I'd better run. That's my —" I stopped

short when I turned to look back at Nellie and realized she'd gone back into her shop and closed the door. Oh, well. So much for our friendly conversation.

I did appreciate the cinnamon and frankincense candle, though. I made a mental note to prepare Nellie a thank-you card. Maybe this incident would be a turning point for Nellie and me. We could become friends. Okay, probably not, but we might at least be more civil toward each other. I'd like to be able to think of Nellie without clenching my teeth.

As I walked the rest of the way to the Seven-Year Stitch, I noticed that Mr. Benton was pushing Mr. Padgett in a wheelchair, and Mr. Padgett had a light blanket lying on his lap. The poor man must have been more infirm than I'd realized. Riley might have been right — Mr. Padgett might be liquidating his assets and preparing for the worst.

I quickly got Angus inside and placed him in the bathroom.

"I'm sorry, baby," I told him. "It's just until Mr. Benton gets Mr. Padgett inside. He might not want to come face-to-face with a puppy dog the instant he gets into the store."

I ran back to the front door and held it

open for the two men.

"Hello, I'm Marcy," I said to Mr. Padgett over the din of Angus's barking.

He extended his hand. "Anderson Padgett. It's a pleasure to meet you, young lady. Simon has been highly complimentary of you."

"Thank you," I said. "And, of course, I appreciate your speaking well of me, Mr. Benton."

He smiled. "Simon, please." He gazed around the shop. "Is Detective Nash here?"

Before I could say no, I spotted Ted on the sidewalk.

"He's just now arriving," I said.

"It sounds as if you have a rather large protector somewhere in the back," Mr. Padgett said with a wheezing chuckle. "I wouldn't have thought you'd need a guard dog in this quaint town."

"He's more of a companion really," I said with a smile.

Ted came through the door and greeted Mr. Benton and Mr. Padgett. Mr. Benton made the introductions and Ted shook hands with Mr. Padgett.

"If the three of you would like to start on down to MacKenzies' Mochas, I'll reset the clock on the door and let Angus into the shop," I said. "I'll join you momentarily."

Ted held the door for Mr. Benton to push Mr. Padgett's wheelchair through, and then he turned and winked at me before going out the door.

I smiled. My heart skipped two and a half beats every time I looked at that man.

I let Angus out of the bathroom, kissed him on the head, and then rushed out the door to catch up to Ted and our dining companions. I wondered for the umpteenth time why Simon Benton had arranged this meeting. I could understand his wanting Mr. Padgett to talk with Ted — he was investigating the museum heist — but why would he want to talk with me?

Whatever the reason, I was glad I'd forgone the jeans and T-shirt this morning in favor of a sleeveless red sheath, kitten-heel strappy black sandals, and a bold silver cuff. All three of the men were wearing suits, a fact that I'd anticipated when I got dressed. There was nothing more uncomfortable than feeling like the "poor relation" in a Victorian novel.

Ted held the door, this time at MacKenzies' Mochas, for the rest of us. Mr. Padgett insisted I go in ahead of him. I appreciated his chivalry, but it did make me feel rather oafish to walk ahead of a man in a wheelchair.

"Hi! Welcome to MacKenzies' Mochas," Sadie said when we walked in. She gave me a quizzical look, and I nodded slightly to let her know I'd fill her in on all the details later. "Will there just be the four of you?"

"Yes," said Simon Benton.

"Right this way." Sadie led us to a table and took away one of the chairs to accommodate Mr. Padgett's wheelchair. She handed each of us a menu and told us our server would be with us momentarily.

Our server was a new waitress named Cheyenne. She was working for MacKenzies' Mochas while furthering her education at the Tallulah County Community College. She was a bubbly redhead with green eyes and a ready smile. Cheyenne took our orders and left us to talk.

"Ms. Singer, did you get to see my collection before it disappeared from the museum?" Mr. Padgett asked.

"I did. My favorite piece was the David and Goliath tapestry," I said. "It's magnificent."

"It is, isn't it?" He drew his eyebrows together. "I hope it hasn't come to any harm."

"I hope so, too." I glanced at Ted, but of course, he could offer no reassurances.

Cheyenne arrived with our drinks, passed

203

them around, said our food would be out in just a few minutes, and asked if we needed anything else. When we all denied needing anything at the moment, she scurried off to refill another diner's water glass.

"I've always enjoyed your Japanese textiles myself," said Mr. Benton to Mr. Padgett. "I absolutely adored that lotus from the Meiji period. It was breathtaking." He shook a finger playfully at Mr. Padgett. "I told you to sell me that one."

"I wish I had," Mr. Padgett said. "The chances of either of us ever seeing it again are slim to none."

"Don't give up hope yet, Mr. Padgett," said Ted. "We're following up on a number of leads."

"And there's a chap here from the Federal Bureau of Investigation as well," said Mr. Benton. "I'm not terribly impressed with him, however. I'd appreciate none of you passing this information along, but I don't feel that Special Agent Brown is as competent as I would have liked him to be."

"I think he's a decent guy." Ted took a drink of his water. "But he has his mind on two major cases at once right now, so he might seem a bit scattered."

"Two major cases? Here in Tallulah Falls?" Mr. Padgett sounded incredulous.

"Yes, Special Agent Brown had been searching for the man who was found murdered on Saturday morning," Ted said.

"The man wrapped in my kilim," Mr. Padgett said. "Do you believe he was connected to the museum theft?"

"It's a possibility," Ted answered. "Again, we're pursuing every lead."

"What was his name again?" asked Mr. Padgett. "The police told me, but it slips my mind right now."

"It was Geoffrey Vandehey." Ted took another drink of his water.

"Geoffrey Vandehey." Mr. Padgett squinted. "I've heard that name before . . . and not in connection with my kilim or the art theft."

"Vandehey is the chap who stole that early Cézanne from that art collector in Seattle two years back," said Mr. Benton.

"No, that's not it," said Mr. Padgett. "I'd heard about that theft, naturally, but I've heard the name Vandehey in connection with something more recent."

"Whatever it was, it's nothing to trouble yourself about, Andy," said Mr. Benton. "If this Vandehey fellow is — or was — connected to the theft of your textile collection, Detective Nash here will get to the bottom of it. I'm as impressed with Detective Nash

205

and his team as I am *un*impressed with Special Agent Brown."

Cheyenne and another waitress came with trays bearing our food. Ted seemed relieved.

After lunch, I went back to the Seven-Year Stitch and began making Nellie Davis a thank-you note for the stress candle she'd given me this morning. I thought that Ted and I might light the candle over dinner or after class this evening. He didn't usually seem uncomfortable being on the other side of the interrogation table, but he had appeared to be today. I wondered why.

I wanted to make Nellie's card as quickly as possible — the thought of feeling indebted to that woman made *me* uncomfortable — so I went to my office and got my ribbon-embroidery supplies. I put a piece of linen fabric in a small hoop and threaded a length of thin yellow ribbon through the large eye of the needle. I made a circle of ribbon loops and left the inside to be filled in later with black embroidery thread. I was making Nellie a bouquet of black-eyed Susans.

I used the yellow ribbon to create three flowers, and then I took some dark green ribbon to make some leaves around them. Finally, I threaded the needle with six-strand black embroidery floss and filled the inner circles of the yellow flowers with French knots.

I was finishing up the last flower when someone came into the shop. He was about five feet five inches tall, had black hair and dark brown eyes. He wore khaki pants and a light blue polo shirt. And he looked tired. There were circles beneath his eyes, his clothes were slightly rumpled, and his mouth was slack. I knew before he even told me that he was George Vandehey, Geoffrey Vandehey's son.

I put aside the embroidery hoop and stood. "Hello. I'm Marcy."

"I'm George Vandehey. I understand you found my father."

"I did." I stepped toward him. "I'm so terribly sorry for your loss."

"Thanks." His voice was barely above a whisper.

"Please sit down," I said. "May I get you some coffee or a soda or a bottle of water?"

"Water would be nice. It's hot out there."

"It is." I went to the office and got Mr. Vandehey a bottle of water.

Angus wandered over, sighed, and placed his head on Mr. Vandehey's knee.

"Angus, no," I said.

"It's all right," said Mr. Vandehey. "I like

him." He stroked the dog's head.

"He knows you're sad." I handed him the water.

"Thank you. And thank *you*, Angus. You're a good boy."

"He is . . . a good therapist, too," I said. I didn't have to wait long for the question I'd immediately known was coming and dreaded.

"Did he appear to have suffered?"

I wasn't sure how to answer that. Of course he suffered! He was shot, rolled up in a rug, and dumped in an alley!

"No," I said. "I don't think so."

"He wasn't a bad man," said Mr. Vandehey, "no matter what you've heard about him."

"Oh, I know he wasn't. I sensed that immediately, Mr. Vandehey."

"Please call me George."

"George," I said. "I did hear about the Cézanne, of course, but I also know about your sister's accident. I believe your father's actions were those of a desperate man."

"That's true. We were all devastated by Libby's accident. She'd been such a vibrant person . . . always on the go . . . riding that bike of hers everywhere." He closed his eyes. "And then she was blindsided by that truck . . . and it never stopped. Witnesses described it as a four-door white pickup truck, but no one got a license plate number."

"The driver of the truck was never found?"

He shook his head and tears escaped from beneath his closed lids and rolled down his cheeks.

Angus licked his hand.

George opened his eyes and patted the dog. "Libby was paralyzed from the neck down. She and her husband had some insurance, but their deductibles and outstanding medical costs were far more than they could pay. Libby's husband, Miles, was planning to file for bankruptcy, but Dad implored him not to. He didn't want their credit to be ruined. Besides, Libby's health care costs would be ongoing for quite some time."

"Is there any hope that Libby will regain function in her limbs?" I asked.

"There's an operation that can be done," George said. "I think that's why Dad was here — to secure the money for that operation."

"Do you think he was involved in the Padgett Collection theft?"

"I don't know. After the Cézanne disappeared, we didn't hear from Dad for a couple of weeks," he said. "Of course, we didn't know anything about the painting. We love art — our entire family always has — but we were in Canada. We didn't hear anything about the art theft in Seattle until after Dad's confession letter was found."

"And then your dad sent money for Libby?" I asked.

"Not exactly. Money just appeared in our accounts. Libby and Miles received a hundred and fifty thousand and I got fifty thousand." He smiled sadly. "He didn't want me to feel left out, I guess. And then he called me at work one day and told me he wouldn't get to see us for a while. I asked what he'd done . . . where the money had come from. He said he'd entered into a transaction with someone, and that the police now believed he stole a valuable painting."

"Wait." I placed my hand on George's forearm. "Your dad *didn't* steal the Cézanne?"

"I don't know what to think," he said. "He said he'd *entered into a transaction*. But where did the money come from?"

"Could someone have paid him to take the painting?"

"That's possible. But it's also conceivable that my father took the painting but didn't want to admit it to us."

I stood and began to pace. "Chad Cummings made twenty million dollars from the insurance company after the Cézanne was stolen. He bragged to me right here in this shop that he made more than ten times what he'd paid for it."

"And you think he might've paid Dad to steal the painting."

"Think about it," I said. "Your dad goes to Seattle at Chad Cummings's bidding to appraise his painting — which had already been appraised for the insurance company. What if Cummings only contacted your father because he'd heard about Libby's accident and thought Dr. Vandehey might be in need of money to help pay for her health care costs?"

George nodded.

"This thought isn't new to you."

"No, it isn't," he said. "In fact, it's the main reason I'm in Tallulah Falls and plan to stay here until Dad's murderer has been caught."

I sat back down and lowered my voice. "You believe Chad Cummings paid your dad to help him commit insurance fraud."

"Yes, I do," George said. "And when we found out about the operation that could help Libby, I think Dad contacted Chad for more money."

"But Cummings blew him off," I said. "He had a letter confessing that Dr. Vandehey had stolen the painting. Any retraction of that confession would be — in Cummings's eyes — the word of a thief versus the word of a respected art collector."

"Not just in Chad Cummings's eyes. Every law enforcement official on the case would have seen it that way, too."

"Like Special Agent Floyd Brown."

"You sound like you've had the pleasure of making Special Agent Brown's acquaintance," said George.

"I certainly wouldn't call it a pleasure." I looked into George's solemn brown eyes. "Do you think Chad Cummings killed your father?"

"I'm almost sure of it."

"We need to call Ted," I told him. "Detective Ted Nash . . . he's my boyfriend. . . . He's the lead investigator on the case. We should let him know about this right away."

"Not right now . . . please. I'm tired, and I'd like to go back to my hotel room and rest."

"Of course. Would you like to come to my house this evening? The two of you can talk privately there."

"Possibly," he said. "I'm afraid any law enforcement officials would ruin my case against Chad until I can gather adequate evidence against him."

"Not Ted," I said, scribbling my address on the back of my business card and handing it to George. "He'll know exactly what to do."

CHAPTER FIFTEEN

I called Ted immediately upon George's departure. Poor little Angus, still empathizing with George's depressed demeanor, went to sigh by the window. Thankfully, he'd never seen a silent movie, or else he'd have been lying on the sofa with one paw up over his head à la Theda Bara or Clara Bow.

"You're missing me already?" Ted asked when he answered my call.

"Yes, but that's not why I'm calling," I said. "I have a new lead on the murder of Geoffrey Vandehey."

"Let's have it, Inch-High."

"George Vandehey came by to see me just now and told me he thinks Chad Cummings killed his dad."

"Because Dr. Vandehey stole his painting?" Ted asked.

"No, because he thinks Cummings paid his dad to take the painting and write the confession so that Cummings could commit insurance fraud."

"I don't know, babe. That could be wishful thinking on George's part."

"But it could also be true," I said. "It's like he said, at this point, no one would have believed Dr. Vandehey had he gone to the police."

"Right. So what was the point in Chad Cummings killing him? Had Dr. Vandehey come forward, he would have immediately been arrested," Ted said. "Now, if you were explaining the motive Vandehey had to kill *Cummings,* that would make more sense."

"Would you talk to George anyway?" I asked. "I invited him to meet with us at my house after class this evening."

"Sure, I'll see what he has to say."

"Thanks. I'm not sure he'll come, but he might. I told him you were wonderful."

He chuckled. "Are you trying to use your feminine wiles on me, Ms. Singer?"

"Mmm-hmm. Is it working?"

"Mmm-hmm."

I laughed. "See you after class."

"Looking forward to that . . . seeing you . . . meeting George Vandehey, not so much."

"By the way, why did you appear to be so uncomfortable at lunch today?" I asked.

"Because Anderson Padgett was right — the chances of him recovering his art collection are slim to none. He's obviously not in good health, and I didn't want to admit that to him."

"He knows, of course."

"He does," Ted admitted. "But I'm going to do everything I can to help him get it back. I'm just not optimistic about my efforts paying off."

"I have confidence in you."

"Even after yesterday?" he asked.

"Even after yesterday."

Sadie came over after the lunch rush. I was writing Nellie Davis's name on the envelope of the ribbon-embroidery card I'd made for her.

"What's up with that?" Sadie asked. "Is there a little spring-loaded fist in there that's going to come up and pop Nellie in the nose when she opens the card?"

I giggled. "No. This morning when Angus and I were passing by her shop, she stepped out and gave me a stress candle."

"A stress-*relief* candle or a stress-*inducing* candle?"

"A stress-relief candle . . . I think. Now that you mention it, I'd better look at the label to be sure." I looked at the label and then turned it toward Sadie. "Yep. See? It says so right there."

"Well, I'll be. What brought that on?"

I explained Nellie's visit to me yesterday. "She acted like she was scared half to death. Ted went over and talked with her, and then Special Agent Brown did, too. She told me this morning that she appreciated Ted's visit, but she hadn't cared for Brown's attitude. I basically told her welcome to the club."

"Yeah, that guy's a jerk. He came to talk with Blake and me Saturday afternoon. He also detained our staff and let business back up while he questioned them, even though the on-duty staff was not the staff that had been working Friday night." She rolled her eyes. "Manu sent his deputies to talk with the people who'd worked the night before."

"I have no idea why Brown won't listen to reason. He seems to have no common sense whatsoever. It's like he wants to rearrange the facts to make them what he wants them to be. Yesterday he said that I *alleged* stumbling over the body." I spread my hands. "Like I . . . what? Killed Professor Vandehey, wrapped him in either a rug that I stole or a stolen rug that happened to be lying around in my alley, and then left him until the next morning when I pretended to stumble over his body? How ridiculous is that?"

"That's pretty out there, Marce. Maybe *Blake* killed the guy, wrapped him in said rug, left him outside your shop so it wouldn't be too close to MacKenzies' Mochas, and waited for you to stumble over the body so you could call Ted, Ted could call Blake, and Blake could come and be surprised."

I laughed. "That is perfect Special Agent Brown logic!"

"So, what was with the old guys you and Ted were lunching with today?" she asked. "They aren't wedding directors or anything, are they?"

"No, they aren't wedding directors. One was Anderson Padgett."

"The guy whose art collection was stolen?"

"The very same," I said. "He was the older one in the wheelchair. The other man was his friend Simon Benton."

"Not that it's any of my business . . ."

"Not that that will stop you from asking . . ." I giggled. "Simon Benton invited us to have lunch with him and Mr. Padgett because he said Mr. Padgett and I could discuss textiles, and they could talk with Ted privately about the case."

"Privately? In a crowded dining room?" She turned down the corners of her mouth. "Makes sense to me."

"Maybe it's Special Agent Brown logic," I said.

She nodded. "That could be it. SAB logic — we now have a new code word for stupidity."

"Guess what." I didn't give her a chance to guess. When Sadie guessed something, it was usually as outlandish a speculation as anyone could imagine. Before she could provide an answer, I said, "I met Ted's mother yesterday."

"Ooh, did you have dinner? Did he take you over to her house? Did he just spring this meeting on you, or did you know about it ahead of time? And if you knew about it, why didn't you tell me?"

"I knew nothing about it," I said. "She came into the shop. And she didn't introduce herself to me, either! I didn't even know who she was until Ted came in and called her 'Mother.' "

"The woman went ninja on you?" Sadie sat on the sofa facing the window and patted the cushion next to her. "Get over here and spill. Blake can handle things for a few more minutes."

I sat down beside Sadie and told her all

about my first encounter with Veronica Nash.

"Well, at least, she stood up for you," she said. "That's something . . . right?"

"I don't know if she was standing up for me or if she was simply showing me that she's adept at putting people in their place." I blew out a breath. "I don't know what to think of her. I mean, she bought a cross-stitch kit and some pattern books and said she might be back today, but I don't know if she's for Ted and me or against us."

"Did Ted know his mother was planning on dropping in on you?"

"No," I said.

"Did he say why he hadn't introduced the two of you before?"

"He said it was because he was afraid his mother would jeopardize our relationship," I said.

"What did Bev say?" she asked.

"I told Mom I was afraid it meant that Ted wasn't serious about me. She told me he's over the moon for me and that she believed him — that he didn't want his domineering mother to intimidate me until we were further along in our relationship," I said. "What do you think?"

"I think your mom is a wise woman. Ted does love you. Besides, it could've been worse. The first time I met Blake's parents, I was wearing a Xena Warrior Princess costume."

"Oh, I remember that! There had been that costume party on campus! And his parents had dropped by to bring him some groceries." I laughed. "You did look beautiful, though! Didn't Blake's dad say, 'Wowza,' and give him a thumbs-up?"

Sadie threw back her head and laughed, too. "Yes! He did! That didn't help me win points right away with Blake's mom, either!" She wiped tears from her eyes. "Oh, my goodness, I hadn't thought about that in forever. I'll have to remind Blake about it when I get back."

"You know he'll want you to dig out that costume again."

"That's all right. I still have it."

"Do you really?" I asked.

"I sure do. And he's got his Hercules outfit, too." She stood. "Don't sweat the mom thing, Marce. When she gets to know you, she'll love you." She gave Angus a quick hug before she left. I could see that she was still grinning as she walked past the window.

Later that afternoon, as I worked on my crewel project, I got to thinking about

George Vandehey again. Was Ted right? Was George's belief that Chad Cummings had asked his father to take the Cézanne nothing more than the hope of a bereaved son? Who could help uncover the truth?

I picked my cell phone up off the coffee table and called Vera. When she answered, I asked if she and Paul were up to some sleuthing.

"Are we ever!" She paused. "At least, I am. I'm not sure about Paul, but I imagine he'll agree. What's going on?"

I told her how George Vandehey had been to see me and that he believed Chad Cummings had committed insurance fraud. "He thinks Cummings contacted Dr. Vandehey after hearing about his daughter's bike accident and asked him to come appraise the painting."

"And when Vandehey got there, Cummings offered him money to take the painting so that he could collect the insurance money," said Vera. "That's brilliant."

"Ted thinks George is doing some wishful thinking," I said. "After all, Cummings *did* present a signed confession to police."

"But that could have been part of the bargain," Vera said.

"Do you think you and Paul could discreetly poke around and see what you can

222

find out?"

"You bet," she said. "I'll call you tonight with a progress report."

"Great. I —"

I saw Veronica Nash crossing the street and heading in the direction of my shop.

"— appreciate that, Vera. Thanks."

"No problem. I'll call Paul this instant."

I was ending the call when Veronica stepped into the shop. Angus raised his head but didn't get up to welcome her this time.

"Hello," I said.

"Don't you look beautiful today?"

Did she have to sound so surprised?

"Thank you," I said.

I started to mention that Ted and I'd had a lunch appointment, but then I decided not to. I'd prefer her to think yesterday was the fluke and that — like her — I always dressed stylishly. Today she was wearing a navy skirt and a paisley tank. She obviously worked out, because her arms were as toned as her legs.

"How did your project go?" I asked.

She joined me on the sofa and took the kit out of her large white purse. "I think I'm doing well. In fact, I stopped by just to show you the progress I'm making." She handed me the hoop.

I looked down at her cloth and saw that

she had indeed got quite a bit done on the open pink rose and rosebud. "You must've worked half the night."

"I worked while listening to some Bach," she said. "I found the stitching to be tedious at first. But when I saw the image start coming together, I didn't want to stop."

"It sounds as if you had a relaxing evening." I handed the project back to her.

"I did. Did you?"

"Yes, thanks."

"I don't want to make you feel awkward," said Veronica. "I know Ted was reluctant to bring you around because I tend to be critical of the women he dates."

For not wanting to make me feel awkward, she was doing a fine job of it.

"I despised Jennifer," she said. "You know about Jennifer, don't you?"

"Yes. She was Ted's first wife."

"Not in my book. In my book, she was simply a mistake." Veronica compressed her lips in anger before going on. "I never liked her, and I didn't try to hide that fact. She was immature and selfish."

"Talk about immature," I said. "You come here, and I have a giant doll in my store."

Veronica laughed. It was a light, tinkling chortle, and I couldn't help laughing right along with her.

"I'm sorry about that," she said. "I was rather snide about that mannequin. I always have met Ted's girlfriends prepared not to like them."

"Even before Jennifer?"

"Yes. Before she came along, I hadn't wanted to cut the apron strings. He was too young. He wasn't ready for a relationship. He had his education to think about. Then he met Jennifer and despite — or maybe because of — my protests, he married her. Two years later, he expected me to say, *I told you so.*"

"But you didn't?" I asked.

"No, but I sure thought it. Mother knows best, and all that jazz."

"I thought it was *father* knows best."

Veronica scoffed. "Every woman knows that's a crock."

We laughed again.

"After Jennifer, he didn't date very much," she continued. "And when he did, he kept the women far away from me."

"I guess he hasn't met anyone special enough to bring home to Mother," I said nonchalantly.

"He hadn't. Not until you. I'd ask him periodically if he was dating anyone and he'd say no. And then all of a sudden, in every conversation I have with my son, I'm

225

hearing 'Marcy, Marcy, Marcy, Marcy.' "

I felt the color rise in my cheeks, and I lowered my eyes.

"And so I asked, 'When am I going to get to meet this Marcy?' And he would be evasive. He'd tell me we would have dinner together soon, but we never made any definite plans. I came in yesterday because I was tired of waiting. I wanted to meet you."

I raised my eyes back to hers. "I'm glad we got to meet."

"I am, too," she said. "Ted has been so happy these past few months. If he's that smitten with you, I'm not going to do anything to risk his happiness."

"He called you."

She smiled. "He did. He said it worried you that I'd barged in —"

"I never said *barged*!"

"I know," she said. "But it worried you that Ted didn't set up the meeting himself."

"It did concern me. I'm happy, too, Veronica. And, like Ted, I've been hurt badly in the past. I was afraid to trust my heart to him, but I finally reached the point where I was afraid not to."

She reached over and briefly squeezed my hand. "So, how long do you think it'll take me to finish these roses?"

"I'd say one more night of Bach will do it."

I'd decided to have breakfast for dinner and was in the kitchen making pancakes when Ted got to my house. Angus was happily romping in the yard. Ted came on into the kitchen. I took the pan off the stove eye and went to stand before him.

"I love you, Ted."

"And I love you," he said huskily as he swept me up into his arms.

The pancakes were cold by the time we got around to eating them, but neither of us minded.

"Did you hear back from George Vandehey?" Ted asked as he poured maple syrup over his stack of flapjacks.

"No. He might not meet with you. He doubts you would believe him."

"I'll admit to being skeptical, but I'm not close-minded. If he can provide me with some proof, I'll take the proper steps to ensure that Chad Cummings is brought to justice."

"I know," I said. "I called Vera this afternoon and asked her and Paul to quietly look into George's contention that Chad Cummings hired Dr. Vandehey to steal the painting."

Ted grinned. "With Ethel and Fred Mertz on the case, what could possibly go wrong?"

I slapped his arm with my napkin. "They might find something. . . . Well . . . Paul might."

"They might," he agreed. "Either way, Cummings is a suspect in Vandehey's murder. He always has been."

"But in your book, *everyone's* a suspect," I said.

"There is that. But if Cummings is guilty, I'll find the proof to convict him."

CHAPTER SIXTEEN

When Angus and I arrived back at the store, Reggie was already there waiting for us. She was leaning against the wall and reading a book.

"Oh, no! Are we late?" I asked.

Reggie smiled. "No. I'm early." She dropped the book into her purse. "The library closes at four thirty on Tuesdays. Manu was still at work, so I grabbed a quick dinner at MacKenzies' Mochas, and here I am."

I unlocked the door. "Come on in."

She wore a white cotton sari with white embroidery — or *chikankari* — on the sleeves and hem. She also had on long blue-and-silver drop earrings and matching bangles that made a tinkling noise when she moved. She said hello to Angus and then sat down on one of the red club chairs and began to unpack her tote.

I got Reggie a bottle of water and set it on

the coffee table.

"Thank you," she said. "How are you? Are you having any nightmares or anything like that?"

"No. I did get a little nervous last night second-guessing myself about whether or not I'd locked the door."

"You should always lock the door as soon as you get inside."

"I normally do," I said. "And I *did*. . . . I just got scared."

"That's normal. I've been concerned about you. You know I'm here anytime you need to talk, right?"

"Thanks . . . and ditto."

Vera rushed through the door in denim capris and a flowing short-sleeved leopard-print top. After looking around to make sure only Reggie and I were in the shop, she pulled me to one side and asked if she could speak freely in front of Reggie about what we'd discussed earlier. I told her she could.

"All right, Paul and I haven't made much progress in the Chad Cummings fraud investigation," said Vera.

"Fraud investigation?" Reggie asked.

I brought her up to speed on George Vandehey and his belief that Chad Cummings had paid his father to steal the Cézanne.

"That's possible," Reggie said. "About

fourteen years ago, an ophthalmologist in Los Angeles was convicted of insurance fraud for arranging to have a Picasso and a Monet stolen from his home. He was trying to collect seventeen and a half million dollars."

"Chad Cummings told me he got twenty million for the one Cézanne," I said. "But George has no proof to back up his allegation that Cummings paid his father to steal the painting. The money that showed up in his and his sister's bank accounts could have been the money he was paid for the painting."

"Yes, George would have a hard time proving any of that," said Reggie. "Now that his father is dead, he should try to put his theories behind him . . . unless . . . ?"

"Unless he believes Chad Cummings killed his father," I finished for her.

She frowned. "That's a stretch."

"That's what Ted says," I said.

"You didn't tell me George thinks Chad killed the professor," Vera said. "But Paul and I discussed it, and Paul thinks it's possible. Chad Cummings is a powerful man, and he wouldn't want anyone making any accusations against him."

We had no time to debate the matter further, because the other students began filing in. One of them was Sissy Cummings.

"Sissy, I'm so glad you could make it," I said. "Please come over and have a seat."

"Thank you. I hope the instructor doesn't mind my sitting in and observing," she said.

"She'll be delighted." I introduced Sissy to Reggie, and they hit it off immediately.

Sissy marveled over the delicate work on Reggie's sari as well as the sample work she was teaching the class.

"It isn't as hard as it looks," Reggie said. "Here. Give it a try."

She led Sissy step by step through one of the stitches.

I mingled among the students asking if they'd like a water, juice, or soda. Angus also mingled, getting petted by everyone. There weren't many classes where Angus wasn't the star attraction, but he was always aware of who welcomed his attention and who did not. He'd given Veronica Nash a wide berth today.

Vera sidled up to me and whispered, "I'll see what I can get out of Sissy Cummings."

My eyes widened. "No!"

I doubted she'd even heard me. She'd already gone over and taken a seat beside Sissy on the sofa.

Reggie noticed my stricken expression and saw that Vera had snagged prime real estate.

She gave me an almost imperceptible shrug and then reengaged Sissy in another stitch demonstration.

It wasn't until after class that Vera got a chance to interrogate Sissy. Everyone had gone except Vera, Sissy, Reggie, and me. I kept wishing Vera would leave before she could say something inflammatory to Sissy. In fact, I was regretting bringing Vera and Paul in on my quest to find information about Chad Cummings. Why hadn't I left the sleuthing to Ted and Manu?

"It's getting late," Reggie said.

"It is," I agreed. "This class has been a pleasure, as always, though. I'm so glad you were here, Sissy."

"Thank you. I enjoyed it very much."

My cell phone, which I had on the vibrate setting for class, rang. I didn't recognize the number, and I excused myself to step into the hall and take the call.

"Marcy, it's George Vandehey. I'd like to meet with you and the detective."

"Great," I said. "Can you be at my house in half an hour?"

"Yes, I'll be there."

I ended the call and texted Ted to let him know the plan.

When I returned to the shop, Reggie was

wide-eyed and Vera was asking Sissy if Chad had been intending to buy anything from the Padgett Collection before it was stolen.

"Yes, as a matter of fact, he wanted to make an offer on the David and Goliath tapestry," said Sissy. "He says he brought me here to see the exhibit, but he was really here because he wanted that tapestry."

"I was interested in one of the Japanese pieces myself," Vera said. "I'd think your husband would be gun-shy after having the Cézanne stolen."

"He says that's what insurance is for." Sissy shrugged. "I thought the tapestry was beautiful, but I can't think of a single place in our home large enough to display it. It's huge."

"You know, even with the insurance reimbursing you for the Cézanne, that had to be quite a blow to wake up and realize it had been stolen," Vera hammered on. "If I had a Cézanne and someone stole it from me, I believe I'd want to throttle him."

"Yes, it was quite a shock," Sissy said.

"How did you guys feel when you found out the man who stole your painting had been murdered?" Vera asked.

"We felt horrible!" Sissy placed a hand at her throat. "The professor might not have been a good person, but his life had value.

All lives have value."

"He was possibly not as bad as you might think," I said. "His son came to see me because I was the one who found Dr. Vandehey. He explained to me that his sister had been in a horrible accident just prior to the theft of the Cézanne. He believes his father stole the Cézanne in order to help pay the medical expenses."

"Oh, my goodness. I had no idea." Sissy's eyes filled with tears. "I wish he'd talked with us about it. I'd have gladly given him some money."

"You have a tender heart," Reggie said.

Sissy wiped away her tears. "Chad says it's *too* tender. He says that if he'd let me, I'd fall for every hard-luck story in the book." She smiled. "I guess it's true. But it sounds as if the professor could have really used our help. I'm sorry he didn't trust us enough to ask for it."

When George arrived, I introduced him to Ted and then left them alone in the living room while I prepared a tray with decaffeinated coffee, creamer, sugar, and the peanut butter cookies I kept in the freezer for unexpected guest emergencies. All I had to do was put them in the microwave for thirty seconds, and they were warm. You'd have thought I just got them out of the oven . . . which — technically, since the microwave is an oven — I did.

I walked into the living room, and Ted stood and took the tray from me. It was as if I were too dainty to carry a heavy tray. *Swoon!* Of course, he could've come into the kitchen and brought it all the way into the living room, but I wasn't complaining. He was still sweet to take the tray, place it on the ottoman, and pour each of us a cup of coffee.

"George was explaining his theory to me about how Chad Cummings set his father up by having his father steal the painting and then write out a confession," Ted said, passing around the cups and saucers. "The only problem is that without any tangible evidence, law enforcement won't believe you. Chad Cummings is holding all the high cards."

"That's true, but my father was smart," said George. "He wouldn't have written that confession without having an ace up his sleeve. I believe he had something — either on his person, in his hotel room, or in a safe-deposit box somewhere — that proves Chad Cummings had Dad steal that painting so he could collect the insurance money."

"I don't believe anything was found on the body," Ted said. "Your father's personal effects are still in evidence. I can go with you to look at them tomorrow."

"Thank you. What about his hotel room? May I see it, too?"

"The crime scene techs have already gone over it and cleared the hotel to rent out the room," he said. "Anything belonging to your father was put into evidence with the rest of his belongings."

"Still, if it's possible, I'd like to see his room," said George.

"You think he hid something in there," I said.

George nodded. "I do. Do you think it would be possible?"

"If you don't find anything when we look through your dad's effects tomorrow, I'll call the hotel," Ted said. "If they haven't rented out the room, we'll go over and take a look."

"Thank you," George said. "My father wasn't a saint by any means, but I know he wasn't the villain Chad Cummings made him out to be."

After George left, I took the tray back to the kitchen and tried to get Angus to come back in. He was enjoying the cool night air, however, and wouldn't budge from his spot on the porch swing.

Ted came up behind me and nuzzled my neck. "Let him stay a while longer."

I leaned back against him. "All right."

He took my hand and led me back to the living room. We kicked off our shoes and cuddled up on the couch.

"It feels so good to be lying in your arms," I said, snuggling against his chest.

He kissed the top of my head. "Let's play hooky tomorrow and go hide out in the mountains."

I laughed softly. "You always want to play hooky when a case isn't going well — of course, you never *do* — and you've promised George he can look through his father's things tomorrow."

"I did do that, didn't I?"

"Which case isn't going well?" I asked. "The murder of Geoffrey Vandehey or the museum theft?"

"Neither is going well. There's a lot of finger-pointing going on at the museum. The board of directors thinks Josh Ingle is at fault. Josh thinks the board has been trying to undermine him for months. One security guard hints that another was lazy, while another says one might have been moonlighting." He groaned. "If we could find one person who would tell us the unadulterated truth, we might be able to solve that one."

"My sweet Diogenes," I murmured.

"What did you call me?"

I giggled. "Diogenes . . . the guy who wandered all over ancient Greece with a lantern searching for an honest man."

"I believe there are honest men in the world . . . just not at the Tallulah Falls Museum." He laughed.

"You don't think Anderson Padgett hired someone to steal his collection, do you?" I asked.

"No. Why? Do you?"

"No. In fact, it had never crossed my mind until George Vandehey voiced his belief that Chad Cummings hired the professor to steal his Cézanne," I said. "Mr. Cummings didn't seem terribly distraught about the loss of the painting, but he was bragging about how much profit he made off it once the insurance company paid up."

"You never can tell, but I'd be very surprised if Anderson Padgett had anything to do with the theft of his collection."

"I would, too," I said. "Sissy Cummings came to Reggie's class tonight. Vera asked her if her husband had been interested in any of the pieces from the Padgett Collection. She said the reason he'd come to Tallulah Falls was to try to get Mr. Padgett to sell him the David and Goliath tapestry."

"Had they talked about it before Cummings came to Tallulah Falls?" Ted asked.

"I don't think so. Remember, during lunch today, Simon Benton mentioned that he'd tried to get Mr. Padgett to sell that tapestry to him. If he wouldn't sell it to a friend, why would he sell it to a stranger?"

"True. And from what you told me Vera said about it, Padgett was only willing to sell selected pieces of his collection, not all of it."

"That's right," I said. "Vera got to talking to Sissy about the stolen Cézanne and asking her how she and Mr. Cummings had felt when they found out that Geoffrey Vandehey had been murdered."

"Good old Vera . . . always subtle. What did Sissy say?"

"She said all life was valuable no matter how bad a person Geoffrey Vandehey might have been. And then I couldn't help myself."

Ted stiffened.

"I told her that Dr. Vandehey's son believes that his father stole the painting to help pay for his daughter's medical care," I said.

Ted relaxed.

"What did you think I was going to say?" I asked.

"I can never tell with you, Inch-High."

"Well, after I told Sissy Cummings about Libby's accident, she got teary and said she wished Dr. Vandehey had simply asked them for help. She said she wished he'd trusted them enough to turn to them."

"So, had they known Vandehey before having him appraise the painting?" Ted asked.

"I don't know. She did say her husband believed her to be too tenderhearted. So maybe Mr. Cummings did know about the accident and exploited it to get Dr. Vandehey to steal the painting for him."

"Maybe. But, again, if George has no proof, we can't go accusing Cummings of anything," he said.

"Let's think about all of that tomorrow." I turned and ran my hand gently down the side of his face. "I believe we've had enough shop talk for tonight."

He smiled. "Indubitably."

I giggled at the pretentious word until he kissed me. Then I completely forgot what had been so funny.

CHAPTER SEVENTEEN

The next morning, I was unpacking a shipment of Christmas ornament kits. It wasn't that I was rushing the season, but in order to get Christmas ornaments completed in time, people needed to start in the summer or early fall. Angus was lying by the window with his Kodiak bear. They were watching the world go by. All in all, it was very peaceful. There had been a few customers come in, and we had made some friendly transactions.

And then Chad Cummings barged into the Stitch. There was nothing friendly or peaceful about him. In fact, Angus jumped up and ran to stand between me and the irate man.

"What did you say to my wife last night?" he demanded.

"Mr. Cummings, I'm not sure what you're talking about. Mrs. Cummings was here to observe the *chikankari* class, and as far as I know, she had a nice time."

"Well, you or someone in your class upset Portia," he said. "She came home in tears over that no-good Geoffrey Vandehey."

"That was probably my fault, Mr. Cummings. I mentioned to your wife that Geoffrey Vandehey's son was here and that he told me his sister had been in an accident around the time the professor stole your painting. I didn't mean to upset her."

"Portia isn't like most people."

"She told me you believe her to be too kind-hearted," I said.

"It's not just that. Portia has some . . . issues . . . mentally. She's . . . delicate."

"She said she wished Dr. Vandehey had trusted the two of you to ask for financial help if he needed it rather than steal the painting."

"Yeah. She liked that painting," he said.

"Mr. Cummings, did *you* know about Elizabeth Vandehey's accident?"

"Sure. That's why I called and asked him to do the second appraisal. I was trying to throw the guy a bone. How does he repay me? By stealing my Cézanne."

"I'm sorry. You must've felt terribly betrayed."

"Damn right I did," he said.

Angus uttered a low growl.

"Look, I'll get out of your hair before your dog goes for my jugular," said Mr. Cummings. "I'm sorry I overreacted, but just please . . . if Portia comes in again, try not to upset her in any way."

"I'll certainly do my best," I said.

Angus didn't move until after he saw Chad Cummings walk past the window in the direction of MacKenzies' Mochas.

I bent and gave him a hug. "Thank you, baby. I don't think he would've done anything rash, but I'm glad you were here just in case."

Christine Willoughby, one of my regular patrons, walked into the shop. "Hey, share some of that puppy love with me, would ya?"

I laughed as Angus bounded over to Christine. The woman was thin, and I was always afraid Angus would knock her over. But she must've been stronger than she looked.

"How are you this morning, Christine?"

"I'm fantastic! Just dropped in for some yarn. How are you?"

"Good . . . well, better, now that a *friendly* person is here. The last guy who came in here wasn't Mr. Congeniality."

Christine put her fists on her waist. "Do I need to have Jared bring you a crowbar?"

Jared, Christine's son, was an auto mechanic.

I laughed. "No. I think Angus let him know we didn't appreciate his attitude."

"Good." She went back to petting Angus and directed her comments to him. "We don't understand why people have to be so mean, do we? No, we don't! No!"

The dog wagged his entire body and reveled in Christine's adoration.

Christine glanced into the box. "What've you got there?"

"Cross-stitch and ribbon-embroidery Christmas ornaments."

She picked up an angel. "This is gorgeous. Do you think I could do it?"

"I know you could," I said. "You can knit like crazy. I'm sure you can cross-stitch and do a few ribbon-embroidery stitches. If you want to try one, we'll sit down over here on the sofa and get you started."

"Are you sure you have time? I know you're busy."

"Never too busy for you." I smiled. "You're one of my favorite customers."

We sat down on the sofa. Angus saw that Christine's attention was momentarily fixated on something other than him, so he lay down at her feet to wait for his turn to come back around again.

"This is a counted cross-stitch project, so there's no design stamped on the fabric," I said. "The first thing we need to do is to find the center." I folded the fabric in half and then folded it again. "See? Your center is now defined by the crease."

"This looks hard," said Christine.

"It's not." I placed the fabric in the small hoop that came with the kit. "Just be sure and count the squares between the holes and not the holes when you're counting stitches. The center is already marked for you on the pattern, so . . . let's see . . . the first color floss we'll be using is white."

I separated two strands of the white embroidery floss sent with the kit and threaded the needle. "We're going to start in the center and go right."

Christine and I spent the next hour getting her familiar with the art of cross-stitch and making a dent in her new project. In fact, she got so involved in her cross-stitch that she would've left without the yarn she'd initially come in to buy had I not reminded her.

Ted brought chicken salad croissants from MacKenzies' Mochas for lunch.

"My favorite!" I exclaimed. "What's wrong?"

"Nothing's wrong," he said. "I mean, not really."

I stopped with my croissant halfway to my mouth. "What do you mean, *not really?*"

"Mother invited us out to dinner on Friday night. We can choose the place." His tone was casual, but he didn't meet my eyes and started eating his croissant as if he were starving to death.

I put my croissant back down on my plate. "Do you want to go?"

"That's entirely up to you."

"No, it isn't," I said. "You weren't ready for your mother and me to meet when she came into the shop the other day."

"True. But I know she's been in again since then, and I think it's probably . . . safe."

"Safe? You sound like we're going to a war zone rather than out to dinner."

He shrugged. "It probably wouldn't hurt to wear a flak jacket, if you have one."

I stared at him.

"I'm kidding," he said. "So, would you like to go, or not? I told her I'd call and let her know this afternoon."

"I'd like to go," I said. Why was Ted so anxious about his mom and me getting to know each other? Wanting to change the subject, I said, "Chad Cummings charged

247

in here this morning angry because I'd upset his wife. Maybe I *could* use a flak jacket."

"Why didn't you call me?" Ted asked.

"He didn't stay that long. He upset Angus, though. He came and got between us."

A muscle worked in Ted's jaw . . . a sure sign he was clenching his teeth.

"Don't do that," I said. "It'll give you a headache. Besides, it was no big deal."

"It *is* a big deal! A suspected murderer comes in here bullying the woman I love —" He put his fist up to his mouth.

"I'm not afraid of Chad Cummings." I got up and went over to embrace Ted. I'd just told a huge lie, by the way. I was terrified of Chad Cummings, especially after Ted classified him as a suspected murderer. "He was angry because I apparently did something to upset his wife, who is a delicate, instable creature. Do you really believe Chad killed Geoffrey Vandehey?"

He scooted back his chair and pulled me onto his lap. "I don't know. But I'm not ruling him out. George is absolutely convinced that Cummings killed his father."

"Did he find anything to support his belief among the evidence this morning?"

"No. But he, Special Agent Brown, Manu, and I are heading over after lunch to check out the hotel room Dr. Vandehey had occupied."

"Why is Special Agent Brown tagging along?" I asked.

"He was at the department this morning as George was leaving. George mentioned his theory to Brown, and so Brown insisted on accompanying us to the hotel."

"What are your feelings on Special Agent Brown?"

"I don't trust him," said Ted. "I don't think he's particularly competent, either. But I guess he's one of those enemies I should keep close during this investigation."

"Just be careful." I kissed him, and then went back to my chair so Ted could finish his lunch and I could start on mine.

"*You* be careful," he said. "And if Chad Cummings ever comes back into this shop again, you call me."

"I will."

I was sitting in the sit-and-stitch square working on the beaded embroidery project I was making as part of tonight's class. It was an adorable cupcake with a cherry on top, and I planned to give it to Sadie when I finished.

My cell phone rang. It was Mom, and the ringtone of the woman's scream pierced the air. Too bad I was the only one there to appreciate it.

"Hi." I giggled.

"What's so funny?" she asked.

"You know how I told you I was going to change your ringtone to a bloodcurdling scream? Well, I did. It's hilarious!"

"Marcella Singer, what if your shop had been filled with customers? Would it have been so amusing then?"

"Maybe not, but it would've been great if Ted or Sadie had been here," I said. "Anyway, I'm really glad you called."

"I just had that feeling, you know? No, actually, you probably don't know . . . but you will someday when you have children of your own. What's going on?"

"Ted's mother has invited us out to dinner on Friday," I said. "She came by the Stitch again yesterday, and she was really nice. . . ."

"But?"

"I don't know, Mom. There shouldn't be a *but.*"

"But there is. You're not sure you can trust her. And that's all right, darling. Trust isn't something you give lightly. It's something that must be earned."

"True. She told me yesterday that it's great seeing Ted happy, but she also told

250

me she detested his first wife."

"From what I've heard about her, she was pretty detestable," Mom said.

"Yes, she was. But I have to wonder if Veronica finds fault with any woman Ted gets involved with."

"Mothers are protective. We can't help ourselves."

"I'm nervous about Friday night," I said. "What should I wear?"

"Something that makes you feel confident."

"I just don't want to get hurt . . . by Ted's mom . . . and especially not by Ted."

"I don't think you will be," she said.

After we hung up, I continued working on my beaded cupcake, and I thought about David — the man who'd literally left me standing at the altar over a year ago. He'd paid me a visit here in Tallulah Falls a couple months ago and wanted to get back together. I'd seen how terribly wrong we were for each other then. In fact, I wondered what I'd ever seen in him in the first place. Ted, on the other hand . . . I found something new to love about him every day.

That thought was interrupted by Vera, hurrying into the shop wearing Bermuda shorts, a bright pink camp shirt, a floppy white hat, oversize sunglasses, and flip-flops.

"I have a development!" She spotted Angus. "Hi, sweetie." She patted his head and then came and sat next to me, taking off the sunglass and hat and placing them on the coffee table.

"What is it?" Her excitement was infectious. Could she and Paul possibly have discovered something that would verify George's claim that Chad Cummings had paid Geoffrey Vandehey to steal the Cézanne?

She took a piece of paper from her purse, unfolded it, and spread it out on the table. "This is a replica of the stolen painting."

It was a still life with apples on a white plate, a knife lying by the plate, a wine goblet, and a skull to the left of the apples.

"Okay," I said, waiting for her to get to the point.

"Now when we find it, we'll know what it looks like."

I smiled. "That's fantastic."

"Isn't it? I just went to the Web site of the auction house where Chad Cummings had bought the painting, got the director's phone number, called him, and had him send a copy of their photograph right over."

"Thank you, Vera. That was a wonderful idea." It wasn't the earth-shattering revelation I'd been expecting, but it wasn't bad.

"It's kind of an odd painting, isn't it? The more you look at it, the more you see."

"I agree. Look at the handle of the knife. See the —"

A scream pierced the air.

Vera and I jumped up. She ran to the window, and I rushed to the door.

When I stepped out onto the sidewalk, I saw Nellie Davis standing just outside her shop. "It's Nellie!" I called to Vera.

I hurried forward and put an arm around Nellie's bony shoulders. "Are you all right? What's happened?"

"That!" She pointed to a dead rat lying on her sidewalk. "It was there when I came back from lunch. There's a note with it."

Vera had joined us by that time, and she gingerly picked up the folded piece of white card stock. " 'Don't be a rat, or you'll wind up like one,' " she read.

I took my cell phone out of my pocket and called Ted. When he answered, I quickly explained the situation.

"Tell Vera to put the note down, and don't let anyone else handle it," he said. "I've got a crime scene unit on the way."

"He said he'd protect me," Nellie wailed.

"He will," I said. "He and some deputies are on their way over here now."

"But somebody knows." Tears wound

253

through the crevices of Nellie's wrinkled face. "Somebody knows, and he's going to hurt me!"

My eyes met Vera's over the top of Nellie's bowed head. I widened my eyes, and Vera widened hers.

What should we do? I mouthed at Vera.

She shrugged her shoulders up to her ears.

"Nellie, would you like to come over to my shop until Ted arrives?" I asked.

"No. I can't leave my shop unattended. Someone will come in and steal me blind."

"Then I'll stay with you," Vera said. "Marcy, go on back to the Stitch before someone comes in and robs you and Angus blind."

I pursed my lips to let Vera know I didn't think she was being very funny. "I'll be happy to stay. I can see the sidewalk from Nellie's shop, and I should be able to tell if someone goes into my shop."

"Nonsense," Vera said. "We'll be fine."

"Yes, Marcy, go on back to the Seven-Year Stitch," said Nellie. "Everything will be all right."

Vera took Nellie and led her inside Scentsibilities. "I'll call if I need you."

"Okay," I said.

I turned and went back to the shop. It was a good thing I did. Angus was pacing and was awfully disturbed because he hadn't known what was going on. I knew the feeling. I hated being kept out of the loop.

I thought about who might've sent the rat to Nellie. It had to have been one of the people who'd dumped Geoffrey Vandehey's body in the alley. Was it possible that someone had seen her here on Friday night?

CHAPTER EIGHTEEN

I saw Ted's red unmarked car and a police cruiser pull up and park. Ted and Manu got out of his car, and two deputies emerged from the cruiser. Ted gave me a wave before heading toward Nellie's shop.

I waited for what seemed like forever until the bells over the door jingled. Then it wasn't Ted but a customer. I had mixed emotions about that. I was always thrilled to have a customer come into the shop, but I was anxious to know what was going on up the street.

The customer needed regular-weight embroidery precut stabilizer sheets. I didn't have any on the shelf, but I had some in my storeroom. I got them for her and asked if she needed any other supplies. She thanked me but said she was good on everything else at the moment. She paid for her stabilizer sheets, I put them in a periwinkle Seven-Year Stitch bag, and she went on her way.

The next person who came through the door was Ted.

"Is Nellie all right?" I asked.

"She's still very shaken up. Manu is worried that she'll have a heart attack or something, and he's trying to convince her to go to the hospital and get checked out."

"Do you think she will?"

He shook his head. "She insists that she's fine and that she isn't going anywhere. Frankly, I think she's too afraid to go anywhere."

"Did the crime scene techs find any prints?" I asked.

"Only Vera's."

"Do you think someone saw Nellie looking out the window of her back door, or do you think word got out somehow that Nellie reported seeing a black van?"

His face hardened. "I don't know, but there'd better not be a leak in our department. I won't just have somebody's job — I'll have his head."

"How's George? Did he find anything at the hotel?"

"As a matter of fact, he did," Ted said, his face becoming more animated as he pictured the scene. "We go in, right? And, as expected, there's nothing. The drawers are all empty. The closet is empty. . . . But then

George pulls out a miniature tool set and starts taking the screws out of this air vent!"

"Are you serious?"

"Yeah! I ask him if he doesn't think he's going a little overboard, but he says, 'I know my dad.' Sure enough, he takes the vent cover off, reaches inside, and takes out a USB flash drive."

I gasped. "What was on it?"

"Unfortunately, we don't know yet. But we *are* optimistic," he said. "See, we took it back to the department and tried to read the flash drive using my computer. But the drive was encrypted. So we took it to one of the tech guys. He said it was really good encryption, but he knew what company made the encryption software. He's getting in contact with the company to have the message decoded."

"That's so exciting," I said. "Do you think the flash drive will have a recording or photos or *something* that will incriminate Chad Cummings?"

"I hope it will," he said. "Not only to bring Cummings to justice but to help redeem Geoffrey Vandehey — if he was, in fact, Cummings's pawn — in George's eyes."

"Either way — I mean, even if Dr. Vandehey did actually steal the Cézanne — he did it for his daughter. I think both children know that. I only hope Chad and the delicate Portia don't leave Tallulah Falls before you find out what's on that flash drive."

"I don't think they will, especially not with Anderson Padgett in town. Padgett is the kind of guy Cummings likes to rub elbows with . . . and he'd love to get his hands on some of the old guy's art." He nodded toward the coffee table. "What's that?"

"It's a photo Vera brought in of the Cézanne stolen from Chad Cummings," I said.

"Would you make me a copy of that, please?"

"I'd be happy to." I scooped up the photo and took it back to my office to make a copy. "Are we having dinner together this evening?" I called over the roar of the copier. "Or would you rather wait until after class?"

"Those pancakes were amazing! Could we have some more of those?"

I laughed as I headed back to the shop with the photo. "Before class or after?"

He bent and kissed me. "Both."

I was still smiling when Vera came back into the shop to retrieve her things.

"Don't you look like the cat who swallowed the canary who has Detective Ted

Nash wrapped around her little finger?" Vera asked.

"That's a twisted simile if I've ever heard one," I said. "Is Nellie feeling better?"

"Yes. I didn't leave her until her sister arrived. The sister is going to stay with her for a few days." She put her floppy hat back on, covering her now-tousled hair. "I saw that card you'd made Nellie thanking her for the candle. You and she might become friends, thanks to this latest drama."

"Don't hold your breath."

Vera chuckled and grabbed her purse. "You can keep the photo. I have a copy of it at home. I'm hoping Paul can get it put on the AP wire."

"That would be wonderful," I said. "Maybe it could help us locate it."

"Not that I'd want to do anything to help that nasty Chad Cummings," she said. "I just get a bad feeling from him."

"I do, too. And you should've been here this morning when he plowed through the door blessing me out for upsetting his delicate wife," I said.

Vera's jaw dropped. "What?"

I nodded. "He said she came home crying over Geoffrey Vandehey's predicament. He said he knew about Vandehey's daughter and that's why he allowed Vandehey to do the second appraisal on the painting."

She narrowed her eyes. "Do you believe him?"

"I don't know. I think that if anything, he knew about the accident and used Dr. Vandehey's financial predicament to get him to steal the painting," I said. "But, of course, to hear him tell it, he threw Vandehey a bone and was repaid for his kindness with the theft of his priceless painting."

"But he admitted to knowing about the accident," Vera said. "Why didn't he share that information with his wife?"

"Apparently, she's too delicate and sensitive. He hinted that she's not mentally stable."

"Ah, well, I have to run. I never intended to stay this long, but I hadn't anticipated Nellie's episode." She waved at Angus, who was lying in front of the counter. "Toodles!"

Before getting back to work on my beaded embroidery cupcake — well, *Sadie's* beaded embroidery cupcake — I decided I should take Angus for a walk. I went to the counter, got his leash, and clipped it onto his collar.

I was afraid that the deputies might still be with Nellie, and I didn't want her to think I was being nosy, so I headed in the direction of MacKenzies' Mochas.

Angus and I were on our way back to the

261

Stitch when we met Simon Benton heading toward the coffee shop.

"Good afternoon," he said. "You're a regal couple strolling along today."

"Thank you," I said.

"I'm popping into MacKenzies' to get an iced coffee. Would you like one?"

"No, thanks, but I certainly appreciate the offer."

"I know you have to get back to your shop," he said. "May I stop in when I'm finished here?"

"Please do."

Angus and I went back to the shop. I unclipped the leash from his collar and put it in a small rectangular basket by the register.

Within fifteen minutes, Simon Benton had joined us in the sit-and-stitch square. Despite my answer to the contrary, he'd brought me an iced coffee. I was glad. It was delicious.

"Thank you, Mr. Benton. I appreciate your thoughtfulness."

"Ah, well, I thought it would be just the thing to rejuvenate you on this middle of the week, middle of the afternoon."

"It really is . . . as is your company," I said.

"Well, I value the compliment, young lady. Mr. Padgett and I were delighted to lunch with you and your beau yesterday," he said. "We'd like to do it again before Mr. Padgett leaves Tallulah Falls."

"We would enjoy that, too. Has Mr. Padgett said how long he'll be in town?"

"No, he hasn't," said Mr. Benton. "I believe he's hoping against hope that some evidence will be found and his collection will miraculously be recovered . . . with the exception of that one Turkish kilim, of course."

"I understand that at one point the museum wanted to offer a reward for information on the return of the collection with no questions asked," I said. "However, the police chief asked them to wait to see if a ransom demand was forthcoming."

"Yes, the board of directors discussed that very fact with Mr. Padgett earlier today. They're going to get Chief Singh's approval, of course, but they are planning to offer a combined reward within the next day or so."

"I hope they get some good solid leads." I sipped the iced coffee. It really did hit the spot.

"I pray they do as well," Mr. Benton said. "Between the two of us, however, I think it's unlikely. I would imagine the thieves are long gone by now, wouldn't you?"

"Probably. Although with the theft being

so recent, the robbers couldn't possibly hope to sell it . . . right?"

He shrugged. "Tallulah Falls is a very small town. The word wouldn't have spread so quickly from here as it would from a larger city like Seattle or Denver."

"True, but this is the age of the Internet," I said. "People with camera phones have opened the doors to an entirely new brand of journalism."

He laughed. "But it isn't always *reliable* journalism, eh?"

"Fair enough. Still, I think word spreads a lot faster today than some folks realize." He was the *folks* I didn't think realized the power of the Internet. "Do you think the murder of Geoffrey Vandehey and the museum theft are connected somehow?"

"It's hard to say." He crossed his legs and sipped his coffee as if he was giving the matter much consideration. "I believe that having stolen art before, Dr. Vandehey might have been involved in the theft of the Padgett Collection, yes. That said, why would his partners take the time to kill him and dump his body before making their getaway?"

"I don't know," I said. "Maybe they wanted his share of the profits. Or maybe he changed his mind and felt bad about stealing from Mr. Padgett."

"Why would he feel bad about stealing from Mr. Padgett if he had no qualms about stealing from Mr. Cummings?" he asked.

"Have you met Mr. Cummings?"

Mr. Benton threw back his head and laughed. "Indeed I have, Ms. Singer, and he is not as nice a person as Andy."

"No, he sure isn't."

"But Dr. Vandehey wouldn't know that, having not made Mr. Padgett's acquaintance, would he?"

"I guess not," I said. "So you're basically saying once a thief, always a thief?"

He inclined his head. "I wouldn't go that far. I'm merely trying to play devil's advocate and come up with a reason his partners would have killed Dr. Vandehey were he part of the plot to steal the Padgett Collection."

"Okay. If you don't think that Dr. Vandehey would have changed his mind about stealing the collection, do you believe his partners killed him in order to get the professor's share of the profits?" I asked.

He set his coffee cup on the coffee table, leaned his elbows on his knees, and steepled his fingers. "The more I dwell on it, the more I begin to reconsider Dr. Vandehey as a participant in the theft. As I said before, why would the other thieves take time from their escape to kill him, wrap up his body, and dump it in an alley? The group would be on the lam. Even if they'd decided to murder Dr. Vandehey, they wouldn't have done it here in Tallulah Falls. They'd have killed him on the outskirts of town . . . or waited until they got to their planned destination."

"That's a solid theory. Do you watch a lot of detective shows?"

"As a matter of fact, I do," he said with a laugh.

"If Dr. Vandehey wasn't part of the museum robbery plot, why do you believe he was murdered?" I asked.

He tapped his fingertips together. "I've met several people here in Tallulah Falls alone who bore a grudge against Dr. Vandehey. Mr. Ingle, the museum curator, resented Dr. Vandehey because the older gentleman was a fount of knowledge, and Mr. Ingle was afraid that Dr. Vandehey was here to take his job and ruin his career."

"But that's not enough to kill someone over," I said.

"Is it not? People have killed for less, Ms. Singer," he said. "Perhaps Mr. Ingle learned of Dr. Vandehey's true identity and wanted to be the person responsible for recovering the stolen Cézanne. That would've made him a hero. He'd get a lot of press over it and, once he'd earned his master's degree, he could've left Tallulah Falls and found a more prestigious position."

"I have to admit, that motive beats the first one."

"Then there's that blowhard Special Agent Brown," Mr. Benton continued. "Dr. Vandehey made a fool of him, got him demoted, and was clever enough to ensure that Agent Brown wouldn't find the Cézanne after searching for it for years. He had a lead and came here to the opening-night gala to search for Geoffrey Vandehey, did he not?"

"He did," I said.

"Did this lead come out of nowhere? Perhaps Agent Brown had been following Dr. Vandehey. Again, this is a small town. What if Agent Brown thought he could get his revenge on Dr. Vandehey and none of these lower-level law enforcement officers would dare question him if he said he had been forced to kill the man in self-defense?"

"These law enforcement officers are some of the best in the country," I said.

"*I* know that, but I daresay Agent Brown did not . . . at least, until he arrived. And he still carries himself with a certain amount of arrogance that is unearned," he said. "I'm not saying Agent Brown is the killer, of course. I'm merely throwing around notions."

"You said you knew of several people in Tallulah Falls who had a grudge against Dr. Vandehey," I said. "So far, you've mentioned only two. What else have you got?"

He smiled. "You're enjoying my stories."

"I am. Have you ever thought of becoming a screenwriter?"

"No . . . but now I might," he said.

"What do you think of Chad Cummings as the murderer?" I asked. "He has a forceful personality, and he definitely held a grudge against Dr. Vandehey."

Mr. Benton took a drink of his coffee, set the cup back down on the table, and leaned back in his chair. "Chad Cummings . . . let me think on that one for a moment. . . . Ah! I've got it. You mentioned the fact that thieves will often ransom stolen art back to its owner. Perhaps Dr. Vandehey approached Mr. Cummings and asked for money to return the Cézanne. Mr. Cummings lost his temper and accidentally killed Dr. Vandehey."

"You're forgetting one thing in all your theories," I said.

"What's that?"

"The rug. If anyone other than one of the

thieves murdered Dr. Vandehey, where would he have gotten the kilim in which he was wrapped?"

Mr. Benton laughed and slapped his open palms on his thighs. "You are the clever one! I'll have to think more on my theories, Ms. Singer . . . unless, of course, one of the villains I mentioned *was* involved in the theft."

"I suppose that's a possibility," I said.

"Everything is a possibility . . . isn't it?"

CHAPTER NINETEEN

Ted and I didn't have pancakes again after all. He came over and we cooked dinner together. We had spaghetti and meatballs, with turtle cheesecake for dessert. It was a quickly put together meal. Nothing was homemade — the pasta sauce came from a jar, the meatballs came from the freezer, and the cheesecake had been thawing in the fridge since last night — but it was fun being in the kitchen, working together, and chatting while we prepared our meal.

Once we sat down to eat, I told Ted all about Simon Benton's theories on who murdered Geoffrey Vandehey.

"He presented fairly convincing arguments for the murderer being Josh Ingle, Chad Cummings, and even Special Agent Brown . . . until I pointed out that the killer had to have been in on the museum heist to have wrapped Dr. Vandehey up in the kilim."

"An excellent deduction, Inch-High."

"You knew all along that the murder of Geoffrey Vandehey and the museum heist were connected, didn't you?" I asked.

"Well, it *was* rather obvious . . . but we don't know *how* the two are connected yet."

"How do you think it's connected?"

"I'm not sure," he said. "It basically comes down to whether or not George is right about his father. I believe that if George is correct in his assertion that his father was paid to steal the painting from Chad Cummings, then Dr. Vandehey likely came to Tallulah Falls to confront Chad and to possibly even blackmail him for more money."

"I know Cummings had a private investigator looking for Vandehey, but how did Vandehey know Cummings would be in Tallulah Falls?" I asked.

"Good question," said Ted. "Maybe Vandehey was keeping tabs on Cummings, too."

"I guess that's possible. If you'd stolen something that valuable from someone, you'd want to make sure they weren't closing in on you," I said. "And if George is wrong about his father being paid by Cummings to steal the Cézanne?"

"Then Dr. Vandehey was in on the Padgett Collection heist from the beginning, and Simon Benton's theory is probably pretty close to the truth. Vandehey's partners murdered him in order to keep his share."

"I hope George isn't wrong," I said. "I feel that, criminal or not, Dr. Vandehey did what he did because he felt he had to in order to get money for his daughter's health care. Plus, I'd hate for George to go the rest of his life being disappointed in his father."

"George will continue believing he's right whether the evidence is there to support his contention or not."

"Then I guess that's a good thing."

"In a way," said Ted. "But I'm not George. I want to know the truth."

His cell phone buzzed. He looked determined to ignore it.

"Answer it," I urged. "It might be important."

He took the phone from his pocket, looked at the screen, and frowned slightly. "Hello, Mr. Padgett. How may I help you?"

He listened for a moment and then said, "All right. I'll see you at your hotel in half an hour."

When Ted ended the call and put the phone back in his pocket, his face was unreadable.

"Good news?" I asked.

"I'm not sure. Mr. Padgett said he remembered where he'd heard the name George Vandehey within the past few days and

272

would like to talk with me about it."

"Then, by all means, go," I said. "I'll straighten up the kitchen and see you back here after my class."

"Leave the kitchen. I'll come back and clean up after I've talked with Anderson Padgett."

I smiled. "You're wonderful, but you're wasting time. Go."

Vera was the first to arrive at class. She'd changed from her Bermuda shorts into a gauzy sundress, and she'd been able to style her hair back into submission.

"Paul put the photo of the Cézanne out on the wire service," she said. "Hopefully, many of the news outlets will run it. I'd love for someone to see it and have it be recovered."

"I would, too," I said. "Although forgive me for saying this, but I'd prefer it go to a museum than to Chad Cummings. He's already made — what did he tell me? — ten times what he paid for it, so I think he's been rewarded enough."

"What are your thoughts on him and Sissy?" she asked. "Do you get the feeling he's abusive?"

"I thought that at first, but now I'm wondering if he isn't overprotective. He gets angry when she's upset. . . . He buys essential oils to help calm her nerves. . . . I don't know."

"It could be that he does those things to control her, you know."

Vera wasn't able to expound on the subject, because a few other students — Julie, her daughter, Amber, and Muriel — arrived.

Muriel was hard of hearing. She typically sat down on one of the club chairs and worked quietly for the duration of the class unless there was something she had difficulty with.

Not today. Today she immediately announced, "I was just in Nellie Davis's shop, and she says you almost got her killed."

"What?" I cried.

Muriel nodded her cottony little head. "She says you told everybody that she saw who killed that professor man that you found lying on a rug out behind the shop."

"I did no such thing!"

Muriel, unfazed by her own declaration, sat down in her usual spot and took her project out of her tote.

"Are you gonna take that from her?" Vera asked. "After you made her a card and everything?"

I crossed my arms and began to pace.

"Why would she think I would tell anyone anything about her?"

Angus, sensing my outrage from across the room and not sure at whom it was directed, decided now would be a good time to get in his bed beneath the counter.

"To get her killed, apparently," said Amber, the precocious teen, with a grin.

I laughed. Leave it to a kid to ease the tension in a room.

Julie shrugged. "If you want to go tell her off, class can wait for a few minutes."

Vera jumped in. "We can all go . . . for moral support."

"You just don't want to miss anything," I said.

"Well, there is that," she admitted.

"Thank you all for your having my back, but I have no need to go rant at Nellie Davis," I said. "She had a rough day, and I suppose she's still reeling from it. If blaming me for her predicament makes her feel better, so be it."

"You're really taking the high road on this," said Vera. "I'd be as mad as a wet chicken."

I was, but I didn't want to show it.

"We aren't going to let Nellie's ravings ruin our class," I said. "Let's see how you've progressed on your projects. Muriel?"

Muriel already had her head down and was working contentedly on her beaded tulip. It was as if she'd never created the furor over Nellie's comments when she walked in the door. I wondered if she even remembered mentioning it.

Since Muriel appeared to be engrossed in her work, I moved on to Amber. Amber was embroidering a kitten with a beaded collar and a metallic ball of yarn.

"This is fantastic, Amber!" I said. "You're almost finished. We'll have to get you another project soon."

Amber beamed at the praise. She was really good at needle crafts. I knew her mother used this as a way for the two of them to bond, but Amber had a knack for it. I hoped she'd keep it up.

Julie, who worked a full-time job in addition to caring for her family, hadn't got very far along on her stargazer lily. Still, she was doing great work, and I told her so.

Before I could look at anyone else's project, Nellie and a heavyset woman with a square jaw and . . . well, pretty much a square everything . . . burst into the shop. She and Nellie appeared to be complete opposites — one tall, one short, one thin, one heavy, one with short hair, one with long hair up in a severe bun — in every way except one. They were both unpleasant. Well, there might be one other way in which they were alike — they hated me.

"You!" The one who wasn't Nellie extended her arm and pointed her index finger at me. "You're the one whose loose lips have put my sister's life in danger!"

I walked over to the women so they wouldn't encroach upon my class in the sit-and-stitch square. "I did nothing of the sort. For one thing, I'd have known nothing about Nellie even being here that night had she not told me so herself. And for another, I didn't go spreading that information all around town."

"Is that so?" the woman I now knew as Nellie's sister asked.

"Clara, I'll handle this myself," said Nellie. Looking at me, she said, "I'd hoped our dual scare would help us to put our past behind us and move forward as friends. I see now that is not to be the case, and I would like you to return the candle I gave you."

I heard someone get to her feet and come scurrying over to stand behind me. I guessed it was Vera. I was right.

"Well, Marcy would like the card back that she painstakingly made for you," said Vera. "Unlike your candle, which was merely sitting on a shelf, Marcy's card was a true attempt at friendship."

Hadn't I told her not to hold her breath on Nellie and me ever being friends?

"Fine," said Clara. "She can have her nasty little card back, but we're here for Nellie's candle and to tell Ms. Motormouth not to spread any more gossip about my sister."

Vera brushed me aside so she could stand toe-to-toe with Clara. "You can have your nasty little candle, and Nellie can keep her card to remind her that she *could've* made a good friend instead of an enemy here today."

"Nellie hasn't made any enemies," I said quickly. I didn't want her to think I was the one who'd left a dead rat outside her door.

"Well, she sure hasn't made a friend," Vera said. She looked around and spotted the stress-relief candle on the counter. She stepped over, got the candle, and shoved it at Nellie. "Here. Take your candle and get back up the street where you belong. Both of you!"

As soon as Nellie and Clara had left, I looked around at the wide-eyed group . . . except, of course, for Muriel. She was sitting with her head bowed over her tulip, working diligently.

"Well, now that the drama is over, let's

get back to work," I said.

When I got home, Ted was already there. He was stretched out on the sofa watching a baseball game. He clicked the television off when Angus and I came into the living room.

"Shame on you," he said.

I groaned. "Did you hear about the Nellie fiasco already?"

"No. I said shame on you because you went ahead and cleaned up the kitchen. I knew I shouldn't have left before helping you straighten up. What's the Nellie fiasco?"

"Let me put Angus out, and I'll tell you."

I followed Angus through the kitchen to the back door and opened the door for him. He bolted out into the backyard, thrilled to be completely carefree for a few minutes.

I went back into the living room and sat on the sofa in front of Ted. I first told him of Muriel's announcement when she arrived at class.

"It made me angry," I said. "But I put it behind me and moved on with class. Well, lo and behold, Nellie and her sister, Clara, came to take back the candle Nellie gave me. So much for my stress relief!"

"I wouldn't say that." He began massaging my neck and shoulders. "I can help with

279

your stress relief."

"Yes, you can."

"So, did you give Nellie back her candle?" he asked.

"Vera did. And then she told Nellie and Clara to go back up the street where they belonged."

He laughed.

"I told you and Sadie that Nellie had been working late that night, but that was it," I said. "You didn't even need her confirmation that a black van had been in the alley. So why would she think I told anyone that she saw something more than that?"

"Who in their right mind can figure out Nellie Davis's thought process?" He continued rubbing my shoulders. "Don't let her bother you."

"If anybody let something slip, it was probably *her,* right?"

"Right." He kissed my neck, and I leaned back against him.

"Did you see Mr. Padgett?" I asked.

"I did."

He was still kissing my neck, and I was beginning to forget all about Nellie Davis and Anderson Padgett and Geoffrey Vandehey.

Then he said, "Mr. Padgett said the name Geoffrey Vandehey was familiar to him because his secretary told him last week that one of the receptionists had taken a call from him in which he said the Padgett Collection was about to be stolen."

I turned to look at Ted's face. "What happened then? Did Mr. Padgett not take the warning seriously?"

"He said he did. He told me he had the secretary relay the information to someone here in Tallulah Falls. He tried to call her but couldn't reach her this afternoon. He said he'd call her tomorrow and see who she talked with."

"Do you imagine she spoke with Josh Ingle and that the extra security he hired was due to her call?"

"Possibly," Ted said. "I talked with Josh after speaking with Mr. Padgett. Josh said he spoke with Padgett's people several times in the weeks and days leading up to the exhibit opening. He said that, naturally, they discussed concerns about the exhibit being damaged or stolen. But he doesn't remember a call in which a specific threat was mentioned."

"Maybe it was intercepted by someone on the board of directors."

"Could be," he said. "I'm going to speak with the museum's receptionist tomorrow to see if she remembers taking the call."

"Mr. Benton said that Mr. Padgett and the board of directors are going to announce a combined reward for information leading to the recovery of the remainder of Mr. Padgett's collection," I said.

Ted nodded. "Manu green-lighted the reward yesterday, but I believe the board and Mr. Padgett were still hammering out the details and deciding what to say in the press release."

"I wonder if offering the reward will pay off."

"I expect it to pay off handsomely," he said.

"Do you really?" I asked.

"I do . . . especially for you and me."

"Why do you say that?"

"Because as soon as the offer of the reward is announced, you will go to the museum and tell Josh Ingle that Nellie Davis saw everything. . . . In fact, since you enjoy gossiping about her so much, you can say you knew she was in on the plot from the beginning. Why, you could tell Josh that Nellie explained to you herself how she stayed late Friday night in order to help her partners in crime wrap Geoffrey Vandehey in the purloined kilim — Ow!"

He chuckled and put his forearm up to block the blows from the pillow I was beating him with. Like the seasoned law enforcement officer he was, however, he quickly disarmed me and tossed the pillow across the room.

We fell off the couch and ended up lying on the floor, laughing helplessly.

"I told you I could help with your stress release," he said.

CHAPTER TWENTY

Angus and I had been at the Seven-Year Stitch just about an hour on Friday morning when Special Agent Brown strode in.

"Good morning, Ms. Singer," he said, unbuttoning his suit jacket and placing his hands on his hips.

That gesture made me nervous. "Hello, Special Agent Brown. What can I do for you?"

"I've just been talking with Nellie Davis. She and her sister called and asked me to come to her shop. Ms. Davis has accused you of spreading rumors about her."

"Oh, for crying out loud! I did no such thing!"

"Relax, Ms. Singer. I don't think you did, either. I merely came by here to appease Ms. Davis and her sister and to give you a friendly piece of advice — stay as far away from those women as possible. I think they're flaky . . . and possibly dangerous."

"What you're saying isn't news to me, and I have no intention of going around either of them again," I said. "While you're here, though, may I ask you a question?"

"I won't guarantee you an answer, but you can ask."

"How did you know Geoffrey Vandehey was in Tallulah Falls?"

"I got a call from someone close to Anderson Padgett," he said. "The guy told me Vandehey had been in touch with Padgett's office and said the collection in the Tallulah Falls Museum had been targeted for a heist."

"That's odd," I said. "How did the guy know Vandehey was actually here in town?"

"He was here, too. His name's Simon Benton. I guess he spotted Vandehey or something."

I didn't mention it to Special Agent Brown, but I wondered why Simon Benton hadn't told me he was the one who tipped Brown off to Vandehey's location.

"I'm sorry you didn't find Vandehey in time to stop the theft of the collection," I said.

"So am I." He shook his head. "I know that boy of his wants to think Vandehey was just a pawn in someone else's game. I can't say that I blame him. Nobody wants to think badly of a parent. But I believe Geoffrey Vandehey was more ruthless than any of us realize."

Then Special Agent Brown told me to have a good day, and he left.

I was too antsy to go right back to work. I didn't want to be accused of spreading gossip or any other nonsense, though, so I decided to go ask Sadie what she thought I should wear to dinner that evening. I put the clock on the door saying I'd be back in ten minutes and headed down to MacKenzies' Mochas.

Blake was manning the counter.

"Blake, can you call Sadie up for me?" I asked.

He nodded and spoke into a headset as he took a customer's money and gave the man change. I was impressed with Blake's ability to multitask.

Within seconds, Sadie came to the counter.

She jerked her head for me to come over to the side with her. "What's up?"

"I need some advice," I said. "Ted and I are going to dinner with his mom tonight, and I can't decide what to wear."

"What did Bev say?"

"She told me to wear something I'd feel confident in. But I need specifics. I'm a nervous wreck about this evening."

"You can borrow my Xena costume." She smirked.

"Be serious."

"I am serious. What an impression that would make!"

"Sadie . . ."

"All right, all right. Let's see. . . . What about your sleeveless navy cowl-neck blouse and your gold-and-navy geometric-print pencil skirt? That outfit is both sexy *and* sophisticated."

"I think that would work great!" I gave Sadie a quick hug. "Thank you."

"You're welcome," she said. "Now . . . low-fat vanilla latte with a hint of cinnamon?"

I grinned. "You know me so well."

I hurried back up the street where Angus was waiting for me in front of the picture window. I unlocked the door and removed the cardboard clock.

"The good news is I know what I'm going to wear tonight," I told the tail-wagging dog. "The bad news is that Ted's mom will be there."

He opened his mouth in a big, goofy dog grin that made it look as if he were laughing. That, of course, made me laugh, too.

A woman with shoulder-length brown hair

and wire-framed glasses stepped into the shop. "This sounds like a fun place to be!"

"We hope it is," I said. "I'm Marcy Singer, and this is Angus. Welcome to the Seven-Year Stitch."

"It's nice to meet you both." She petted Angus and then began browsing the shelves.

"Is there anything in particular I can help you find?" I asked.

"Actually, I'm looking for some small, folk art cross-stitch patterns."

"Holiday or all-occasion?"

"I'm primarily looking for small Christmas designs I can make as ornaments or put with gifts," she said. "I wouldn't mind finding a couple of Halloween designs to make to brighten up my desk at work, though."

I walked her over to the Christmas display and showed her a selection of the Prairie Schooler cross-stitch folk art designs.

"This company has a wide assortment of both Christmas and Halloween designs," I said. "Their Schooler Santas are five-inch-by-seven-inch cards. They do a different card each year and have been doing so since 1984."

"That's cool." She picked up the *Nordic Holiday* book. "I love this one. It looks like the patterns only use three colors — red, green, and white — and they look simple to do. I'm not a very experienced cross-stitcher . . . at least, not yet."

"I think you'll do a great job with these. And if you need any help, just come back by. We'll figure it out together."

"Thank you," she said.

"I know springtime has already passed, but I love the *Bunnies* book," I said.

"Bunnies? Do you have one of the books in stock?"

"I do."

I retrieved the book for her and she wanted it, too.

"Okay. Let me look at the Halloween stuff . . . and then get some embroidery floss . . . and then I've *got* to get out of here before I spend all my money!"

I laughed and led her over to the Halloween display.

"These are all so cute," she said. "I don't want to start something big, though, because I don't know whether or not I'll have time to finish it."

She finally decided on a couple small, inclusive Halloween cross-stitch kits.

"These are perfect," she said. "Now, if you can just get me the thread — I mean, the floss — I'll need for the Christmas patterns, I'll get started on those."

I looked at the pattern book, found the

floss numbers, and rounded up the corresponding skeins. As I rang up her purchases, I told her about the classes offered on Tuesday, Wednesday, and Thursday evenings and that I was putting a flyer with more information in her bag. It was really good to run across someone new to stitching who was so excited about it.

Ted brought Caesar salads for lunch.

"I thought we'd better try to behave ourselves with lunch so we can overindulge over dinner," he said.

"Okay. I talked with Sadie, and at least, I know what I'm going to wear now — my navy blouse and blue and gold skirt."

He nodded. "Sounds great."

Of course, I could've said *my potato sack dress and furry bedroom slippers,* and he'd have said it sounded great.

"I spoke with the receptionist at the museum this morning," he continued. "She said that on the day she got the call about Vandehey having knowledge of the heist, Mr. Ingle had a lot going on. Before she could talk with Ingle about Vandehey, Simon Benton walked by. She asked Benton if he'd ever heard of Geoffrey Vandehey, and he said he had. She then explained the phone call she'd received from Anderson

Padgett's secretary. Benton told her not to trouble Mr. Ingle with the information — that he'd handle it personally."

"Well, that certainly lines up with what Special Agent Brown told me earlier today," I said.

"Brown was here?" Ted frowned. "What did he want?"

"Nellie and her sister had called him to complain about me divulging Nellie's secrets."

He rolled his eyes. "Those two need to —"

"Not a big deal," I interrupted. "He said he was only here to appease them but said they were flaky and that I should stay away from them. I told him he didn't have to tell me that. Anyway, I asked him where he got the tip that Vandehey was in Tallulah Falls, and he said it came from Simon Benton. I didn't say anything to Brown, but I wondered why Simon Benton failed to share that information when he was discussing murder theories with me yesterday."

"That's something I intend to find out right after lunch," Ted said. "I have an appointment to talk with Benton at one thirty."

"I just think it's weird that he was throwing out all those theories and neglected to mention that he's the one who tipped off

Brown." I shrugged. "I guess he was just being flippant with the theories — and I took them as such — but still . . ."

"I'll let you know what he says about calling Brown. I plan on asking him why he didn't divulge that information to us — local law enforcement, I mean."

I grinned. "I knew what you meant. I didn't expect you to go ask, 'Hey, why didn't you tell Marcy and me you called Special Agent Brown about Geoffrey Vandehey?' "

He laughed. "You never know. I might ask him in just that way." He made his voice a falsetto. "Hey!"

"Ha-ha. You think you're so funny."

"You think I am, too," he said.

"Yeah . . . I do." I sighed. "I'll need you to make me laugh after dinner this evening. I'm so nervous about that."

"Ah, don't be. Didn't I tell you? Mom said I could choose the restaurant. I thought you might want to dine on familiar ground — Captain Moe's."

My jaw dropped and I laughed. "Are you kidding me?"

"Nope."

"She'll be appalled," I said.

"Maybe, at first . . . but she'll come around. Captain Moe is a charmer."

I laughed again. "I love you so much."

"I know."

After lunch, the shop got very busy for a little while. Customers came in for hoops, frames, cloth, floss, and needles. And then the slump hit. During the school year, there was a slump every day around three or three thirty. I thought maybe that's when children were getting out of school, so parents and grandparents were either picking them up or making sure they were home when their children arrived. Yet, even now in the summer, the three o'clock slump persisted. Was it merely coincidental that the slump was during the school dismissal hour? Or was the slump at that time because even in the summer, the ingrained routine remained? I was pondering this deep question of the universe when George Vandehey came into the shop.

"Hi, George," I said. "How are you?"

"I'm better today than I was when I saw you last." He sat down on the sofa and began stroking Angus's wiry fur. "Manu called me this morning and told me that the flash drive had been decoded. I went by the police station and copied the information onto another drive so the original could stay with the police."

"That was a good idea."

"I agree. It was actually nonnegotiable since the flash drive I found in the hotel room is evidence in . . . well . . . you know." He gave me a slight smile. "Anyway, even though the information is no longer encrypted, it's still encoded."

"It is?" I asked. "How can that be?"

"Dad used his own versions of shorthand and cryptic messaging to protect his notes," George said. "Manu thought I might be able to help his technicians decipher Dad's code."

"Are there any audio or video files on the flash drive?"

"Sadly, no. But there are photos I hope will prove to be helpful."

"I hope they will, too," I said.

"I'm absolutely convinced that there's enough evidence on that flash drive to convict Chad Cummings of insurance fraud."

I said nothing. I didn't want to discourage him, but how could a jury believe George or the police computer technicians could crack Geoffrey Vandehey's code when none of them had a master key to go by? Chad Cummings's lawyers would have that thrown out immediately.

■ ■ ■

I was putting the finishing touches on my appearance when Ted arrived to pick me up. I'd already fed Angus and let him out (and back in). I slipped on platform nude pumps and diamond stud earrings. Then I applied a swipe of berry lipstick and fluffed out my hair again. I'd taken the time to curl it, and it was a little bigger than I was accustomed to. Still, I did look more polished when I took the time to style my hair and take pains with my makeup.

Ted gave me a wolf whistle when I came down the stairs.

"Look at our girl, Angus," he said. "Isn't she beautiful?"

Angus woofed. He was either in agreement or simply in the mood to bark. I preferred to think he agreed.

"Thank you both," I said.

"Are you ready?"

I took a deep breath. "No . . . but I suppose I might as well be."

He kissed me. "Just be yourself."

"What if she doesn't like myself?"

"She'll love yourself," he said.

"George Vandehey came by the shop today," I said once we were in the car. "He said he'd made a copy of the flash drive."

"Yeah, I took a look at it after I got back to the office this afternoon. If all the files are properly decoded and transcribed, the prosecution might very well be able to put together a case against Chad Cummings."

"But aren't George and the computer techs grasping at straws?" I asked. "If they don't have a master key to work from, how will they possibly be able to decipher the notes?"

"For one thing, I don't think the cipher is as complex as George might have led you to believe," he said. "And for another thing, if the two techs and George all come back with the same code, then they must be right."

"I guess."

"Of course, the strength of the evidence will depend on what's contained with the files . . . but there are several files."

"Did you speak with Simon Benton?" I asked.

"I did. He said he didn't mention his call to the Federal Bureau of Investigation to local law enforcement at first because he didn't want it to appear that he thought us incapable of handling the matter," said Ted. "He also said that we locals had no reason to arrest Vandehey, while Special Agent

Brown did."

"Wait. Vandehey was a fugitive," I said. "He could have been arrested by any law enforcement officer, right?"

"Right, but it appears Benton's heart was in the right place initially. After the robbery, he was simply too embarrassed to tell us."

"Why?"

Ted shrugged. "It was apparently because his instincts proved wrong. He should have come to us rather than taking the matter to Special Agent Brown, who he thought would be able to arrest Vandehey and get him out of the way before he could move forward with any plans to rob the museum."

"But if Vandehey was involved in the heist, why would he call and warn Anderson Padgett?" I asked.

"That, Inch-High, is the million-dollar question."

CHAPTER TWENTY-ONE

When Ted had mentioned that his mother lived in an upscale condo, I wasn't expecting something so luxurious. This place was gorgeous. It looked like a resort hotel.

Ted pulled around to the front door. I got out of the passenger seat in order to let his mom have the front seat. A doorman immediately came out and asked who we were there to see.

"Hey, Bill," Ted called. "We're just here to pick up my mom. We're taking her to dinner in Depoe Bay."

Bill, the doorman, beamed. "Wonderful, Mr. Nash. I hope you have a fabulous meal!"

"I'm sure we will. By the way, Bill, this is Marcy Singer."

Bill gave my hand a genteel shake. "A pleasure to meet you, Ms. Singer."

"It's a pleasure to meet you, sir," I said.

Then I slipped into the backseat of Ted's car.

"I see your mother coming now," Bill told Ted. To Veronica, he said, "You're looking lovely this evening, Ms. Nash. Enjoy your evening out."

"Thank you, Bill." She got into the car and turned to look into the backseat. "Oh, there you are. For a minute, I thought you'd bailed out on us."

"Not a chance," I said. "Ted told me he chose my favorite restaurant."

"Well, I'm looking forward to that, then."

It was obvious from the way she was dressed that Veronica thought we were going somewhere *tres chic.* She wore a black silk suit, black pumps with red soles, a triple strand of pearls and the necklace's matching bracelet, and pearl cabochon earrings. I was glad I'd stuck with my original plan and worn my navy blouse and geometric-print skirt.

Did I mention that Ted looked gorgeous, by the way? He was wearing dark blue dress pants and a blue-and-white-striped button-down. I liked to think he'd been listening when I'd mentioned I was wearing my navy ensemble and that he dressed to complement my attire.

During the half-hour-or-so drive to Depoe Bay, Veronica talked to me about her cross-stitch project, which she was doing very well on. And she talked with Ted about work.

"Have there been any leads in recovering the textiles stolen from the museum?" she asked.

"No."

"Well, hang in there, dear. You'll find them."

He rolled his eyes at me in the rearview and I nearly giggled.

I would have loved to be able to see Veronica's expression when we pulled up in front of Captain Moe's.

"Is this it?" she asked.

"This is it," Ted said. "Everybody sit tight. If Captain Moe is peeping out a window and sees a lady get out of my car on her own, he'll most assuredly rake me over the coals."

He got out and came around to my door first. I grinned mischievously as I took his hand and stepped out of the car. He then opened his mother's door and helped her out. He offered each of us an elbow to hold on to, and he ushered us to the door.

I could hear the jukebox playing a loud rock song circa 1989 from halfway across the parking lot. I squeezed Ted's arm. He looked down at me and winked.

I was happy to be here at Captain Moe's. Ted and I hadn't been here in a couple weeks. And I was thrilled Ted had brought me somewhere that he knew I'd feel at ease.

Captain Moe flung the door open just before we got to it. "I knew I recognized that strapping young man with the beauty on each arm!" He held open his arms, and I stepped into an encompassing Captain Moe bear hug.

For the world, Captain Moe reminded me of Alan Hale Jr., who played the skipper on television's *Gilligan's Island.* He was tall and barrel-chested, and he had snowy white hair. Unlike Mr. Hale, however, Captain Moe had a neat, trim beard.

After hugging me, Captain Moe shook Ted's hand.

"I know wee Tinkerbell here, but who is the other lovely lady you're dining with tonight?" Captain Moe asked Ted.

"This is my mom, Veronica Nash," Ted said.

"Delighted to make your acquaintance, Ms. Nash," Captain Moe said, taking her hand and bowing slightly. "Welcome to my establishment."

Captain Moe was Riley Kendall's uncle. He and Riley's father had both referred to me as Tinkerbell for as long as I'd known them. I didn't know if this was due to my hair color, my stature, or my impish nature. Or maybe they just couldn't remember my given name. I didn't mind. Having a nickname was cute — it made me feel as if I belonged.

The diner had a counter down the middle of the back part of the room, and there was additional seating in the forms of booths and tables. Captain Moe showed us to one of the only empty tables in the place.

"You're busy tonight," I said.

"Never too busy for you, Tink. Your usual?"

"Please." I grinned.

"Ted, your usual?" he asked.

Ted nodded. "Please."

"And, Ms. Nash, would you like to see a menu?" Captain Moe asked.

I could tell Veronica was struggling to adjust to this unexpected turn her evening had taken. She'd thought she was going to a high-class restaurant, and instead she was in a diner. It was a first-rate diner, mind you, but it wasn't the Four Seasons.

"Captain Moe makes the best cheeseburgers on the planet," I told her.

"I haven't had a cheeseburger in ages," said Veronica. "Give me one of those,

302

please . . . and some fries . . . and a chocolate shake."

"So . . . three usuals," said Captain Moe with a chuckle.

He went over to the counter and got our drinks. When he brought them back, he asked about Angus. I told him Riley was in the shop Tuesday evening.

He nodded. "She comes there to hide out, you know."

"She can hide out at the Stitch anytime," I said.

"Ted, I saw the press conference earlier," Captain Moe said.

"Press conference?" Ted echoed.

"Yeah . . . Josh Ingle and that Padgett fellow were on the news offering a million dollars for any information leading to the recovery of the stolen artwork," he said.

Ted raised his eyebrows in my direction. "A million dollars? Whoa, *Nellie!*"

As we drove home, we discussed how well the evening went.

"I was surprised at how well your mom adapted to Captain Moe's," I said. "I mean, she'd obviously been expecting a four-star restaurant instead of a tiny diner back away from everything."

"She loved that burger, though," he said.

"She didn't leave a crumb!"

I laughed. "Thanks for thinking of Captain Moe's. I believe we were all more comfortable there than we would have been at a fancy restaurant."

"I totally agree. With me, you get the brawn *and* the brains."

"Speaking of your brains and your use thereof, when you said that about Nellie, I nearly fell out of my chair," I said.

"Hey, we could do a lot with a million dollars."

We turned onto my street, and Ted suddenly became serious.

"What?" I asked. Then I realized there was a strange car in my driveway.

Ted pulled into the drive. "You stay here."

"Wait," I said. "It's hard to be sure in the dark, but that looks like the rental car George Vandehey has been driving."

"Either way, I want you to stay in here with the doors locked until I assess the situation." He reached into the glove compartment and got his gun. "If anything happens, call nine-one-one."

Before I could respond, he'd locked the doors and was moving around to the side of the car. Sometimes it scared me when Ted went into supercop mode. I had to admit it *was* sexy, though.

Ted eased up to the rear driver's side of the four-door sedan and yelled for the driver to get out of the car with his hands up. This set Angus to barking so loudly I could hear him from inside the car . . . and he was inside the house.

George Vandehey got out of the car. His arms were trembling, and his face was ashen. Ted lowered the gun and motioned for me to come on. I got out of the car and hurried toward them.

"We should get inside before Angus goes ballistic," I said.

The three of us went inside, George explaining as we went that he'd gone to the Seven-Year Stitch looking for Ted and me and then looked up my address in the phone book and come here when he'd found no one at the shop.

"I wouldn't have come by without calling . . . and I probably should have waited until tomorrow . . . but I was so excited. This can't wait," he said. "It's about what I found on the flash drive my father had hidden in his hotel room."

Angus was still agitated, so I asked Ted to let him out into the backyard.

"I'll run up to the office and get my laptop," I said, taking off my shoes and carrying them with me.

"I'll put on a pot of coffee after I let Angus out," Ted said. "George, decaf or caffeinated?"

"Either," said George. "Actually, make it regular. I'm so excited, there's no way I'll get any sleep tonight regardless."

When I returned with the laptop, I could smell the coffee brewing. I headed for the living room but realized that Ted and George were in the kitchen. I went in there, set the laptop on the table in front of George, and booted it up.

He took the flash drive from his pocket and plugged it in. "Okay. Let me show you the first photo and the corresponding note." He pulled up a photo of the Cézanne painting in which the photographer had zoomed in on the apples. "The note for this photo was a single ten-letter word." He looked at Ted and me expectantly, as if one of us was going to call out the word like contestants on a game show.

I shook my head.

"Temptation," said George. "I'll admit I studied on it, but I couldn't come up with a ten-letter word to describe apples. So then I opened a search engine and typed in a query asking what apples symbolize. Apples represent forbidden fruit. The ten-letter word is temptation."

"And finding that word helped you break the code?" Ted asked.

"Precisely! See? *Temptation* has several of the major letters: *t, e, a, i,* and *n.* From there, it was easy to fill in the blanks on most of the other words. If you have a three-letter combination beginning with *in,* the other letter is more than likely a *g.*"

"So *temptation* provided you with the beginning of a key," I said.

"Right." George pulled a folded-up sheet of paper out of his pocket and handed it to me. "I wrote out all twenty-six letters of the alphabet with a grid below each letter. In the grid, I placed the symbol that Dad had created to correspond with the letter."

I unfolded the paper and looked at it before giving it to Ted.

"As you can see, I didn't fill in all the blanks," George said. "Most . . . but not all. For example, there were no *J*'s in Dad's notes." He pulled up another photo. "This one is the entire image of the Cézanne. The corresponding note says *Tried to buy from Cummings for the amount he paid for it. Cummings laughed. Said the Cézanne is worth what he paid many times over.*"

Ted and I exchanged glances. It was apparent that neither of us saw what George was getting so excited about. So far, the photos and notes he'd shown us proved nothing.

"Now take a look at this one," said George.

A photo depicting a close-up of the knife filled the screen.

"I took the knife as a sign of treachery," he continued. "And the note that goes with this image indicates that Cummings wanted Dad to exaggerate the painting's worth."

"But Chad Cummings had already told your father that it was worth what he paid for it many times over," I said. "His wanting its worth exaggerated doesn't make sense."

"It does when you consider the paltry amount Cummings paid for it," George said. "Keep in mind that when he first bought the painting, no one realized it was an early Cézanne."

The next photo was a close-up of the glass of wine. "The note that corresponds to this photo says *So says a German proverb — wine and women make fools of everybody.* I'm guessing Dad's referring to his love of Libby here. It's a veiled reference telling why he was willing to go along with Cummings's scheme."

George's voice broke, and I patted his shoulder.

"Who's ready for coffee?" I asked.

"Not yet for me, please," George said. "I'm afraid I'd spill it in your laptop."

"None for me, either, thanks," Ted said.

"I feel that these next two photos — and the notes that go with them — are the most damning." He pulled up a photo of the Cummingses' home security alarm keypad. "The note says *Code 093072 — I am to go in on Tuesday evening when the family will be attending a play at the son's school. The nanny will also be in attendance, and the rest of the staff will be given the night off. I've been told to take only the painting and my compensation of two hundred and fifty thousand dollars. If I take anything else, or if the painting is recovered prior to the insurance payout, my daughter will suffer the consequences.*"

I gasped. "Oh, my gosh! Cummings threatened your sister?"

Ted merely stared at the computer screen. I could tell the gears were grinding in his head, but I had no idea what he was thinking.

"Let's see the next one," Ted said.

George brought up an image of the confession letter. I'd seen a copy of it at one of the online news sites.

"The corresponding note says *I was made to sign this. I notice with some satisfaction that something I'd said about the painting be-*

ing unappreciated except for its monetary value was added to the letter." George looked at Ted. "What do you think? Does this prove I'm right about Chad Cummings paying my father to steal his painting?"

Ted took a deep breath. "It comes close. Have you spoken with Manu about this yet?"

"No," he said.

Ted took out his cell phone. "Let me step here into the living room and call him. I'll be right back."

While Ted went into the living room, I poured each of us a cup of coffee. George asked for sugar but no cream. I set the cup near his right hand.

He raised his eyes to mine. "What do you think?"

"I think this is incredible," I said.

"It proves my dad was forced to steal the Cézanne, right?"

I nodded slightly, and then went to let Angus back inside. It did appear that the flash drive contained evidence exonerating Dr. Vandehey, but I didn't know if it would be enough to convict Chad Cummings of insurance fraud.

Angus greeted each of us and then went to the living room to find Ted.

When Ted returned, he confirmed my fears.

"The good news is that Manu's men found the same thing you found," he said to George. "This means that two independent cryptology teams — you and our tech guys — deciphered the code within the flash drive and got the same information. However, it will still come down to Chad Cummings's word against that of a . . ."

"Of a dead man," George finished.

"I'm afraid so. Your father can't explain his actions to a jury, and Chad Cummings's attorneys would present the argument that Dr. Vandehey created the flash drive after the fact in order to cover his tracks if and when he got caught," Ted said.

George sighed. "I guess that's it, then."

"Not so fast. In the morning, Manu and I are going to bring Special Agent Brown up to speed on the information found on the flash drive. Then we're bringing Chad Cummings in for questioning."

"Do you mean it?" George asked.

Ted smiled slightly. "Yes. But don't get your hopes up."

"Let's say for the sake of argument that Chad Cummings is forced to admit that even one thing — that he gave Dad the security code, for instance — is true. Do

311

you think that proves . . . ?"

"Proves that Chad Cummings coerced your dad into stealing the Cézanne?" I asked.

George shook his head. "Do you think it could prove that Cummings killed him?"

"Let's just see what tomorrow brings," said Ted. "All right?"

"Okay," said George.

CHAPTER TWENTY-TWO

I kept looking at the clock in between customers Saturday morning. I knew Ted and Manu were questioning Chad Cummings, and I was anxious to know what was going on. I hadn't deluded myself into thinking that Mr. Cummings would break down and admit that everything on the flash drive made sense and was true. In fact, some of the things Geoffrey Vandehey had alluded to hadn't made a bit of sense as far as I could see. But I did hope that if Mr. Cummings was guilty of insurance fraud, the truth would come out somehow.

A young woman and her little girl came into the shop. The little girl immediately squealed with delight and went to hug "the pony."

Her mother looked slightly horrified until I assured her that Angus — who was taller on all fours than her toddler (and a head taller than me on two feet) — was as gentle as a lamb and wouldn't hurt the child. In fact, Angus lay at the girl's feet so she could pet him easier.

The woman appeared to be relieved, but she kept a watchful eye on the two of them.

"I'll be glad to put him in the back, if you'd prefer," I said.

"No, that isn't necessary. I'm sure they'll be fine," she said. "I just get so nervous."

"That's all right. You can't be too careful where your children are concerned."

"Do you have any?" she asked.

"Not yet," I said. Naturally, her question conjured up a lot of what-ifs and maybes, which I didn't need to dwell on right at that moment. "Is there anything I could help you find?"

"I'm actually looking for children's crafts," she said. "She's so creative, and I'd love to get her interested in embroidery . . . but I don't want anything she could get hurt on or that would be over her head."

"Of course. If you'll step right this way, I have a good selection of children's needle-point kits. They come with a stamped plastic canvas, the yarn needed to complete the project, and a large plastic blunt-tipped needle."

"That sounds like exactly the type of thing I'm looking for," she said.

After taking her over to the children's section, I allowed her to browse and said I'd go back and make sure Angus and her daughter were all right.

The woman quickly came over with her hands full of needlepoint kits. "Hey, Janilyn! Do you like these, sweetie?"

The little girl lifted her face off Angus's neck so she could see what her mom was talking about. She giggled. "Monkey!"

"Yes, I knew you'd like that one," said her mom. "What about these others? Do you like the puppy dog?"

Janilyn nodded her curly blond head.

"Angus is a puppy dog," I told her.

The child chortled. "No. He's a pony!"

"These kits are designed for children a little bit older than Janilyn," I said. "But I'm sure you'll watch her carefully."

"Definitely. When I'm not around, I'm putting the needle somewhere that she can't get hold of it and put it in her mouth."

Janilyn gazed up at her mother. "I won't eat it."

"I know. . . . I just like to be careful."

"Mommy careful," Janilyn told me.

"I'd be careful with you, too," I said.

Janilyn's mom decided to take the monkey and the puppy kit and see how the child fared with them. "If she likes them, I'll be back to get more."

"Thank you," I said. I rang up her purchases.

As they left, Janilyn waved to Angus. "Bye, pony!"

Sissy Cummings came through the door as Janilyn and her mother went out.

"How adorable was she?" Sissy asked. "She makes me want another one!"

"Is Chad Jr. an only child?"

"He is. And it always seems that when I think I'm in the mood to have another, Chad isn't. And when he wants another one, it's not the right time for me." She shrugged. "Maybe Chaddie is supposed to be an only child." She sighed. "Anyway, I really enjoyed watching your friend do the *chikankari* work the other night. I think I might like to give it a try. Do you have any books on the subject?"

"I do have a couple *chikankari* books I ordered when Reggie and I decided to do the class," I said. "They're right over here."

Sissy followed me to the books and got both of the ones on *chikankari*. "These can be an early birthday present — from me to me."

"Oh, when's your birthday?"

"It isn't until the end of September, but I buy myself early birthday gifts all summer long." She laughed. "It's the perfect excuse to indulge myself once in a while."

Once in a while? I considered three months to be more than once in a while, but what did I know?

As she paid for her purchases, Sissy said, "By the way, the police asked Chad to come down to the police station to talk with them this morning. Do you know anything about that?"

"I imagine it has something to do with Geoffrey Vandehey," I said. "Wouldn't it be wonderful if they had information that would lead to the recovery of your Cézanne?"

"Frankly, no. Please don't tell my husband this, but I despised that painting from the moment he bought it," she said. "I understand that it was a fabulous investment — and I'd begged Chad to sell it — but I always thought that painting was downright ugly."

"As they say, art is subjective."

"It certainly is. Well, I'm off. Thanks, Marcy."

"Thank you, Sissy. If you need any help with the *chikankari* in the book, please let me know," I said. "We'll call Reggie."

After Sissy left, I went to the sit-and-stitch square to work on my beaded-cupcake project. Sissy had seemed relaxed and calm for someone whose husband was being questioned by the police. Of course, she didn't know *why* they were talking with him.

My mind drifted back to the information on George Vandehey's flash drive, and I remembered the security code: 093072. That was most likely Sissy's birth date. I wondered if Chad Cummings used it as the code so he wouldn't forget the date. But then, if Sissy was buying herself gifts three months before her actual birthday, it seemed to me her credit card bill would be enough of a reminder.

I hadn't realized how hungry I'd become until Ted arrived with soft steak tacos, chips, and *queso*. The tantalizing aroma immediately made my stomach growl.

"Goodness, Angus, you must be starving," Ted said, winking at me.

"We both are," I said.

"Then it's a good thing I brought an extra taco."

I quickly put the cardboard clock on the door and gave Ted and me thirty minutes. We went into my office, and I took a couple sodas from the mini fridge and set them on my desk while Ted opened the boxes containing the chips and *queso* and the tacos.

"How did the interrogation go?" I asked.

"As expected, Cummings denied everything. He said he had no idea how Geoffrey Vandehey got the code to the family's private home security system, and then he demanded a lawyer be present while he was being questioned."

"Just any old lawyer or his lawyer from Seattle?"

"I suppose any lawyer will do at this point, but it isn't going to be easy to find one on a Saturday," said Ted. "While Cummings goes through the directory trying to get an attorney who will answer the phone, Manu and I opted to take our lunch break. Brown stayed with Cummings. His loss."

"I hope it doesn't turn into a long day for you," I said.

He arched an eyebrow. "Do you have plans for me?"

"Maybe. I think a homemade veggie pizza, a bottle of wine, and some kind of silly TV marathon might be good for both of us."

"That does sound nice," he said, "unless, of course, you're trying to make a fool of me."

"What are you talking about?" I asked.

"The German proverb in Vandehey's notes — wine and women make fools of everybody?"

319

"Oh, right!" I laughed. "Well, I promise, I'm not trying to make a fool of you. By the way, Sissy Cummings was in here this morning. She mentioned something about her birthday being the end of September. I think it's the code — 093072."

"I'd say you're right." He dipped a chip in the warm *queso.* "You know, it probably wouldn't hurt for us to question the wife, too."

Simon Benton strolled by after lunch. He'd been to MacKenzies' Mochas and was drinking an iced coffee.

"I love these things," he said. "If I don't get back to Denver soon, I'm going to gain twenty pounds."

"I don't think they're *that* fattening, are they?" I asked.

"Who knows? Furthermore, who cares?" He chuckled and sat down on the club chair near me. "Hello, young man," he said to Angus.

Angus wagged his tail but stayed over near the window with his Kodiak bear.

"He's busy watching the world go by," I said. "He does that some days."

"It makes him appear most contemplative." He took a sip of his coffee. "I want to apologize for not being forthcoming with you yesterday about my telling Special Agent Brown that Geoffrey Vandehey was in Tallulah Falls."

"Oh, that's quite all right," I said. "We were only having a bit of fun theorizing about the identity of Vandehey's killer. I didn't actually think we'd solve the crime."

"Neither did I. Were I that clever, I'd be at 221B Baker Street in London, right?"

"Right."

He leaned over to see what I was working on, but before he could comment, Angus began barking.

"It's okay, Angus," I said. "Everything's fine."

Nellie Davis had been walking down the street toward MacKenzies' Mochas and stopped to peer into our window. When she realized Simon and I were looking back at her, she turned and practically ran back in the direction of her own shop.

"Who the devil was that?" Simon asked.

"Her name is Nellie Davis, and she has been a thorn in my side ever since I moved to Tallulah Falls."

"Does she always behave so irrationally — watch you through your storefront window and then run away when you catch her?"

"No, that one is a first," I said. "She has told me — and others — that the Seven-

321

Year Stitch is cursed. She has tried to get me to leave so her sister could lease my shop . . . that was, of course, before the one between our stores became vacant. But the most out-of-character thing she'd ever done was this week. She appeared to befriend me."

"And now she's stalking you?"

I laughed. "No. She came over and expressed concern because I'd found Dr. Vandehey in the alley. She told me to be careful and even gave me a stress-relief candle a day or so later. Then she came and took back the candle and told Special Agent Brown that I was trying to get her killed."

"It sounds as if that wretched woman is destined for the loony bin."

"Agreed."

"Why on earth would she tell Brown such an egregious tale?" he asked.

"She believes I betrayed her confidence over something. . . ."

"Over what?"

"A black van, of all things," I said.

He took another sip of his coffee. "I have no clue what that means."

"Join the club. With Nellie, you never know what anything means. I simply know that she hates me and is out to get me. Other than that, your guess is as good as mine."

After work, I changed into a pair of shorts and a T-shirt. I was glad to see that Ted had also changed into comfortable clothing before coming over.

He held up a bottle of white zinfandel. "I didn't know what would go best with veggie pizza. Will this work?"

"It sure will." I was busily chopping the broccoli and cauliflower while the pizza crust browned.

"What are our television marathon options?" He took out an ice bucket, filled it, and put the wine in the bucket to chill.

"Let's see. . . ." There was a long list of options of shows I enjoyed or had been meaning to check out. "We could watch *Longmire, Arrow, Burn Notice, Supernatural, Psych, Damages, Justified —*"

"Let's watch *Justified,*" he said. "We can raise a glass to the late, great Elmore Leonard."

"Deal. So how'd this afternoon's interrogation go?"

"I feel fairly sure that Cummings and his wife were involved in insurance fraud." He came up behind me and wrapped his arms around my waist. "We don't have enough to prove it, though, and I expect the thieving couple to flee Tallulah Falls immediately. On the plus side, Special Agent Brown will be on their heels."

I put the knife down and turned to face Ted. "He will? Isn't Brown more interested in who killed Geoffrey Vandehey than he is in a painting that disappeared over two years ago?"

"No, babe. Brown specializes in stolen art and art fraud. To him, that takes precedence over the murder. He'll go to Seattle and question everybody with regard to the Cummings case and leave us to investigate the homicide."

"You're glad he's getting out of your hair, aren't you?"

"Delighted," he said, dropping a kiss on my lips. "He'll likely come back about once a month or so until either we mine some viable leads in the theft of the Padgett Collection or he decides it's a lost cause."

"Speaking of viable leads, have any good ones come in yet?"

"No, they have not, and that's entirely your fault."

"My fault?" I asked.

"Yes. You haven't turned Nellie Davis in yet and collected our reward money."

I giggled. "I might have to do that after this afternoon. She was creeping around the

Seven-Year Stitch — I thought at first she was going to MacKenzies' Mochas — and then she came up to the window and looked in. When we saw her — Simon Benton was there, too — she turned and practically ran back to Scentsibilities."

He laughed. "That's one strange old bird."

"Yes, she is. And I doubt she'll ever pass by my shop again," I said. "I suppose I lost Sadie and Blake a customer."

"They're sure to go bankrupt now . . . which is another good reason for you to go ahead and turn Nellie in so we can get our cool mil."

CHAPTER TWENTY-THREE

On Sunday afternoon, Ted and I left Angus at home in the air-conditioning, and we braved the heat to go play miniature golf. We went to the indoor arcade at the mall outside of town. The facility had an eighteen-hole pirate-themed mini golf course, laser tag, and arcade games such as pinball and air hockey.

I wasn't great at mini golf, but sometimes I got in a lucky shot or two. Ted, who also played regular golf, could have gone on the pro-mini-golf circuit if there was such a thing. Lucky for me, though, we didn't keep score. Ted won a free game by making a hole in one on the last hole, but we decided to keep the pass and play again another day. I wanted to beat him in a game of air hockey.

When we walked into the arcade section of the game center, we immediately spotted Josh Ingle and Kelly Conrad. Josh waved as soon as he saw us and started over. Kelly acted a bit sheepish, but she came along with Josh.

"Hi, guys," I said.

"Hey," said Josh. "What are you doing?"

"We just finished up a game of mini golf," Ted said. "We won a free game. Would you like our pass?"

"Sure," Josh said. Then he glanced at Kelly. "If you'd like to play, that is."

"Yeah, that sounds like fun," she said.

Ted handed the pass to Josh.

"Thanks," said Josh. "Would you guys like to get something to drink before Kelly and I go play golf?"

Ted and I said we would, and we went into the small food court. Kelly and I found a table while Ted and Josh went to buy the drinks. I didn't want to be nosy, so I waited for Kelly to acknowledge the elephant in the room.

"This is our first date," she said shyly.

"Are you having fun?" I asked.

She nodded. "I went to see Josh on Tuesday afternoon, and he was so discouraged and upset over the robbery. I gave him my number and told him to call me if he needed to talk with someone. And then I took your advice and spoke with my sister."

"Apparently, that went well."

"It did," she said. "I told her I'd gone by

the museum to see how Josh was doing. Of course, she'd heard all about the Padgett Collection being stolen and all that, and she said it was nice of me to be concerned about him. I told her I kinda liked him but that I didn't want to pursue a relationship with him because they had dated." She glanced down at her folded hands. "She told me not to be ridiculous — that she and Josh only went out a time or two and had nothing in common. So here we are."

"I'm glad," I said. "Whether things work out for you and Josh or not, I would imagine your conversation opened up a new line of communication between you and your sister."

"It did. She couldn't believe I'd held a grudge against him all this time for asking me out after dating her first." She smiled. "It's funny how you can completely misunderstand things and blow them out of proportion in your mind when you don't attempt to discover the truth . . . or when you think you know the truth but neglect to confirm it. . . . You know what I mean?"

"I know exactly what you mean," I said.

The guys returned with drinks: water for Ted and me, a diet soda for Kelly, and lemonade for Josh.

"How are you holding up, Josh?" I asked.

"I know you're still concerned about the robbery, but hopefully, the reward will be the incentive someone needs to come forward with some valuable information."

"I'm praying that will happen," he said. "And I'm doing all right. Kelly is helping me in that department. She has been wonderful to talk with me and encourage me."

Kelly blushed. "It isn't that big a deal. I'm glad to help."

"I've run into more — how can I put this nicely? — *eccentrics* this week than I ever have at one time in my entire life," said Josh. "First of all, that Special Agent Brown is like Inspector Clouseau . . . only not as competent! Sometimes I watched him interview people and could've sworn he was *trying* to botch things up! He's unbelievable."

"I was afraid that his grudge against Geoffrey Vandehey would jeopardize his entire investigation," Ted said. "That's why I was so glad that some of our guys were there just about every step of the way with him."

"They certainly needed to be." Josh shook his head. "It would've been comical to watch him work had it not been so important to me that the collection be found and the thieves brought to justice. If neither of those things ever happens, I'll lay the blame squarely at the feet of Special Agent Floyd Brown."

"Tell them about Anderson Padgett," Kelly prompted.

"He's another oddball," said Josh. "Don't get me wrong — the guy is as nice as he can be. . . . He's simply . . . different. Ever since he's been in town, he has come to the museum at least once a day and looked at every single exhibit. If there's anything in the exhibit he can touch — like the stuffed bear in the wildlife exhibit — he does. I took him on the tour the first couple of times, and then he said he was fine going through on his own."

"There seems to be something very sad about that," I said. "It's like he's lonely."

"I believe he is lonely." Josh took a drink of his lemonade, grimaced, and added two packets of sugar. "You'd imagine that someone with as much money as Anderson Padgett has would have more friends than the Queen of England. And maybe he does in Colorado."

"I ran into him in the museum one day, and he seemed sweet," said Kelly.

"We had lunch with him, and he struck us as a charming man, too," I said.

"What about Chad Cummings?" Ted asked Josh. "What kind of vibe did you get from him and his wife?"

"At first, I thought he was sort of bossy with her," Josh said. "But then I started watching them more, and it seemed like he wasn't bossy so much as he was — What's the word I'm looking for? — *accommodating*. I came to the conclusion that she was the pants-wearer, not him."

"I don't know," Kelly said. "I only met her once, but I got a different feeling than that. She struck me as very down-to-earth. I felt like Mr. Cummings was one to throw his weight around and brag about how much money they had and stuff like that."

"I agree with Kelly," I said. "Mr. Cummings gave me the impression he was a showoff. I won't be sorry when he leaves Tallulah Falls in his Bugatti's rearview mirror."

"I won't be sad to see Simon Benton leave, either," said Josh. "There's something about that man and his highbrow language. He's treated me like the prime suspect in the Padgett Collection heist from day one. I believe he'd hang that crime on me in a minute if he could."

"Your uncle won't let that happen," Kelly said softly.

"If the board decides to get rid of me, there's not anything he can do about it," he said. "He helped me get the job. I can't ask any more of him than that."

"But the theft wasn't your fault," she told him.

"Are you about ready to play that game of mini golf?" he asked.

I was rather glad he changed the subject. Being privy to what should have been a private conversation was starting to make me uncomfortable.

Ted and I took the long way home. It was a beautiful day, and we were enjoying the drive. We were listening to an oldies station and singing along — badly and with incorrect words — to some of the songs.

We turned down the street on which MacKenzies' Mochas, the Brew Crew, Scentsibilities, and, of course, the Seven-Year Stitch were located. MacKenzies' Mochas was bustling, the Brew Crew was — like the Stitch — closed on Sundays, and . . .

"Oh, my gosh!"

"What the — ?"

We saw it at the same time — a police cruiser with its lights flashing parked in front of Scentsibilities. Ted pulled in behind the car.

"Wait here," he said. "I'll leave the engine

running."

"No!" I protested. "One, I want to know what's going on; and two, I want her to know that whatever it is, I didn't do it!"

"All right."

We got out of Ted's car and hurried into Nellie's shop. Officer Audrey Dayton, her auburn hair in a ponytail, was taking notes and trying to console a weeping Nellie.

As soon as she spotted me, Nellie's sister, Clara, pointed a long, crooked finger and hissed, "You!"

"I have done absolutely nothing," I began. "I —"

Ted held up a hand. "Please, babe, let me handle this. Officer Dayton, what's going on here?"

"Ms. Davis received a threatening phone call," she said. "The caller used a voice-distorting device but made it appear to Ms. Davis that he or she was somewhere inside the shop. I've gone over the premises, and the only people here are Ms. Davis and her sister."

"What was said during the call?" Ted asked.

"According to Ms. Davis, the caller threatened to kill her if she doesn't get out of town immediately," said Officer Dayton.

"Did you call her?" Clara's venom-voiced

question was directed at me.

"No, she did not," Ted answered on my behalf. "Ms. Singer has been with me all day. She has neither made nor received any phone calls." He turned back to Officer Dayton. "Number blocked?"

She nodded. "May I talk with you outside for a moment, Detective Nash?"

They stepped outside, and I hurried after them. No way was I staying inside with the Wicked Witch of the East and the Wicked Witch of the West. I felt it was no co-incidence that I was wearing my ruby red sandals today.

"I'll get back in the car and let you two talk privately," I said.

"Don't," said Officer Dayton. "It's not that private, and I don't want you to have a heatstroke sitting in the car. I just wanted to ask Detective Nash if he feels the threat against Nellie Davis is legitimate."

"Yes, I do," he said. "First, someone tried to scare her with the dead rat, and now they're calling and giving her an ultimatum. She saw something more than a black van in the alley that night. She needs to tell us what."

"All right. I was going to advise Ms. Davis to take the threat seriously either way," she said. "I believe it's always better to err on the side of caution. But if there's something she's holding back — something that could help us to help her — then she needs to come clean."

"Agreed."

Ted went back into the shop, and Officer Dayton and I followed. Well, she followed. . . . I more or less straggled along behind.

"Ms. Davis, you previously stated that on the Friday night or the early-dawn hours of Saturday morning when Geoffrey Vandehey's body was discarded in the alley that you saw a black van driving away from the scene," said Ted. "Isn't that correct?"

"I did say that, but now I'm not sure," Nellie said.

"You made that statement on two separate occasions to two separate law enforcement officers," he said. "Are you now recanting that statement?"

"No . . . maybe . . . I don't know," Nellie said.

"Can't you see she's scared half to death?" Clara asked. "Stop badgering her!"

"I'm trying to get to the truth," Ted said. "Until we know exactly what Ms. Davis saw happening in the alley, we can't protect her. Now, Ms. Davis, tell me what you saw."

"I saw — I saw the black van," said Nellie. "I really did, but now I wish I hadn't said anything. I told *her* about it first, and look at where that's got me! I'm gonna be next!"

"You aren't going to be next, Ms. Davis." Ted kept his voice calm and even. "We're here to protect you."

"You can't protect me!" She covered her eyes with her hands. "You can't be here all the time! I never should've said anything, and then no one would have ever known I saw . . . the van."

"You saw something more than a black van, didn't you?" Ted asked.

"I don't know what you're talking about," she said.

"Please level with me, Ms. Davis. You saw someone or another vehicle or you saw the tag number . . . *something.* You know it, I know it, and the person who called you knows it."

This sent Nellie into a sobbing fit, and Officer Dayton and I shared a look of alarm. It was apparent to me that she and I agreed that Ted's telling Nellie Davis the equivalent to *I Know What You Did Last Summer* might not have been the best idea. Although it wasn't Nellie who'd *done* something last summer — or, rather, last Saturday at dawn — but had *witnessed* it . . . Still, reminding

336

a hysterical woman that a crazed killer was gunning for her might not have been Ted's finest moment. I understood why he did it — to scare her into telling him the truth. But it hadn't worked and very well might've had the opposite effect.

"I've been ordered to get out of town or suffer the consequences," Nellie said when she was finally able to take a ragged breath. "And I'm leaving."

"She'll stay with me for a few days," said Clara. "You people do your jobs and get this murderer off the streets."

"I can't do that when I don't know who I'm looking for." Ted turned his icy blue stare on Nellie until she was forced to avert her eyes.

She remained stubborn, though, and didn't tell him what she knew. I had to grudgingly, but silently, give her props for that.

CHAPTER TWENTY-FOUR

Before I went to work Monday morning, I was thinking about what Josh Ingle had said about Mr. Padgett coming to the museum every day and how I'd thought he must be lonely. I called Mr. Padgett at his hotel and asked if he'd like to have coffee with me this morning.

"I have an idea," he said. "Why don't you bring the coffee, and I'll grab a cab and meet you at the museum?"

I said that would work for me. He gave me his coffee order, and we hung up.

I didn't want to wear jeans for my meeting with Mr. Padgett, but I didn't want to dress up, either. I compromised and wore a pink sundress with a braided white-and-pink belt and white sandals. Then I put on a tinted moisturizer with sunscreen, some blush, mascara, and lip gloss as I tried to explain to Angus why he couldn't go with me just yet.

"For some silly reason, dogs aren't allowed in the museum," I told him. "But I'll come back and get you in time to go to work with me."

He sighed and flopped down on the floor in a dramatic display of despair. That, or else he was just hot. Anyway, I took it as despair.

"Trust me, you wouldn't even *like* the museum, anyway. There is no food there. . . . Well, maybe in the gift shop they have candy bars or something, but nothing you'd be particularly interested in," I said. "No granola bones, no peanut butter dog biscuits . . . They don't even have squeaky toys in that place!"

Angus rolled his eyes up at me and then looked back down at the floor.

"If you don't believe me, ask Ted. I wouldn't even be going if I didn't feel sorry for Mr. Padgett."

He sighed.

There was no consoling him whatsoever. I'd be sure and give him a treat after we got to work. Realistically, I knew he'd sleep the whole time I was gone, but I could easily imagine that he would feel alone and left out. Did I mention my mother was a Hollywood costume designer? And that I'd seen too many talking-animal movies?

I hurried off. I didn't have time to stop at MacKenzies' Mochas, so I ran through a fast-food drive-through to get coffees for Mr. Padgett and me. Add to my Angus guilt Blake and Sadie guilt.

I got to the museum at just before nine. That gave me about forty-five minutes to spend with Mr. Padgett before I had to get back home, get Angus, and return to the Stitch.

Mr. Padgett was waiting for me just inside the door. I walked in and handed him his coffee.

"Don't you look lovely and refreshing?" he asked.

"Thank you." I hesitated, wondering if I should push his wheelchair. But then he put his coffee in the cup holder and began pushing himself.

"I love a museum in the morning. Don't you?"

"I have to admit I've never been here in the morning before," I said. "It is a lot different from the weekend and during events. It's so quiet."

"It's reverent, isn't it?" he asked.

"It is."

He rolled over to the wildlife exhibit. As Josh had said he'd done in the past, Mr. Padgett reached out and gently stroked the bear's paw.

"Feel that," he said.

I tentatively touched the animal.

"That was a powerful, majestic animal once," said Mr. Padgett. "Now here it is on display."

"Do you think that's sad?" I asked.

"To a degree. But I also feel that it can live on somehow in this venue . . . being admired by schoolchildren." He smiled up at me. "And doddering old men."

"You are not one of those," I said.

"You're not fooling either of us by saying that," he said. "Denying the truth doesn't make it less so." He rolled on into an area of the museum dedicated to the Pacific Northwest Native American tribes. He gestured toward a basket. "Look at that. It's a coiled basket."

"It's beautiful," I said.

"These types of baskets were unique to the Pacific Northwest and were made by stitching flexible material around a core. Each row is joined to the previous one, and it forms a continuous spiral."

I stepped closer so I could see the intricate work. The top of the basket had an open-worked rim. "What workmanship."

"I knew you'd appreciate it," said Mr. Padgett. "Not everyone does. Many people

341

look at a piece of art and wonder what it's worth — monetarily speaking. They don't even care what it's worth in terms of time spent on creation, the thought that went into it, the craftsmanship, the beauty, the fact that there's not another piece exactly like the one you're seeing."

"I saw a quote once where the author said she trembles when she thinks of everything her quilts must know about her. I believe each artist feels that way about his or her creation."

He reached out and squeezed my left hand. "I wish my children and grandchildren could understand art the way you do."

"They don't get it?"

"Not at all," he said.

"Is that why you were planning to sell some of your textiles to the museum?" I asked. "Because you didn't feel your children would keep them?"

"That's part of it," he said. "They don't fully appreciate art for art's sake. I know few people who do. Not even Simon appreciates art irrespective of its monetary value." He sighed. "I don't feel that I'll be around much longer, Marcy. Now, don't look that way. We're speaking frankly, and my doctor says my ticker isn't keeping time as well as it used to. Before it was stolen, I was considering gifting the collection to the Tallulah Falls Museum and Historical Society."

"Gifting it? Really?"

"Cross my heart and hope . . . Well, not quite yet." He winked.

"Mr. Padgett, you're going to have to stop joking like that."

"Ah, my dear, as author Elbert Hubbard once said, 'Don't take life too seriously. You'll never get out of it alive.' "

I laughed. "You're incorrigible!"

He turned serious again. "I do hate that the collection was stolen. Now no one will get to appreciate it."

"I remember Geoffrey Vandehey saying something similar in the confession letter he signed after taking Chad Cummings's Cézanne," I said.

"I saw something about that when it happened," said Mr. Padgett. "I never met Dr. Vandehey, but from what I've read about him — combined with what I've come to know of Mr. and Mrs. Cummings this week — I do feel that Dr. Vandehey took the Cézanne from the Cummingses' home because it wasn't valued there."

"I never met him, either," I said. "I found his body, and sadly, that was the only encounter I ever had with the man. But I feel that he was unjustly vilified in the matter of the Cézanne. I believe he was a good man at heart."

"I imagine you're right, Marcy."

I didn't have time to go back and get Angus before I went to the shop. I felt bad about it, but by the time Mr. Padgett and I had looked at everything in the museum, I barely made it to the shop by ten o'clock.

I rushed inside and was making sure the Stitch was tidy and that the shelves and bins were properly stocked and in order when someone came in. I turned to see that it was Simon Benton.

"You look a bit flushed," he said. "Are you all right this morning?"

"I'm fine. Just running late. I had coffee with Mr. Padgett before coming to work, and I lost track of time."

"That's easy to do with Andy. He's quite the talker," said Mr. Benton. "I was on my way to MacKenzies' Mochas and thought I'd drop in and see if you'd like anything."

"I appreciate your offer, Mr. Benton, but I'm fine."

"Where's your companion this morning?"

"He's at home," I said. "I'm hoping to run back and get him later. It can be lonely here without him."

"I imagine so. I see your neighbor began taking her threats seriously and flew the coop. I don't want your dog to desert you as well."

"My neighbor?" I asked.

"Ms. Davis."

"Oh! She's always closed on Mondays," I said. "But I do believe she took some time off to spend with her sister."

"Well, I won't keep you. I'll go on down to the coffeehouse and get my usual. See you later!"

"Take care, Mr. Benton!"

Before I could get back to business, Ted called.

"Hey, babe. I was thinking about you and wanted to tell you this weekend was wonderful," he said.

"Thank you, sweetheart."

"What's up? You sound a little down."

"I started thinking about Mr. Padgett this morning and how he's probably lonely, so I called and asked if he'd like to have coffee," I said. "He asked if I'd bring the coffee and meet him at the museum. I did, and we walked around looking at everything, and I stayed too long to go back home and get Angus . . . and I'd already *told* Angus I'd be back to get him, so now I feel like a liar."

345

Ted gave a low chuckle. "I'll go get him and bring him to the Stitch at lunchtime. Will that work?"

"Are you sure you don't mind?"

"Not in the least," he said.

"Thank you, thank you, thank you! I'll get us something from MacKenzies' for lunch so we can eat when you get here," I said. "What are you in the mood for?"

"Can't say . . . This might not be a secure line."

I laughed. "How about pasta salad?"

"Not exactly what I had in mind, but it'll do," he said. "And hey, I'm really glad you finally met my mom. I'd been dreading that and had put it off for far too long. I was afraid you'd hate her and tell me to get lost."

"I liked her," I said. "But even if I *had* hated her, I wouldn't have told you to get lost . . . unless you'd take me with you."

"I'm not planning on going anywhere."

As we were talking, I saw Special Agent Brown walking up the street.

"Huh," I said.

"Huh, what?"

"Special Agent Brown is still here. You must've been mistaken about his plan to take off to Seattle after Chad and Sissy Cummings."

"That's one of those curiouser and curi-

346

ouser conundrums," he said. "They're still in town, too."

"I really did think they'd leave in a huff after they were both hauled in for questioning," I said.

"Yeah, so did I. Gotta run. See you at lunch."

We said our good-byes.

A delivery truck stopped outside, and the guy dropped off a box of stamped tote bags a local church had ordered for their youth group to make for a fall festival sale. I called the youth director and left a message on her voice mail, and then I slid the box into my arms and set it on the floor.

The bells over the door jingled. I straightened and saw that Special Agent Brown had come up to the counter.

"Good morning, Ms. Singer," he said. "Are you doing all right today?"

"Yes. I'm fine, thanks. How are you?" I doubted Special Agent Brown had come by merely to engage me in small talk, so I immediately followed up with "What can I do for you?"

"I wondered if you might have a key to the Scentsibilities shop."

I did a double blink. "You think *I* might have a key to Nellie Davis's shop?"

"Well, oftentimes neighbors do that, don't

they, give neighbors spare keys in case they lock themselves out, or forget something, or the place catches fire?"

"Is Nellie's shop on fire?" I automatically sniffed to see if I smelled smoke. I did not. I wondered if a fire in an aromatherapy shop might smell different from, say, a fire in the Seven-Year Stitch, where there weren't all those distinct odors.

"No, Ms. Davis's shop is not on fire." He huffed. "Do you or do you not have a key?"

"Of course I don't have a key," I said. "Neighbor or not, Nellie Davis would absolutely not trust me with a key to her shop. Why do you need one?"

"Because it's locked, and she isn't there," he said.

"Which raises the question, why do you need to go into her shop when she isn't there?"

"I need to look around. I want to —" He broke off, then came back with, "It's none of your business."

"Your best bet is to call Nellie at her home or at her sister's home," I said. "I believe she intended to stay with her sister for a few days, but you never can tell how quickly Nellie is going to change her mind on something." Like giving you a candle and then taking it back.

"Yeah. Thanks. I'll call her." He turned around and stalked toward the door.

"All right. I do think that's your best bet."

He didn't answer and he didn't turn back. He just went out the door and once again headed toward Nellie's shop.

I immediately called Ted. As soon as he answered, I told him about my visit with Special Agent Brown.

"Why he thought Nellie and I were Mr. Rogers and . . . whoever Mr. Rogers's neighbors were is beyond me," I said.

"Why he feels the need to go into the woman's shop without her being present is beyond me," he said. "Special Agent Brown is getting ready to have some backup whether he wants it or not. Sit tight and stay in your shop. Manu and I are on our way."

CHAPTER TWENTY-FIVE

I saw Ted and Manu arrive at Nellie's shop.
I so wanted to know what was going on. I
hurried to the bathroom and got a paper
towel and some window cleaner. The door
was so smudgy! Well, it *was*!

As I cleaned the window — I *did*! — I saw
Nellie and Clara arrive at Scentsibilities. I
wondered who'd called them, Special Agent
Brown or Manu and Ted.

"Good morning, Marcy!"

It was Christine Willoughby coming from
the direction of MacKenzies' Mochas.

"Hi!" I went back inside and held the door
open for her.

"What's going on up there?" she asked.

"Oh, is something going on?" I took one
last look in the direction of Nellie's shop. "I
have no idea."

"But you're dying to know, aren't you?"

"Yes!" I said.

We both started laughing.

"I came to get a couple more of those angel ornament kits," she said. "I got the hang of it and really enjoyed it. In fact, I finished it up last night and wanted to get one the same style to make for my neighbor and a different one for myself."

As Christine was picking out her ornaments, George Vandehey came in.

"Hi, George. I'll be with you in just a minute."

"Thanks." He went to the sit-and-stitch square and sat down. "Where's Angus?"

"I was wondering that very thing," Christine said.

I explained to them that I'd had somewhere to go before work this morning and didn't have time to go home and get him. "Ted said he'll pick him up for me at lunchtime."

Christine paid for her angels, told me to hug Angus for her, and then she left.

I joined George in the sit-and-stitch square. "How are you this morning?"

"As a matter of fact, I have some exciting news. I went by the police station before coming here, and I was told that Manu and Ted were out," he said. "When I saw Ted's car, I hoped he was here."

"He and Manu both are up the street at Nellie Davis's shop at the moment. I'll text

351

him and ask them to come talk with you when they finish up."

"Thank you. I appreciate that."

I took out my phone and sent the text.

George leaned forward. "There was something else on the flash drive . . . something I'd dismissed before."

"Having to do with the Cézanne?"

"No. It had to do with the theft of the Padgett Collection." He spread his hands. "Here's what happened. I opened the file when I first started decoding the information on the drive. It was all text, and I went on to the photographs. I was so eager to find something to at least partially exonerate my father that I latched onto the photos and the coded messages that corresponded to each one."

"Of course," I said. "That's perfectly understandable."

"But then last night as I was thinking I needed to get back home, I missed Dad so much. I wanted to remember him and dwell on some of the good memories we had." He paused, collecting his emotions. "Anyway, the message in that first file was composed using a double-transposition cipher."

"I've never heard of that."

"It's one of the most difficult ciphers to decode, but Dad taught me and my best friend how to do it when we were in middle school." He smiled. "It let us send notes to each other about girls without the fear that anyone other than the two of us would know what was being said."

"That's cool."

"It is. In fact, my friend and I still send Christmas greetings to each other using the cipher every year. But I'm getting myself off track. I immediately recognized Dad's message as a double-transposition cipher. It took a few hours, but I was eventually able to crack the code."

"What does it say?" I asked.

"It's odd. With the exception of the title, the message is actually a series of quotes from Act III, Scene I of Shakespeare's *Julius Caesar.*" He took a folded piece of paper from his pocket. "Here. Take a look."

At the top of the page was written *Treachery — Anderson Padgett Textile Collection.*

Beneath that was this passage:

Caesar: *The ides of March are come.*
Soothsayer: *Ay, Caesar; but not gone.*
Caesar: *No, not gone, Langford.*

I frowned. "I don't remember a *Langford* being in that play."

"I looked it up. The entire line is bogus,"

said George. "My sister *does* live in Langford on Vancouver Island. That's why at first I thought this message pertained in some way to the theft of the Cézanne, even though the title makes it clear it refers to the robbery of the Padgett Collection."

I was still wondering why Geoffrey Vandehey would have added an extra line to his message as I read the next passage.

Caesar: Et tu, Brute?_____
Brutus: *Where's the teacher?*
Cinna: *Here, quite confounded with this mutiny, as are Beatrice, Benedick, and the guard.*

" 'Where's the teacher?' is a misquote," George said. "In the original, it says, 'Where's Publius?' "

"So when he says 'the teacher,' he's talking about himself," I said. "He's telling us that Anderson Padgett was betrayed by his friend . . . Simon Benton."

"But how could Dad possibly know that?"

"There is no Beatrice or Benedick in *Julius Caesar,*" I said. "Beatrice and Benedick were tricked in *Much Ado About Nothing* when they overheard that each was in love with the other." I paced as I thought. "I think your dad is telling us that during one of his visits to the museum, he overheard Simon plotting with one of the security guards. They were both spending a lot of time there prior to the exhibit opening."

"You're right!" George exclaimed. "Dad had to have overheard that other man plotting against Mr. Padgett."

I saw Simon Benton getting ready to come inside the shop. "Mr. Benton!"

"Yes . . . yes, that's it," George, whose back was to the door, said as Mr. Benton walked inside. "Mr. Benton must've stolen his friend's collection with the help of at least one of the security guards."

"You must believe yourself to be very astute," said Mr. Benton.

George stood and whirled to face him. "I know what you did! You stole from someone who considers you a friend, and you killed my father!"

"You have no proof," Mr. Benton said.

"I'm getting ready to talk with Chief Singh and Detective Nash, and they're going to find enough proof to put you away for a long time," George said. "In fact, they're at Nellie Davis's shop right now. What did you leave there when you threatened her? Does it have your fingerprints on it?"

"She saw you," I said. "That Friday

355

night . . . Nellie looked out into the alley, and she saw you. That's why she acted so weird every time she caught the merest glimpse of you. She recognized you."

"You couldn't simply let well enough alone, could you, Mr. Vandehey? Neither could your father." He took a small pistol from the pocket of his linen jacket. "And now you've dragged poor Ms. Singer into your misfortune. Ms. Singer, if you please, stand and precede Mr. Vandehey to the back door of your establishment."

"Let's talk this over," I said. "Neither Mr. Vandehey nor I want this to go badly."

"Please don't insult my intelligence by promising not to tell," said Mr. Benton.

He waved the gun in a gesture that I knew very well meant that I was to stop talking and start walking. I got up and began slowly moving toward the back door of the shop. I knew that George and I were in a no-win predicament. If we cried out in the hope that Ted and Manu would hear us two buildings away, we risked getting shot and having Simon Benton escape out the back. If we did nothing, we would assuredly be shot at some remote location where help was much farther away than Nellie Davis's aromatherapy shop.

"You don't want to be rash, Mr. Benton,"

I said. "Please take us somewhere, lock us up, and then escape. At least, give us a fighting chance."

"That much I can do," he said. "Now, let's go."

I wasn't foolish enough to think he'd actually give us that fighting chance. I lifted up a silent prayer that either George or I would figure out a way to get us out of this predicament alive.

Suddenly, from the direction of the counter, a woman screamed. In my hysteria, my first thought was that it was Jill and that she'd come to life to save us.

The woman screamed again. It was Mom. She was calling me.

As Mr. Benton spun around to see who was at the counter, George Vandehey saw his opportunity to wrap his arms around the slender man, pinning them to his sides. They continued to struggle as I tried to both stay out of the way of the gun and find something with which to disarm Mr. Benton.

In the meantime, the phone kept screaming.

I ran to the door and screamed, "Help us!" as loudly as I could. Ted came running, and Manu wasn't far behind.

Ted drew his gun on Mr. Benton. "Drop

357

your weapon. Now! Don't make me shoot you."

Mr. Benton dropped the gun onto the floor.

"Mr. Vandehey, get over here out of the way, please," Manu said as he walked over to Mr. Benton. He brought Mr. Benton's hands around to his back and handcuffed him while Ted kept the gun trained on Benton.

As Manu walked Benton outside and put him in the car, Ted holstered his gun and pulled me to him.

"Are you all right?" he asked.

"I am now."

EPILOGUE

It was my first trip to Vancouver Island. Langford was a beautiful wooded area, and the rehabilitation center where Elizabeth Vandehey Hart resided was secluded and peaceful. Ted and I had gone to visit Libby at George's invitation.

The three of us stepped into the great room, where Libby awaited us. Classical music played softly over a speaker system. There was no television in this room, but George told us that the center had a projection room where residents could watch movies two or three times a week. It was believed that most of the patients would find news programs upsetting, so regular television was prohibited. George was glad of that. His sister had never learned of their father's theft.

That's probably why no one at the Ridgeview Rehabilitation Center appeared to realize that the painting that hung on the wall

359

behind the baby grand piano was a priceless Cézanne. Since the painting was stolen from an individual, and since said individual had agreed that the rehabilitation center could keep the painting, it would — at least for now — remain where it was.

As I looked at the Cézanne, I took Ted's hand and thought of Mr. and Mrs. Cummings . . . and Mr. Padgett . . . and Dr. Vandehey, who knew how much his daughter would love this painting.

Sissy — or Portia — Cummings had been convicted of insurance fraud. It had been she who had given Dr. Vandehey all the details of the night they would be at Chad Jr.'s recital, the code to the security alarm, and the money. She really had detested the painting and had hoped Chad would take the insurance money and replace the Cézanne with something she found more aesthetically pleasing. There wasn't enough evidence to convict Chad Cummings of any wrongdoing. I wasn't sure whether or not he'd been complicit in the theft, but I was happy that Chad Jr. didn't lose both his parents. Sissy was currently serving sixty months in federal prison while Chad was left to pay the fines and restitution. Since he allowed the painting to remain in the possession of the rehab center, he was given a lesser amount of restitution.

Under interrogation, Simon Benton had admitted that one of the security guards had facilitated his theft of the Padgett Collection. The collection was found intact, with the exception of the kilim rug in which Dr. Vandehey's body was wrapped, in a storage locker owned by the security guard.

After adding his final message to the flash drive, Geoffrey Vandehey had gone to the museum to try to convince Simon Benton not to steal from his friend. As he'd done with George and me, when threatened with exposure, Benton had pulled out a gun. He'd shot Dr. Vandehey in the heart. The professor had been killed instantly. It just so happened that Mr. Benton and the security guard had been about to roll up the kilim rug and Dr. Vandehey fell onto it. They rolled him up in it and dropped his body in the alley behind the Seven-Year Stitch. They'd planned to take him farther but were afraid that his blood would leak onto the other textiles, making them worthless.

Once the Padgett Collection was recovered, Anderson Padgett donated it to the Tallulah Falls Museum and Historical Society. Josh had been given a raise and had finally stopped being so paranoid about losing his job.

Ted and I talked with Libby for a little while and then left her alone with her brother. We were walking hand in hand along a nature trail near the rehab center thinking about how good life was when a sudden shrill scream erupted.

It was Mom. She was calling to see how we liked Vancouver Island.

ABOUT THE AUTHOR

Amanda Lee lives in southwest Virginia with her husband and two beautiful children, a boy and a girl. She's a full-time writer/editor/mom/wife and chief cook and bottle washer, and she loves every minute of it. Okay, not the bottle washing so much, but the rest of it is great.

The employees of Thorndike Press hope you have enjoyed this Large Print book. All our Thorndike, Wheeler, and Kennebec Large Print titles are designed for easy reading, and all our books are made to last. Other Thorndike Press Large Print books are available at your library, through selected bookstores, or directly from us.

For information about titles, please call:
(800) 223-1244

or visit our Web site at:
http://gale.cengage.com/thorndike

To share your comments, please write:
Publisher
Thorndike Press
10 Water St., Suite 310
Waterville, ME 04901